King Cobra

Nothing's sexier than seven men with hot rods.

After Eli's mother died, his father honored her life's mission as a social worker by taking in several kids from the wrong side of the tracks. Not all of them stuck, but those who did became Eli's quasi family.

Their bonds, forged in fires set by their personal demons, are unbreakable—or so Eli wants to believe. Especially since he and Alanso, his best friend and head mechanic, witnessed the overpowering allure of polyamory while visiting the Powertools crew.

Much as Eli would like to deepen the relationships among his foster brothers and sister in the Hot Rods Restoration Team, he's hesitant to risk everything on a quick romp behind a stack of tires.

But when Eli catches Alanso exploring their mutual fantasy at a known hookup spot in a public park, all bets are off. And Eli must decide if it's time to jump in full throttle—and trust his instincts to guide him through the night. If the pair can dodge the potholes in their own relationship, maybe they can race together toward the unconventional arrangement with Mustang Sally they both desire.

Warning: Fasten your seatbelts, this is going to be a wild (and naughty) ride!

Mustang Sally

Two men will give her the ride of her life.

Salome "Sally" Rider is flooring the gas pedal of her pink '69 Mustang, desperate to outrun the memory of two of her fellow mechanics getting busy with some bar skank on the hood of a classic car. On *her* custom paint job.

For years her emotions have withered while her lost boys, her Hot Rods, have grown closer than brothers. Maybe some downtime with the Powertools sexperts will help her figure out why Eli and Alanso went looking for some stranger when Sally was waiting right at the ends of their grease-smudged noses.

Sally is dead wrong about what she thought she saw, and Eli "King Cobra" London and the rest of the thoroughly rattled Hot Rods are determined to prove it. They'll show her in the sexiest possible way that she's not merely an interchangeable part in their well-oiled machine.

Yet just as Eli gets up the nerve to make a very indecent proposal, a ghost rises from her painful past. Threatening to slam the brakes on their future before they can get it in gear.

Warning: A sexy car wash complete with lots of studs may not be enough to clean up the pages filled with massive ménage scenes starring extra-dirty mechanics.

Look for these titles by
Jayne Rylon

Now Available:

Nice and Naughty
Where There's Smoke

Men In Blue
Night is Darkest
Razor's Edge
Mistress's Master
Spread Your Wings

Powertools
Kate's Crew
Morgan's Surprise
Kayla's Gifts
Devon's Pair
Nailed to the Wall
Hammer It Home

Hot Rods
King Cobra
Mustang Sally
Super Nova
Rebel on the Run
Swinger Style

Play Doctor
Dream Machine
Healing Touch
Developing Desire

Compass Brothers
(Written with Mari Carr)
Northern Exposure
Southern Comfort
Eastern Ambitions
Western Ties

Compass Girls
(Written with Mari Carr)
Winter's Thaw
Hope Springs
Summer Fling

Print Anthologies
Three's Company
Love's Compass
Powertools
Two to Tango
Love Under Construction

Hot Rods

Jayne Rylon

Samhain Publishing, Ltd.
11821 Mason Montgomery Road, 4B
Cincinnati, OH 45249
www.samhainpublishing.com

Hot Rods
Print ISBN: 978-1-61921-963-2
King Cobra Copyright © 2014 by Jayne Rylon
Mustang Sally Copyright © 2014 by Jayne Rylon

Editing by Amy Sherwood
Cover by Angela Waters
Cover Photo by Sophia Renee

This book is a work of fiction. The names, characters, places, and incidents are products of the writer's imagination or have been used fictitiously and are not to be construed as real. Any resemblance to persons, living or dead, actual events, locale or organizations is entirely coincidental.

All Rights Are Reserved. No part of this book may be used or reproduced in any manner whatsoever without written permission, except in the case of brief quotations embodied in critical articles and reviews.

King Cobra, ISBN 978-1-61921-338-8
First Samhain Publishing, Ltd. electronic publication: April 2013
Mustang Sally, ISBN 978-1-61921-339-5
First Samhain Publishing, Ltd. electronic publication: June 2013
First Samhain Publishing, Ltd. print publication: May 2014

Contents

King Cobra
~11~

Mustang Sally
~129~

King Cobra

Dedication

For everyone who's gotten a speeding ticket.
Especially if you *really* deserved it.

Also to Ivelisse Roberts, Kim Rocha and Pilar Cruz for making sure I curse like an authentic Cuban. I love the random skills I develop as an author!

Chapter One

Eli London stared at the drop of sweat gathering on the shoulder of one of his mechanics, Alanso. He flexed his fingers around the torque wrench he'd retrieved for the man, refusing to let go and trace the path perspiration took over deceptively wiry muscles.

Inked artwork brightened as the bead dampened several tattoos. First a tribal scribble, then a portrait of Al's long-lost mom, and finally the top of an intricate cross that disappeared beneath the bunched fabric clinging around his waist. Torn and oil-stained coveralls hugged a high, tight ass.

All Eli could think of these days was that goddamned ass, which Alanso now shoved out in his direction while the bastard tuned some rich kid's engine. With hardly any effort at all, Eli could smack it. Or bite it. Or fuck it.

Son of a bitch.

Nothing good could come of this obsession. Damn his cousin Joe for putting crazy thoughts in his brain. The guy was a member of a construction crew that liked to work hard and play harder together. Their polyamorous bedroom gymnastics had become obvious when Eli and Alanso had walked in on a scene he couldn't forget. But just because that bastard had been lucky enough to find a whole team of fuck buddies his wife adored—no, loved—didn't mean such a wild arrangement could work for everybody in the world.

Eli had no right to wish for the same. Yet lately, each time he looked at the half dozen guys and girl he considered his grease monkey family, he found himself sporting a hard-on stiff enough to jack up a tank with. Thankfully, the oblivious gang hadn't identified the source of his recent frustration. Though they certainly had borne the brunt of his bad temper, adding guilt to the unslakable arousal stripping his gears, leaving him spinning his wheels.

Stuck and stranded. Alone with his dirty little secret.

Except for Alanso.

Why had that mechanic been the one to witness Joe and his crew's alternative loving along with Eli? Probably because they went most everywhere together. Eli shoved the memory of his right-hand man's right hand from his mind. Or at least he tried. The guy had tortured Eli's cock with greedy pumps of his trembling fist while the crew's foreman, Mike, demonstrated just how hot it could be to take on one of his own. By fucking Joe while the mechanics had stared, in awe of the power exchange.

Grunts had spilled from Joe's mouth, which knocked against his wife's breast as he took everything Mike gave him then begged for more. The audible decadence echoed through Eli's mind day in and day out. In perfect harmony with the memory of Alanso's answering cries as he witnessed the undeniable claiming.

Eli knew that if he slammed Alanso against the 426 inch engine block of that 1970 Dodge Challenger R/T coupe, the man would spread and welcome him.

Boss, friend...brother.

And that's where the fantasy turned to battery acid, burning Eli's insides with the bitter taste of responsibility and logic.

How could he want a guy he considered family? How could he violate that trust?

He couldn't afford to lose Alanso.

Not from his business, definitely not from his life.

So he could never seize what he craved. Frustration bubbled over.

"What's taking so long, Diaz?" Eli knocked thick, bunched biceps with the tool he carried. "We're trying to make a profit here, you know?"

Alanso couldn't seem to wipe his glare away as easily as he

rid his brow of the moisture dotting it. He snatched the wrench from Eli and returned to his task without taking the bait. If Eli couldn't fuck, the least the guy could do was give him the courtesy of engaging in a decent fight. His teeth ground together.

"You hear me, *huevón*? This isn't some charity case. Hot Rods is a business. Don't spend all day on a five-hundred-dollar job." Eli thumped the hood, knowing how the impact would reverberate.

Alanso's shoulders tensed. The clench of muscles along his spine altered the shape of his tattoos. Still, he said nothing about the low blow—or how he'd repaid the Londons a million times over for their hand-up through a solid decade of friendship and loyalty—and continued about his job. One he was damn fine at performing. No one could make an engine purr like Alanso.

"You want half-assed, go hire a motorman from the chain in town." He didn't bother to acknowledge Eli with a look.

Still, as Alanso's boss and best friend, Eli knew that tone well enough. It'd be accompanied by Al's tattooed middle finger sticking up along that wrench, he'd bet.

The defiance made Eli long to grab the other man's chin and force him to gaze up. Maybe then Alanso would see the desperation making Eli more unhinged than Mustang Sally during a particularly bad bout of PMS. God help them all.

He'd never wanted something he couldn't have so badly before. Except maybe to heal his mom during those horrid weeks she'd spent dying.

Terror and a soul-deep pain that never entirely faded turned him into something no better than a cornered animal. Eli lashed out. "Good idea. Maybe they'd spend less time checking me out and do their goddamned work."

A *clang* surprised him. He didn't quite realize what had happened until a spark flew from the metal tool where it connected with the concrete floor of the garage. Alanso had winged the thing an inch or less from Eli's thankfully steel-toed boot when he spun around.

He wouldn't have missed by accident.

"*Para el carajo!* Maybe I should've done more than look. You're obviously too hardheaded to man up and come for me. So the deal's off the table. I've wasted too much time on a dude who's in denial. You're right about that." Alanso sneered. "I'm tired of waiting for you to grow some *cojones.*"

"Keep your voice down." Eli checked over his shoulder. Kaige and Carver didn't so much as glance in their direction, but the stillness of their bodies made it clear they caught at least wisps of the conversation. Years of tough living had taught the men to tread lightly in conflict. At least until swinging a punch became necessary. Then it was likely to become a free-for-all.

"*Joder! Now* you want to shut me up. *Come mierda.*" Alanso scrubbed a hand over his bald head, leaving a streak of oil that tempted Eli to buff it away, maybe with his five o'clock shadow. "Wouldn't want the rest of the Hot Rods hearing about the good life and how we're not living it, right? They might revolt."

"Hey, I've never kept anyone against their will. You all chose to stay here. With me. The door's open." Eli waved toward the enormous rolling metal sheets that protected the garage bays at night or when the weather turned cold. Through them, the pumps of the service station his dad had started were visible.

A flash of something miserable twisted Alanso's usually smiling lips into a grimace. The gesture had Eli thinking of something other than what it would feel like to get a blowjob from the man. That was a first after weeks of studying that mouth.

He reached out, but it was too late. Alanso dodged, taking a step back and then another.

"You know what, Cobra." He grabbed his crotch hard enough to make Eli wince. "You can suck it. Or, then again... No, you can't. That fucking checkered flag has dropped, *amigo.*"

Reflex, instinct, dread—something—inspired Eli to lunge for the man who turned away. Warm, moist skin met his palm.

"Get your fucking hands off me." When the engine guru

pivoted, the unusual chill in his brown eyes froze Eli in his tracks. "You had your chance. You blew it. For us both. I'm out of here."

"You're quitting?" Eli gaped as the bottom fell out of his stomach. "Wait—"

"Hell no. I told you I'm over that bus-stop phase." Alanso sliced his hand through the air between them. His knuckles skimmed Eli's chest. They left a slash of fire across his heart. "I've got places to go and people to do. There are things I gotta learn about myself. And for the first time since we were fifteen, you're not going to be a part of that with me. Your loss."

"Shit. I-I'm sorry." Eli couldn't find a way to say what for. For violating their friendship, for wanting to destroy what they had or for acting like an ass by postponing the inevitable—he couldn't make up his mind. "Don't go."

They'd drawn a crowd. Even Roman inched closer now. The tough yet quiet guy stared openly at their spectacle. Charged air had somehow tipped off Sally too. She emerged from the painting booth, crossing the bays at an alarming rate. If she got tangled up in this, Eli would never forgive himself. Of all their gang, he knew better than to trample on her emotions. Her heart would rip in two if she had any idea of the rift opening at his feet right now.

Just like his chest was hewn.

"I'm not *leaving* leaving, Cobra." Alanso lowered his voice. "This is my home. I hope some things haven't changed. Let me know if I'm no longer welcome and I'll pack my shit. But I can't fucking do this anymore. Not for another damn minute. I have to know what it's like. To be honest about who I am and what I want. Before I lose any more respect for either of us."

"Fine then." Eli leaned forward before he could stop himself. The awful sensations sliding through his guts had to stop. Fast. Before the rest of the garage got caught in their crossfire. He shoved Alanso hard enough the man stumbled across the threshold before catching his balance. It felt like forcing a baby bird from the nest. He only hoped Al spread his wings fast enough. "Get the hell out. Do what you gotta do."

17

Alanso mouthed a plea out of sight of the guys now wiping hands on coveralls and milling near in a semi-circle. "Come with me."

Eli slammed his fist on the big red button on the doorframe beside him. With an ominous rattle, the metal door began to lower between them, severing all communication as completely as if the aluminum were a drawbridge over a monster-filled moat.

The scream of a crotch rocket taking off at an unwise speed ricocheted through their space. Gravel *pinged* when it slung against the barrier he'd erected.

"What the fuck did you do to him, Cobra?" Sally canted her head as she laid into Eli. "You've really been acting like a snake lately, ever since Dave's accident. Hissing at anyone who comes near. We get that you're afraid of losing people important to you. The crew's near miss seems to have scared you stupid. I get it, I do."

He closed his eyes, trying to block out the concern she voiced for all the rest of the guys staring at him.

"But keep going like you are and you'll drive him away."

"Stop talking, *Salome.*" He knew better than to tell her to shut up, even if she didn't understand how her insight cut him. Hopefully using her full name would be enough to convey how serious he was. He couldn't dive into the details.

No way could he admit what he and Alanso had seen. What they'd done.

"You better not have let your fear hurt him. Tell me you didn't." Her emerald eyes begged much more softly than her steely tone.

Eli didn't bother to lie.

The hand she let fly didn't catch him by surprise. She loved Alanso. They all did.

Which was why he didn't bother to duck. He deserved the stinging impact of her open palm on his cheek. That and more. Because even as his head whipped to the side, he admired the stretch of her petite frame when she stood on her tiptoes, her raven hair and the glint of her fancy-painted fingernails, one of her pride and joys.

If he'd only wanted Alanso, maybe the two of them could have explored the possibility. But he was going to hell because he lusted after all of the Hot Rods.

The gang held their collective breath, waiting to see how he would react to Sally's uncharacteristic act of violence. Roman stiffened, prepared to spring to her defense.

All the fight leeched out of Eli.

No matter how bad it got, they didn't have to be afraid he'd attack one of their own. Then again, hadn't he done just that?

The damage he'd wrought would be far worse than the impact of a fist.

His shoulders dropped and his head hung. "I'll get him back."

"You'd fucking better." Mustang Sally shook her hand before propping it on her hip and pointing to the door. "Don't come home without him."

The five remaining guys closed rank around their littlest member. They knew she'd hate for Eli to see her tears or her alarm. He didn't waste any time offering comfort she wouldn't welcome. Kaige, Carver, Holden, Roman and Bryce would take good care of her.

They didn't need him.

But Alanso might.

Chapter Two

Eli punched one of the three metal supports on his Shelby Cobra's steering wheel. The solid construction of the original part ensured it wouldn't bend beneath his punishment. It hurt the hell out of his knuckles, though. Pain obscured some of the alarm bubbling through his gut.

This was the last of the bars in a twenty-mile radius of the Hot Rods garage. Alanso's current crotch rocket—a Honda REPSOL 600RR with a ridiculous #69 racing decal—was nowhere in sight. The neon orange body and wheels would have been impossible to miss, even at night.

He'd hoped to sit shoulder to shoulder with his best friend and drown their sorrows together. Then they could have called Sally to pick them up and things would have been back to normal by the time they commiserated over their killer hangovers in the morning.

Wasn't much a bottle of Southern Comfort mixed with a few drops of cola couldn't fix. At least, that's how they'd gotten through most of life's disappointments in the past.

Well, once they'd been old enough. Or bold enough to sneak some of Roman's stash. The guy was four years older than Eli and had a couple more on Alanso. They'd roped him into the group when he'd been twenty-going-on-forty. He'd spent so much time wasted he'd never seemed to mind picking them up an extra bottle from the liquor store.

Eli's dad, Tom London, had reined in Roman and the rest of the Hot Rods, never letting their habits get them in too much trouble. He'd walked a fine line, mentoring the damaged kids while allowing them to make their own mistakes. Somehow he'd managed to keep from scaring them away from the safe haven he'd created as a legacy to his late wife, despite his own often-crippling agony.

Hell, more than once Tom had decided if he couldn't beat 'em, he should join 'em and put down his fair share of liquid fire, bonding them closer with every drink. It might not have been a recommended approach by *Parenting* magazine, but it worked for them.

And now Eli had jeopardized one of their own.

He squeezed the chrome knob on top of his shifter, out of ideas. All but one.

It was a long shot, but he had nowhere else to turn.

Parking at the far edge of the lot, away from people or other cars, he withdrew his phone from the pocket of his jeans. To extricate the device he had to lift up slightly in the leather bucket seat of his restored Shelby Cobra. Damn Salome and her fashion advice. Hot or not, these jeans didn't leave a lot of room to maneuver. Plus, he felt like he might display some coin slot when he bent over in the low-rise denim. Being a typical mechanic didn't suit his style.

He cursed as he wriggled.

By the time he swiped open his contact list, he grimaced. Confessing his stupidity wouldn't be easy. He gritted his teeth and poked the icon of his cousin Joe smiling like a lunatic next to his gorgeous wife, who cradled their son.

The picture was a few months old. Eli took a second to wonder at how much the little guy had grown in even that short period of time. Like a weed, and bulkier every day. Hopefully the kid liked football. It'd be a shame to waste a build like that. They had a pretty good idea of how gargantuan he'd turn out to be.

After all, their friend Dave was the largest of Joe's crewmates. Considering baby Nathan's dove gray eyes and the shade of his dark hair—which exactly matched his honorary uncle's mop—it was pretty clear who'd contributed the winning swimmer to the crew's effort to give Morgan a baby when Joe hadn't been able.

The crew had survived some serious issues, navigating

tricky waters. Nothing had been handed to them on a silver platter. Maybe Eli should pull his head out of his ass and quit moping long enough to formulate a roadmap to his dream destination.

Lost in thought, it wasn't until the third ring that Eli considered the time. *Fuck!*

They'd been working the later hours their customers loved when Alanso had split. It had to be... A glance at his watch confirmed—after eleven o'clock. Add another hour for the time difference and he winced.

About to hang up, Eli jumped when Joe's voice came across the line.

"Hey." His cousin's answer sounded a little gruff.

In the background, a baby cried.

"Oh shit, sorry." Eli let his head fall back against the leather rest. "I didn't think about how late it is. Did I wake Nathan up?"

"Nah. He's being fussy tonight. The last few days, actually." Joe groaned. "It's not like him. He's usually so quiet, perfect. It's making Morgan nervous that he's not feeling well. Kay and Dave are here too, calming us down. Or trying, at least. Their theory is Nathan's getting his first tooth. Dave said his little sisters got theirs around six months too."

"Ah, damn. I'm sorry to hear that." Eli ran his hand through his short hair. "I'll let you get back to your family, then."

"Honestly, I'll give you ten bucks if you don't." Joe sighed. "I need a minute to myself. Besides, you *are* family."

"If you're sure—"

"Don't make me beg, asshole." His cousin raised his voice a bit. "Hey guys, it's Eli. I'm going to step out on the landing for a few."

"King Cobra!" Dave rumbled a hello while two feminine greetings mingled in the background. "Hey Nathmeister, tell Uncle Eli his truck's running great."

"Of course it is. We don't build shit at Hot Rods." And

Alanso had personally attended to every detail of the project after *that* night. The night they'd seen how badly Dave's injury impacted the rest of his crew. The night they'd watched the guys and their female soul mates comfort each other in their friend's absence.

"Are you going to pay his speeding tickets too, Cobra?" Kayla sounded half-annoyed, but even the chastisement couldn't hide her affection for her husband. Not since a freak accident had nearly stolen him from her.

"I can't be held responsible for his actions. Though I heartily approve." His soul lightened in seconds. *Tough times are temporary.* That's what he'd always told himself and the rest of the Hot Rods when someone had a bad night.

"All right, Eli. I'm heading outside." The ambient sounds got less amplified. "You're off speaker. What's up?"

"Maybe I called to see how you're doing." It didn't seem fair to add to Joe's burdens.

"Eh, we'll be fine. It's just the joys of parenthood. Thank God for the crew. I don't know how Mo and I would do this alone. We're spoiled, I know. Stronger together in the group. But even still it's a lot sometimes." Joe paused. "It's a ton of responsibility to care for another person. An innocent. Seeing Kate and Mike going through the same helps some. Hell, Mike carries all of us on his shoulders sometimes, like you do for your gang. But every once in a while I have to take a step back or I'll drive myself nuts, you know?"

"Of course. You worry so much because you love them." Eli was suddenly glad he'd reached out tonight. He should do it more often. For both their sakes. Why couldn't the crew live closer? "If you didn't you wouldn't deserve them. We both know the world isn't always perfect. Shitty things happen to good people. Look at Dave."

"And your mom," Joe's voice was low, but it carried across the two states between them.

"Yeah." Eli silently added Alanso to that list as well. He had to make this right.

"When I think back on that summer—" Joe didn't need to

spell out which one. Eli would remember it for the rest of his life. In grotesque detail. "It's still not quite real to me. Sort of like a movie. I can see myself, you, your dad. Like zombies. Staggering around, trying to figure out how to make it to the next day and the next. And then the shit with Dave last year... Well, it made me not want to fuck around ever. I tell my family, all of them, how much I love them. Every day. I'm terrified of losing them."

"I hear you. The ache never goes away." Eli rubbed his chest. "But what can you do? Lock yourself out of life to spare yourself the pain?"

"Personally, I wouldn't advocate that plan, no." His cousin bit the statement off.

"Am I missing something here? We're talking about you, right?" Narrowing his eyes, Eli stared into the darkness.

"Not anymore." A sardonic chuckle rang across the airwaves. "You do realize Alanso's been videochatting with us a lot—almost every night for the past month now, right? Hell, I think him and James talk more than a couple of teenage girls."

"What?" Eli sat up straighter. "Why?"

"I'd assume because his best fucking friend is making him uncomfortable with sharing too much. Or maybe refuses to discuss certain issues at all. Probably because the one guy he should be able to trust with his insecurities and hopes seems to have forgotten that not everyone gets a tomorrow. And there's no going back."

"Son of a bitch!" Eli's heart pounded as he took the lashing from his cousin. Sickness washed over him as he recalled the last time he'd seen his mother. Surrounded by flowers from the uncounted people she'd helped in her social work, she'd cautioned him to always lead with his heart before slipping peacefully from the world.

Would she respect him for keeping his hands off the guy he was closer to than a brother? Or would she shake her head at his callous treatment of another human being? Deep down, he knew the answer. Failing her shredded his insides.

"Even Kate said she's disappointed in you, Cobra."

Refusing to pull his punches, Joe let him have it. "Are you that fucking scared?"

First Sally, now Joe. Screw them. "I'm not—"

"Yeah, you are." A snarl from the usually laidback man surprised Eli. When Joe broke their mutual silence, he spoke with a hell of a lot more kindness. Eli might have preferred poison to the pity he sensed now. "You don't have to lie to me. I was there. I know what it did to you when your mom died. But I'm telling you now, you're making a mistake. If you don't fix this, you'll be saying goodbye to Alanso too."

"Fine. I hear you." The phone trembled in his hold. "I just don't see how this can work. If I fuck it up, he'll leave. We won't have even what we do now. How can I take that chance?"

"He can't settle for friends without lying to himself. Hell, to you both. Don't make him do that. He won't last. Neither of you will."

"But Joe..."

"What, E?"

A deep breath delayed his response. "It's not just Alanso. I want what you have. Fucker."

Joe laughed. "I don't blame you. And I think you've got a shot. I remember those stories you told about the wild nights some of the guys have had. They're open to unconventional. Plus, you know your Hot Rods. Deep in your gut, you understand what they need. I can't imagine how your pasts affect you individually, let alone together, but I gotta think you wouldn't have stuck together so long if you didn't rely on that bond to make it through."

"Yeah, the Island of Misfit Mechanics. That's us. So how the fuck do I deal with seven guys and one chick in some crazy-ass relationship? I've never even had a steady girlfriend for Christ's sake." He might grow his hair longer just so he could pull it out. He had a feeling he might find the option handy in the coming months.

"I'd recommend starting slow. Walk before you run and all that shit. Go get Alanso out of that hellhole. Make things right with him. In the crew, it all began with Neil and James. They showed us what we were missing. It didn't take long to catch on, though. Start the fire, Eli. Let it burn."

"Wait." Hope rose in his soul. "You know where Alanso is?"

"I might." Joe laughed. "Depending on if you're going to keep being a toolbox or not."

"You said 'hellhole'." No more kidding for Eli. "Is he in trouble? Damn it! Don't fuck around if he is."

"Nothing he can't handle…probably." A hint of unease colored Joe's statement. "Promise you won't march in there and drag him out just because you think it's the right thing for him. He didn't make this decision lightly. You have to support him. As long as he's not being hurt, you can't get your tighty-whiteys all in a bunch over his little experiment after you refused to play along."

"You mean there's a chance he *is* being hurt?" Eli pinched the bridge of his nose. "What the fuck, Joe? You know I'd do anything for my guys. And Mustang Sally. Tell me where he is. I'll go to him. I'll…try."

"About the best we could hope for, I suppose." A door shutting was followed by Nathan's sobs. They'd slowed and muted but hadn't disappeared entirely. Eli could relate. "Mo, what's the name of the park I wrote down over there?"

A *park*? What the fuck—?

"Chestnut Grove." Eli didn't hesitate. He fired up the engine with a flick of his wrist and slammed the shifter into reverse. "He went to a pick-up spot? Sex with strangers? Jesus."

Morgan echoed the name, confirming his fears.

"Go gentle on him." Kayla called in the background. "He needs you."

"You've got this, King Cobra." Dave added his support.

"We love you," Morgan called.

"And so does Alanso," Joe added. "Don't let him down tonight."

"It's going to take me at least twenty minutes to get there. He left hours ago. What if I'm too late? What if someone's taking advantage of him?" Eli fishtailed as he zipped onto the road and gunned it.

"More likely he's having a helluva good time." The smile coloring Joe's tone faded a bit. "But just in case, maybe you'd better drive it like you stole it."

"I got that." Eli short-shifted into fourth and pressed the pedal to the floor. His Cobra cornered like a champ on the new suspension Kaige had installed last week.

"Right. So time to hang up. Keep calm, lead with your heart and have fun." Joe's smile rang through his tone. "Call us when you can, so we know you're both all right and we can say we told you so."

"Hey, Joe." His cousin surely expected an insult. "In case this is *my* last day...I love you too. Thanks."

He disconnected the call, tossed his phone onto the passenger seat and watched the speedometer climb.

Chapter Three

"You like what you see?"

Alanso checked over his shoulder to confirm the older Latino dude wearing lots of chains had actually intended for him to answer. He thought he'd lurked far enough in the shadows to escape notice.

Maybe he'd made a sound when a couple of the younger guys milling around had approached, scuffling for the honor of kneeling at the man's feet. Each guy offered his mouth to give the bear one hell of a lube job.

Gracious, the guy welcomed them both. With a hand on each of their heads, he drew them closer to his crotch even as he smiled at Alanso.

"Yeah. I'm talking to you, baldy." His laugh held a bit of an edge. "You know it's pitchblack out here. You can lose the pretty sunglasses. Unless you're famous and wandered into 'Nut Grove by accident. Afraid people'll recognize you?"

Alanso shook his head.

"You aren't married, are you? I don't screw around on people's promises. You'll find some here that do if that's your thing. Somebody for everybody pretty much. Not us, though."

"Nah. Nothing like that." Alanso peeled his shades off and tucked one of the arms into the V of his white T-shirt. He liked the way his tattoos showed through the thin cotton. Each inked symbol helped keep him focused on a life motto, lent him strength or illustrated a badge of courage he'd earned.

He rubbed his thumb back and forth over the *R* on his right index finger—part of the Hot Rods label he'd indelibly inscribed on his body. A car drove across his left pinky followed by one letter on each finger, a permanent reminder of the group that had imprinted themselves on his soul.

Tonight, for the first time in over a decade, he embarked on a journey without one of his garagemates. He frowned and rubbed the marking faster.

He'd survived some rough times before stumbling across Eli and his dad at the youth center. As a child he'd drifted from couch to couch owned by gracious members of his Cuban-American extended family until he realized how he burdened families with enough mouths of their own to feed. After that, he'd survived on the streets in gangs of transient teens—most of them orphaned by deported parents—not so different from himself. Except that crime didn't appeal to him as a profession.

Still, he hadn't had to watch his own back in long enough that he felt soft. But he could hold his own. The knife in his pocket was a last resort kind of insurance. His brawling skills would probably render the precaution unnecessary.

"Quit biting that lip and get your sexy *culo* over here. Phil and Ronnie will make room for you, won't you, boys?" The top knocked his boot into the sides of their knees, urging them apart.

The guys must have liked the way the ringleader's cock tasted because they didn't stop licking it long enough to complain about sharing the adequate, but not overly impressive, hard-on. Alanso imagined they were as desperate as he was, waiting for their bimonthly clandestine fix.

He'd heard rumors about this place and the things that happened on a random night every couple of weeks. Luck had been in his favor when he'd overheard some guys passing the news of the next date while he'd used a bar bathroom a few days ago. Adrenaline had run rampant through his system since. Could he go through with a visit?

Excitement and a little bit of terror had left him no choice but to check it out. He worried this could become a habit.

He had every kind of intimacy with the Hot Rods he could want—love, laughter, shared pain, pride in their workmanship. All but one. Sexual. He couldn't do without that final gear anymore. Riding shotgun while they stalked women had quit being fun when he admitted to himself that none of the garage bunnies who threw themselves at Middletown's infamous bad boys stacked up to Sally. And that was even before his eyes had opened to other possibilities.

Hopeless ones.

King Cobra would never let him risk their friendship—his and Eli's, theirs and Sally's or the various combinations of the larger group—on a romp. Despite the fact that some of the guys had teamed up before, it'd always been a fling, nothing serious. Definitely not a relationship like the crew had built. That was risky. If something went wrong it could tear them apart. So he stalled.

As much as Alanso wanted both Eli and Sally, he couldn't stop dreaming about the complex polyamorous relationship he'd witnessed thriving in the crew. And if he couldn't have that unbound wild love with his gang, he at least had to know if his recent distaste for a night of no-strings fucking had to do with the gender of his mattress buddies.

So why couldn't he force his boots to unglue from the matted grass?

"I'm not sure sharing is my thing." *Liar!* His brain shouted at him, knowing full well that if the trio on display before him were Cobra, Kaige and Bryce—or any other combination of Hot Rods—he'd skid across the mostly cleared area beneath the makeshift pavilion like a World Series player stealing home.

"Trying to play it cool, are you?" The man jerked his chin in Alanso's direction. "I can spot that bulge from here, even in this shitty light. Impressive for a Mexican."

"*Pendejo*, I'm Cuban." Alanso tried to keep from letting this fucker get his hackles up. That wasn't the part of either of them he cared to rouse tonight.

"No kidding." The guy rolled his eyes. "Your accent is pretty distinct. My grandmother's from Matanzas. But I did get you to come closer, didn't I?"

"I don't have an accent." He tipped his head.

One of the guys—Ronnie, he thought—still sucking away,

choked, as if on a laugh.

Alanso glared at him.

"Hey now. We're an equal opportunity kind of gathering here." The guy smiled a bit, his face starting to relax as the men teasing him proved they were good at what they did. Maybe they'd teach Alanso a thing or two. "Come on, kid. I'm not going to last forever. Take what you want. At least let me get a better look at you while I cream their faces."

The top grunted. The guys at his feet braced his thighs.

Alanso swallowed hard and glanced away.

White Christmas lights decorated the stand of trees that sheltered like-minded men who had nowhere else to turn for what they needed. It was almost romantic and utterly heartbreaking simultaneously. He wished his first intentional male-on-male experience could have happened somewhere he felt more comfortable.

Like maybe Eli's desk in the garage office or up against a stack of tires.

He didn't count the day he'd actually touched the person he wanted most. Okay, fine, *one* of the people. Damn Joe and the crew for poisoning his brain with dirty possibilities. They'd guaranteed he was unsatisfied with anything short of a tender gangbang. Meanwhile, Eli had obviously been too shocked to listen to his better fucking judgment in the heat of the moment, but he'd snapped into shape as soon as they'd hit the highway toward home. Refusing to talk about what'd happened, he had slammed the door on any relapses.

At least Alanso had experienced heaven once. The memory of Eli's moans—and the heat of his come pouring over the Hot Rods tattoos on Alanso's knuckles—would fill his mind as he fooled around with another man tonight. His imagination was strong enough to superimpose the crucial details over his make-do experience.

Vivid enough they'd drive him to ecstasy or at least action.

Going home without having taken his bisexuality for a test drive was not an option. Sure, he liked fooling around with women plenty. But now that he admitted to himself he'd always been kind of curious about men, he felt like he'd starved that part of him for far too long. The pussy he'd scored since the eye-opening round with the crew just hadn't satisfied him.

The urge to fuck—to be fucked—had grown in him until it hurt.

And Eli hadn't been there to take away the ache this time.

No more.

But he could use some help getting started. He hadn't dared stop for a fortifying drink. Not when he was riding his motorcycle, and definitely not when he was flying solo over new territory. "Look, I—uh, I've *mostly* never done this before."

"Sure you haven't." The guy snorted. "It's been my first time every other week for the last decade too."

So long in a meaningless cycle. Why hadn't this guy found a lover? One he could take in the light of day? Was Alanso doomed to hiding in the shadows if he did this tonight? No, it was just a trial. A way to find out what he really wanted before he gambled with bigger stakes.

"I thought I could watch this time around." And if it got him hot enough, maybe he'd do a little taste testing of his own.

"Sorry, kid. That's not how it works. No play, no stay." The veteran shrugged somewhat apologetically. "Otherwise, how do we know you're not going to narc on us? Or take incriminating pictures or some shit? Get dirty like we do or go back to momma."

"That *puta* left me behind years ago." He slipped his fingers through his belt loops to keep from stroking the tattoo of her on his shoulder. "Kicked out of the country. Sent back to Havana. Couldn't be bothered to lug a brat with her."

Why the hell was he telling a stranger that?

One of the cuties, Phil, manipulating the standing guy paused. He pressed a kiss to the side of the ultra-stiff shaft in his fist and peeked up at Alanso. "No one's rejecting you tonight. Come over here."

Alanso clenched his jaw and nodded once. "Maybe."

The second man on his knees lifted his head and winked up at the guy he serviced. "He's cute. Can we keep the new guy, Links?"

"It's up to him." Links held out his hand as his playthings adjusted their places. Chains rattled as they brushed against his cargo pants. "You want to play with us, *cariño*?"

"I think I do. Yeah." Alanso scrunched his eyes closed a moment before stepping forward. He hadn't realized he'd crossed the space until one of the men pressed his palms to Alanso's thighs.

"We'll go easy on you." He nuzzled the crotch of Alanso's jeans. The deep breath Ronnie drew made him self-conscious for not making a pit stop at the apartment above Hot Rods, which he shared with the rest of his garagemates, to change before heading out. Had he hesitated, even for a moment, he wouldn't have been able to go through with this. As it was, he'd driven around for hours before pointing his bike in this direction.

"I'm pretty sure I'd prefer it if you didn't." He held out his hand, feeling ridiculous. "I'm Al."

"A pleasure." Phil smiled while Ronnie growled and tugged the waist of Alanso's jeans.

"Help us with Links. Or get your peeking in while we work. I'm suddenly hungry for dessert."

Alanso allowed his knees to collapse. A puff of dirt rose around him. His shoulders bumped into the guys now flanking him. The heat they radiated was welcome.

"Ain't that a pretty sight?" Links thrust his hips forward, rubbing his cock over Phil's cheek before presenting his tool to Alanso. "Go ahead. Try it. You might like it."

"That's what I'm afraid of." He looked inward, measured the pulse of excitement flooding his veins and decided this was it.

Time to find out once and for all.

"One thing...I'm doing this the safe way or not at all." Alanso wouldn't budge on that requirement. If he ever did get another shot with Eli, or Sally, or any of the other guys, he refused to put them in danger.

"Damn, I'd like to be in your mouth bare. But I get you don't know us. Yet." Links dug in his pocket and withdrew a couple of condoms. "Mint or cherry?"

"Go for the mint," Phil advised. "It's like brushing your teeth. Covers up the rubber taste."

He nodded.

Links ripped the foil and sheathed himself so fast Alanso figured he'd done it a million times before. The guys beside him each wrapped an arm around his waist, drawing him into their fold. They helped him lean forward despite the pebbles gouging his knees. Links brushed the pad of his thumb over Alanso's lips, triggering his reflexive opening.

The three men fed him his first taste of male flesh.

His eyes went wide, and his gaze locked on Links'.

"Mmm, you like that? Yeah. I knew you would." The guy splayed his fingers on Alanso's bald head and rubbed the shiny surface of his scalp.

Alanso weighed the plump, if not huge, cock on his tongue. He suckled lightly, then a bit harder. It felt nice in his mouth. Warm, firm and full. His eyes drifted closed as he went for another nibble.

"You're fucking hot. A waste to never have had this mouth fucked before."

The guy was getting into it now. Really.

"Enjoy while you can, Al," Ronnie cheered him on. "Links is close already. We got him good and riled for you. Maybe next time you'll taste him. A little sweaty, a little salty."

"Shit, Phil." Ronnie ground against Alanso's left side, prodding his hip with a thick shaft encased in denim. "Cut that out or you're going to make me come in my pants again."

"I have a feeling we'll both be up for more than one round after this." He smiled at his friend.

"Probably true." The guy practically vibrated where they fused together.

Alanso could relate. His tongue lapped along the coated

underside of Links' erection, making him half-freak-out and half-celebrate. He was doing it. Really doing it. And *coño*, it felt good. Right.

Almost perfect.

Alanso relaxed his jaw, permitting himself to take Links farther into his mouth. He didn't stop until the head of the guy's cock stabbed the back of his throat and he choked. The men on either side of him pulled him off.

"Don't get all crazy now, Al." Phil rubbed his shoulders. "You'll have plenty of chances to practice if you want them. Go slow tonight. Enjoy this."

He moaned. The vibration had Links' cock jerking on the tip of his tongue. He craned his neck and sucked harder.

"Careful. Teeth," the guy panted.

Alanso thought of all the sloppy BJs he'd had from too-drunk chicks and tried to focus. When he did, he swirled his tongue around the ridges made by the veins now standing out on Links' shaft. He worked up the length, learning the textures and shapes along the way until he got to the plump head.

Alanso closed his lips around the tip of Links' cock and suckled. He flicked his tongue through the indentation made by the slit at the top, smearing superslick precome from the divot onto the reservoir of the condom. A shiver ran down his spine as he imagined the bulge filling with seed.

"Goddamn," Links growled.

"He's a natural." Phil patted Alanso's ass.

"Go ahead. Take him deeper. Slow this time," Ronnie coached him. "Be ready. You probably won't get far before he goes off."

The four men braced each other in a ring, each of them fully engaged in the moment.

Alanso felt part of something…bigger…than his simple arousal.

What if it were Carver, Holden and Eli sharing the moment with him? Sally and Roman? Bryce? Kaige? Something this powerful would forge an unbreakable bond. He'd never have to worry about losing them again. Not like his mom.

Desperation forced him to suck harder than intended. He sealed Links' fate.

"Oh shit, yeah." The man's fingers dug into Alanso's shoulders. The tiny pain was welcome.

"Keep going," Phil encouraged. "Drain him dry."

His throat flexed as Links shouted and squirmed. The minty cock in his mouth swelled then jerked as Alanso's first satisfied customer filled his condom with a thick load. For Alanso. He'd pleased a man. An experienced, kind of jaded guy.

Phil tapped his chin. "Okay, Al. Let him go. He's spent."

He opened his mouth. A whimper escaped along with limp flesh when Links' cock slipped free. Alanso's hand flew to his jeans and ripped them open before jamming his fist inside.

"Oh hell no." Ronnie tugged his wrist.

Alanso nearly decked the man. He could come with a few good jerks.

Links hit the dirt on his knees just as Phil and his partner colluded to shove Alanso backward. He fell to the ground, his shoulders slamming into the clearing. For one tiny second, fear shriveled his balls.

"Shh. Nothing to fight here, Al." Phil held him down gently. Alanso could have broken the hold at any time. "Let us take care of you like you deserve."

"Me?" He hadn't considered that.

"Yeah." Phil grinned, a wolf's smile. "It's your turn."

Chapter Four

Eli balled his fists to keep from charging into the clearing and taking a swing at the men who dared to put their hands on his best friend. But Joe's warning rang in his mind. He had no right to interfere. He'd rejected Alanso's advances. Given up the chance to be the man reveling in the seduction of Al's innocent mouth on his cock.

What a fucking moron.

Except he wouldn't have worn some nasty fucking condom. Alanso knew where he'd been. Hell, they'd been there together most of the time.

Jealousy burned through him, nearly as hot and bright as desire.

About the time Alanso really got into his amazing-looking blowjob, Eli unknitted his zipper and withdrew his cock. He took himself in hand, stroking in time to the uneven lunges of Alanso's mouth on the guy they'd called Links' shaft. The flex and play of muscles around the edges of Alanso's T-shirt only fired him up more.

Eli wished he could feel the strength there as Alanso submitted to him. Not because he had some sick urge to lord over the guy. But because he had waited so long for Alanso to trust that his friends would always care for him, wounded or not. Once and for all, maybe he'd believe that none of his friends would ever choose to leave him behind.

Yet, in some ways, wasn't that exactly what he'd done by refusing to walk beside his best friend on this journey?

His cock wilted for a split second until Alanso's science project lost his control. The man broke, grabbing Al's head and anchoring him in place as he rode the open, succulent mouth in front of him and shot his come into the condom in spasm after spasm of what looked like a world-class orgasm.

Eli half-expected the guy to drop dead on the spot.

He wanted to hate the bastard. But he was thankful that Links had given Alanso what he needed when Eli couldn't. That the stranger had respected Al, taking pleasure while giving plenty in return. Fuck them.

All three of the apparent regulars now hovered around Alanso. His cheeks were darker than usual, a flush on his tan skin, and his chest rose and fell rapidly. The nice one, Phil, petted Alanso as if he were a stray dog to be tamed. Meanwhile, his accomplice shimmied those hot-as-hell jeans then a pair of bright yellow-and-black boxer briefs over Al's trim hips and down his powerful thighs.

Eli leaned against a tree so he wouldn't crash to the forest floor at the sight of Alanso's dick, rock-hard. Sure, they'd shaken the ketchup bottle together plenty of times as teenagers. All of the Hot Rods except Sally had whipped it out periodically during those hormone-laden years when Roman would bring home a porno or one of the other guys had gotten lucky in the storeroom of the garage.

But he swore he didn't remember Alanso's cock looking like that.

It shamed Eli that he hadn't noticed the heft and impressive girth of Alanso's hard-on when he'd clasped it in his fist the day they'd discovered just how close the crew really was. To be honest, he'd been too mesmerized by Mike fucking Joe and overwhelmed by the possibilities to take it all in.

Plus, if he'd allowed himself to concentrate on Alanso's cock spewing all over his hand, he never could have returned to normal once they'd left the fantasyland of their mutual masturbation and returned to the garage. *Fuck.* Had he gotten this entirely wrong from the start?

Maybe he should have done exactly the opposite.

Months and months of torture could have been alleviated for them both.

Because Eli knew as he watched the three men in the grove undress Alanso—slowly yet deliberately—that he would have to do the same someday before he died. Or he'd regret it with every breath he took.

Bronze skin coated in a light sheen of perspiration glinted in the twinkling lights wrapped through the bushes. Alanso looked like a sacrifice staked out on the turf. Or maybe a god surrounded by devotees.

Eli could understand.

He leaned forward as Phil dropped down to tease Alanso's beaded nipple and the stainless steel barbell running through it. Eli had imagined doing that no less than a thousand times and could almost guess what the heated metal would feel like on his tongue. Or against the back of his teeth as he tugged lightly on the embedded adornment.

Links tucked himself into his pants and unclipped a length of chain from one of a dozen pockets.

Eli tensed, preparing to tear all three of the fuckers limb from limb if they so much as hurt one of the nonexistent hairs on Alanso's head. Instead of anything sinister, Links let the length fall, heavy, onto Alanso's biceps then drew it upward until it draped over his wrist. The implication of restraint was all that was required.

"Stay still, *cariño*. Let my boys treat you nice."

As if the chain weighed a ton, Alanso obeyed, not moving a fraction of an inch. To see the fiery man yield made Eli's dick drip. Slickness eased the shuttling of his fist over his length. Too much of that and he'd shoot all over the weeds at his feet before they'd even gotten to the juicy shit.

"Come on," he whispered.

Alanso's hips lifted, begging for something he likely didn't understand. Links had no trouble diagnosing a case of unrequited desire. "Phil, put your hand on his cock. Squeeze him nice and tight. You can stroke him a little. Don't you dare get him off yet."

"Yes, sir." The dude seemed to enjoy taking orders as much

as he would relish being the recipient of the prescribed treatment. Eli's cock leaked, the droplet splashing into the soil.

"And Ronnie, push those legs wide as they'll go, considering our slut still has his pants around his ankles and those hot fucking motorcycle boots on. I bet you really ride, don't you?"

Alanso nodded. His eyes scrunched closed as his new cohorts assaulted him with pleasure. Knees splayed, soles of his feet touching, he gave them plenty of room to operate.

"That's it." Links tweaked Alanso's other nipple before returning his hand to Al's head and stroking him lightly enough to belie his gruff commands. "Now, Ronnie, get your face in those balls. Don't be prissy either. Fucking slather them with your tongue. Soak him. Let your spit run down his crack. Get his hole nice and drenched."

Eli thought someone had knocked the wind from him. What if they tried to fuck Alanso? Was he ready for that? Would they hurt him?

Could Eli stand by and watch them penetrate his best friend?

Something in him roared. That right should have been his.

Except he'd wasted the opportunity.

If he could do it all over...

Alanso writhed when Ronnie slurped his sac into his mouth and pulled lightly. Phil's fingers rhythmically squeezed and released Alanso's cock, teasing the bottom of his fat head.

From his outpost, Eli could detect the flaring of Alanso's nostrils. A tiny smear of blood emerged on his lip when he gnawed a section between his teeth. Probably trying his damnedest not to shoot.

Phil took it upon himself to nuzzle Alanso's belly. The chiseled abs couldn't have provided much pillow for the slender man's cheek. He watched up close and personal as his buddy followed instructions. Ronnie buried his nose beneath Alanso's heavy *cojones*. He went to town on the sensitive spot between the delicate orbs and Al's ass.

In the moonlight, Eli watched saliva drip toward the

shadows between Alanso's thighs. He imagined the impromptu lube coating his rear entrance.

"Just do it already," Alanso barked.

The desperation in his directive startled Eli. Who could resist that invitation? Apparently, he had. What a fucking idiot. Why had he done that again?

He swore he couldn't remember a valid fucking reason.

Not one.

But he'd had so many.

Hadn't he?

Shit, this was bad.

"You're not ready to be fucked." Links squashed the flicker of hope in Ronnie's eyes. He almost seemed to glance in the direction of Eli's hiding spot. King Cobra froze, his hand grinding to a halt on his cock.

Until the older man returned his laser intensity to the guys he orchestrated once more.

"Don't tell me what I can take." Alanso practically spit at them. "I've had enough of other peoples' judgments on my sex life. If I say I want to be fucked, that's what I want. What does a guy have to do to get a dick in his ass? *Me cago en diez!* Doesn't anyone want me?"

Eli tipped forward. The hand not cradling his erection landed on his knee for support.

The plea sliced through his guts like a rusty knife.

He deserved a thousand more cuts if he'd inflicted that clear pain on Alanso without even realizing it. Of course that's what Alanso would assume. That he was unwanted. Again. Shit. Fuck. Damn.

"You come back in two weeks, you'll have all the cock you can handle. Including mine." Links shook Alanso's shoulder. "*After* you've worn a plug a few days and maybe tried a smaller toy. No way am I letting your first time rip you up so you decide you don't like it. Sorry, *cariño*. You're going to have to settle for Ronnie's finger tonight."

"Argh. Fine. Fuck. Something. Whatever. Now. Please."

Alanso had abandoned all semblance of grace. Raw desire ripped through the glade. The threat of a forest fire was high as he scorched everything, and everyone, around him with his passion.

"A little treat to warm you up." A smile tipped up one corner of Links' mouth. "Ronnie is great with his tongue."

"Down there?" Alanso's eyes widened.

Eli would have chuckled if he weren't so afraid of ruining the moment or causing an accidental misfire. Riding the edge of arousal, he couldn't take much more stimulation. The sights and sounds were nearly enough alone.

"You have no idea..." Phil petted Alanso, keeping him mostly in place when Ronnie's tongue licked a path from his balls to his ass.

"*Dios Mío! Dios! Dios!*" To hell with stealth. The park rang with Alanso's prayers. For more, Eli was sure.

Moist slurps accompanied the stream of mangled Spanish spilling from the guy who surrendered to his fantasies. So fast and furious, Eli couldn't keep up. He got the gist of the litany as Ronnie wiggled his face between those tight cheeks.

"I can feel him getting harder, Links." Phil paused his manipulation of Alanso's cock. The skin there had passed blush and moved on to an almost-painful-looking purple. "Don't disappoint him. He's not going to make it much longer."

"Go ahead." The man nodded to Ronnie. "Work your pinky in him."

"No. Bigger." Alanso gasped.

"Fine. You stubborn little *maricón*." Links shook his head with an affectionate grin on his face. "Give him your middle finger, Ronnie."

Alanso grunted when the man between his legs wasted no time in complying. A hiss escaped his clenched jaw and the white teeth he bared.

"Take it." Links didn't cut him any slack. "You're going to get what you wanted. And then some, I think."

There it was again, a peek in Eli's direction. *Shit!*

Stopping then would have been impossible. He choked up on his cock and refused to break his stare. Not from Links and certainly not from the gorgeous sight of Alanso's awakening.

"Damn, he's tight." Ronnie grunted. "Been a long time since I had an ass like that."

"Hey." Phil shot him a glare.

"No worries, I like your ass plenty." He beamed up at his partner. "In fact, I'm about to show you how much. Give me two minutes."

"More like thirty seconds," Links amended.

"If that." Phil returned his attention to Alanso. He waited until Ronnie signaled him with a nod.

"I'm in as far as I can go." He glanced up at the other two guys. "Gotta really work."

"Good." The encouragement spurred all three men to please Links more. "Ronnie, fuck him. Nice and slow. In and out all the way. Phil, lean in closer. You know you like a nice facial. I bet this is going to be the best you've had. Start tugging on him. Just a little."

Alanso made noises Eli had never heard from him. Not even the time an entire case of motor oil had toppled from a cabinet and smooshed his hand between it and the frame of a vintage Corvette, breaking several bones in the process.

"That's right, *cariño*." Surprisingly tender, Links encouraged Alanso to surrender. "You're safe here. Let it all out. We understand. No one's going to make you hide again, are they?"

"No!" Alanso roared into the night.

Phil's hand rippled along the shaft in his grip and Ronnie went double time.

They all held their breath for a split second. Then Alanso exploded. He screamed, "Eli! Sally!"

And those two little words ripped Eli apart from the inside out.

He shuddered and his cock lurched. His balls felt as though they might flip inside out, they drew so tight to his frame.

The iron tang of blood flavored his mouth. He kept silent despite the tsunami of pleasure, longing and fear laying waste to everything in its path, leaving his insides hollow. His future uncertain. Jet after jet of come poured from him, shooting hard enough from his dick to get lost in the brush.

They came together, even if Alanso didn't know it.

All along, Alanso shuddered. His body jerked as though he'd been electrocuted. He shouted, cursed, prayed, gave thanks and supplied inarticulate expressions of his ultimate relief.

The sight brought Eli to his knees.

His head hung. Moisture scorched his eyes.

He'd reduced his best friend to yielding to a stranger's touch. This couldn't possibly be right. And now he'd probably fucked things up beyond repair. Struggling to get his breathing under control, he listened to the men emerging from their trance, less than ten feet away.

"I wondered for so long. But shit, I never imagined it could be *that* good." Alanso threw one arm over his face. His chest billowed as if he'd unloaded the entire week's supply shipment by himself, in record time.

If Eli didn't know better he might have thought he saw the sheen of tears in Al's eyes before he obscured them.

"Welcome to our world." Phil rubbed Alanso's shoulder. "You did great for your first time. If you find yourself in the neighborhood again..."

Eli regained his feet and took a few steps forward, unable to stay away. *No*. Next time it would be his finger in Alanso's ass. Or better yet, his cock.

"Thank you," Alanso murmured. He deflated as if every bone in his body melted in the wake of his release. How tightly had he been strung that Eli hadn't even realized...

"So, who's Eli?" Phil asked quietly. "And Sally?"

"Huh?" Alanso peeked from below his arm, blinking out of his daze.

King Cobra

"You called for them when you busted." He smiled softly. "Whoever they are, I hope they figure out how lucky they are before it's too late."

"I know." Eli cleared his throat.

Alanso shot up like a rocket. He scrambled to draw his clothes into place.

Links, Phil and Ronnie formed a wall between him and Eli. The man could win over even the toughest crowds in a matter of minutes. Jesus, he was amazing. And he didn't get it. Never had fully.

"It's okay, guys. He's a friend." Alanso cleared his throat. "My best friend."

Eli hated how Alanso cowered when he approached. He didn't hesitate to offer a hand. He hated looming over the guy.

When Al's chocolate gaze flicked upward from Eli's boots, it paused. His pupils dilated even further than the night had mandated.

Eli glanced down and spotted a thick, pearly strand of come he must have launched onto the thigh of his jeans. *Shit.*

Alanso reached up. He hesitated, as if Eli might run again, before touching the tip of one finger to the wet line. He swiped a trace of the fluid from the leg of Eli's pants and brought it to his mouth. A purr escaped from his throat as he tasted Eli's desire.

"Can we talk about this at home?" Alanso gained his feet and stared directly into Eli's eyes. He didn't blink once as Eli tried to put everything he felt into words yet failed miserably.

All he could do was nod his head.

When a couple of creases appeared at the corners of Alanso's eyes, Eli reacted on instinct. He thrust his hands out and cupped the shorter man's cheeks. He drew the guy to him and crashed their mouths together.

Their teeth clicked once before they found their rhythm, both used to leading. Alanso whimpered into Eli's mouth. He couldn't help but try to soothe the frantic questions he'd unintentionally inspired.

Eli forced himself to slow down. For Alanso's sake. He used

every sliver of self-control he had to harness the energy sparking between them as if they stood at the center of an enormous Tesla coil.

Tempering urgency with richness, he glided his mouth over Alanso's.

The vague mint taste didn't stop Eli from detecting the distinct zest of his best friend. Or the delicious flavor of the promise they sealed with their very first kiss.

How different it was to make out with a guy. This man.

And yet the same.

But way better than anything he'd felt before.

They made a few more passes of lips over lips. Until Eli's lungs burned and the edges of his vision turned blacker than the night could account for.

Reluctantly, they split. Alanso's mouth made one last bid for attention, nipping Eli's lower lip as he retreated.

They stared at each other.

"I'm sorry," Eli breathed against Alanso's mouth, hating the remnants of latex he tasted on his friend's lips. "I'll make this right. I swear."

"*Hijo de puta*, you'd better," Alanso snarled before stepping away, a glint of mistrust in his eyes.

"I guess this means we won't be seeing you again." Phil kicked a rock idly.

"I hope not." Alanso grinned and fist bumped Links before jogging up the hill toward his bike. He called over his shoulder, "Thanks."

Eli groaned. It was going to be a long ride home, watching that tight ass fly down the road in front of him.

Chapter Five

Alanso swung his leg over his bike and clomped up the metal stairs at the rear of Hot Rods without waiting for Eli to park his Cobra in the personal bays the rest of the group reserved for their rides. His bed called loud and clear. Given the chaos of his thoughts and the ragged emotion chasing on the heels of his experiment, he thought it'd be best if he avoided a confrontation tonight.

God only knew what he'd say when all of his insides were laid bare. He felt like he was turned inside out and everyone could see his guts, what made him tick and the dumb hope causing his heart to pound.

He had to think.

Or maybe getting in his head too much was the fucking problem. Deliberating hadn't done him any good over the past several months.

Seriously, there was no mistaking the tongue Eli had shoved in his mouth before spinning on his heels and commanding Alanso home.

But he hadn't been exactly affectionate either, had he?

Begrudging intimacy wasn't going to cut it anymore. He refused to settle. Or walk around feeling like he'd done something wrong.

Links had it right. Alanso didn't plan to hide ever again.

Except maybe just this one night. Until he figured out what to say to the five guys and one smoking hot woman staring at him as he opened the door to their common room a teensy bit too fast. The knob slipped from his grasp, allowing the door to hit the wall as he flew inside. A black-and-white picture of their first restoration job fell off the wall. The glass cracked as it hit the hardwood floor they'd installed a few years ago.

Just like that, something inside him shattered along with it.

His eyes flickered first to Sally. Worry lines around her pretty green eyes only amped him up more. This tension between him and Eli had affected the entire group in some way. From where he lounged on the couch beside her, Carver put his hand on her shoulder.

The movie they'd been watching droned in the background.

Roman, Holden, Kaige and Bryce set their cards on the table despite the large pot resting between them. Big, usually quiet, Bryce broke the silence. "You okay, Alanso?"

"No."

Roman's eyes widened and Holden scooted his chair around so he could catch the show too. In an instant, Sally rose and started to cross the sweeping area. The second floor of the garage was enormous. A complete blank slate had allowed them to slice the space into the rooms they needed to house them all while leaving a big-ass kitchen and this common ground.

Fortunately, the size of the living room gave Alanso opportunity to evade Mustang Sally's outstretched arms. He put a beat-up leather recliner between them.

"Don't." He shook his head. She couldn't touch him after where he'd been. What he'd done.

Tears shimmered in her eyes, obscuring jade behind pools of crystal. "What happened? What's wrong? Where's Eli?"

Relief washed through the gang when the door opened for the second time in as many minutes and their King Cobra came home.

"Who broke the picture?" He stepped toward the shards on the floor. Would he sweep them up? Alanso didn't think he could. None of them could put it back together now. It was too late. The damage had been done.

"I did." Alanso didn't recognize the tone of his own voice. "Leave it. I'll get it before I head out in the morning."

"What?" Sally rounded the chair. "Where are you going?"

Alanso kept pace, never letting her close the distance. "It doesn't matter. But I'm tired of pretending to be something I'm not just to fit in."

Sally propped her hands on her hips. She looked damn cute when she got pissed. Not that it happened often. "The hell're you talking about? Did *he* tell you to get out?"

She jabbed a finger in Eli's direction.

"You know better than that, Sally." Eli's response came quiet yet sure.

"Shut up." Her snap at the garage owner raised a few brows in the room. "You've fucked up enough already, haven't you? Somebody damn well better tell us what's going on. Keeping us in the dark is a shitty thing to do. Since when do we hide stuff from each other? Afraid we're going to kick your ass, Eli? I'm starting to think you really deserve it."

Alanso appreciated her loyalty. No questions asked. She'd always have his back.

Which is why he felt extra lame when he rounded on her as she crept closer.

But having her near confused him all over again, just when he'd thought he'd found some answers.

"Stop! Don't you get it? I don't like *chocha*." He drew a ragged breath, knowing he had to say the word. For himself. "Sally, I'm gay!"

Holden laughed first.

He flat out snorted as he rocked in his chair. Several beer bottles scattered on the table in front of him when his arm knocked into them. The clatter echoed off the high ceilings with exposed metal beams.

Sally froze. She tipped her head as she scrutinized him. Her gaze roamed over him inch by inch, as if one of his tattoos had secretly proclaimed his orientation all this time and she'd missed it.

Roman shot up from his chair. He paced behind the poker table. As usual, he didn't say anything right away, but Alanso could practically hear the wheels turning in his mind. What conclusion were they working toward? Would he accept a gay guy in their mix?

Carver piped up from the couch. Not in disgust. With pure curiosity, which was harder to drum up protective anger toward. "I'm confused, Al. It was less than six months ago that I walked in on you, in our laundry room, fucking that check-out girl from the grocery store. There wasn't any faking the way you pile-drived her."

"Hell, this place isn't soundproof. We've *all* heard you making women scream. And that damned Spanish. Wraps them around your dick every time. What's this really about?" Kaige grinned, his golden dreadlocks dancing around his head as he shrugged. "Dude. You almost had me for a second there."

"I'm not joking, *cabrón*." He scrubbed his hand over his head. "Okay, maybe not *maricón*. What do you call it? Bi. Something. Whatever. I sucked a guy's dick tonight and I liked it. Label that whatever the fuck you want."

"You should have waited outside for me," Eli murmured. "This isn't the time or place for this discussion. Let's take a walk. Cool off."

"Fuck you." Alanso wrenched away from Cobra. "I've had enough of secrets. They deserve to know why I'm not welcome. Why everything went to hell."

"You're always welc—"

"No, I'm not." Refusing to settle for half-alive wasn't an option anymore.

While he was distracted, Mustang Sally snuck in. He flinched when she wrapped her arms around his waist and laid her cheek between his shoulder blades. "We love you, Alanso. It doesn't matter who you choose to have sex with. Why would you think we're so judgmental?"

Whether it was the heat of her embrace or the enormous open heart she flashed them all, arousal—the same familiar longing that had plagued him lately in the presence of his de facto family—flared around him. The inappropriate thoughts heated his cheeks and had him staring at the floor.

Not one of the guys uttered a peep.

"Because Eli is." He hated the trembling in his worn-out muscles. It transmitted his exhaustion and fear to Sally as clearly as if he'd painted the torment in the bright colors she loved so much. "He's been keeping me gagged for months."

And didn't that image rouse his cock? Damn thing wouldn't behave. Seriously? After the best fucking night of his life? Well, second best if you counted the session with the crew.

"What?" Roman stood farthest away, but there was no way he had misheard.

"You're ashamed of him?" Bryce took a step closer, cracking his knuckles. "Cobra, what the fuck?"

"Hell, no." Eli rounded on the beefy guy. "You don't understand the situation."

"Of course not, *coño*. Because you haven't shared any of it with them. How could they know what we saw? What we did?" Weeks and weeks of rage exploded from Alanso at once. "You refused to be honest about it. You're a fucking coward. I didn't imagine your cock in my hand or your tongue in my mouth, did I?"

"Holy shit." Kaige plopped into his seat. "Is this the Twilight Zone or something?"

"No. You did not." Eli stepped closer.

Alanso couldn't have retreated even if he'd wanted to with Sally plastered to his back, sobbing quietly. He knew how much conflict upset her. Still, he couldn't stop the snowball they'd set rolling down this mountain of angst.

"Well, at least I'm not crazy *and* gay," he spat.

"Look, if you keep saying that like it's a bad word, you're going to be fighting with more than Cobra." Holden surprised them all by getting fired up. The usually affable guy rarely took a stand on serious issues. "You're not the only one in this room who's hooked up with a dude. I just never had some kind of emo crisis about it. Do what feels good and fuck anyone who tells you not to. What the hell's so hard about that?"

Alanso's stare whipped to his friend. Could it be true? All

this time he'd spent not confiding in them he could have had an ally. It was partially his fault. Not everything could be blamed on Cobra. That asshole.

"Nothing." He cleared his throat. "It's how I plan to live from now on. Like from right this second. And it's how the crew does it too."

"The crew?" Sally tensed around him. "Joe and his guys? What do they have to do with this?"

"Alanso…" Cobra hissed out a warning.

"Quit that." Bryce winged a clay poker chip at Eli. It bounced off his corded biceps. "Let him talk."

Alanso swallowed hard. "When Dave was in the accident and we went down to help, the crew was a mess. Kate and Morgan were pregnant and having a rough time. They were all torn up. Terrified he wasn't going to make it. We finished with the insurance paperwork earlier than expected so we met Joe, Morgan, Kate and Mike back at their house where the women were resting. Or so we thought."

Eli hadn't blinked once. It was as if he could visualize the scene they'd walked in on as clearly as Alanso could. The day replayed like a movie on endless loop in his mind.

"Cobra didn't want to wake them. Morgan had practically passed out at the hospital and the guys weren't hanging in there much better. So he picked the lock. We snuck in." Alanso couldn't stop himself from licking his lips. "Joe was fucking Morgan on a mattress. Right there on the floor of the living room."

"Guess she was feeling better." Kaige's eyebrows wiggled.

"They were helping her get there." Alanso nodded. "Taking away some of the fear and comforting her."

"Who's *they*?" Roman spoke up.

"Kate watched while Mike and Joe got it on with her." Alanso couldn't help the boner that started to rise. He hoped they wouldn't notice.

"Damn." Bryce rubbed his chest. "That's fucking hot. Kate was cool with it?"

"Hell yeah." He thought back to the serene smile on her face. "She wasn't up for sex with Mike just then. But she didn't want him to suffer. I could see how much she loved him. All of them. While she cheered them on."

Eli still hadn't budged. Light brown hair stuck out in a messy array, courtesy of his convertible. He breathed hard at the memories. He stood rigid as Alanso spilled his family's secrets.

Alanso had talked to the crew enough lately to know they didn't mind him sharing the details of their alternative lifestyle. Hell, they'd threatened to call the garage and enlighten the rest of the Hot Rods if he didn't do it soon.

"I always knew Morgan was a lucky bitch," Sally whispered, squeezing him tighter. If she didn't let up he might suffocate. He wouldn't mind. Her hug soothed his heart.

"I assumed because of your moms..." Alanso paused.

"After how I grew up, it seems kind of normal to have more than one partner." Sally hardly ever talked about her childhood in rural Utah. "That wasn't why I ran away. I didn't like being brainwashed. Or forced."

He dropped his shoulder, allowing her to swing around to his side and tuck under his arm. Holding her in return helped him finish. Especially when Kaige asked, "What does any of this have to do with you being gay?"

"Cause what we busted in on was only the beginning." Eli's raspy answer startled them all, if the dead silence was any indication. "Go ahead. You've gone this far. Finish it."

Alanso certainly didn't argue. "After they'd satisfied Morgan, you could tell Mike hadn't had enough. You know how everything falls to him."

Though he spoke of the head of the crew, Alanso stared into Eli's eyes as he elaborated.

"He takes on tons of responsibility. Protects them. Worries. Loves them all." A deep breath stretched his ribs.

Sally rubbed his back with one hand.

"Mike asked Joe if he could fuck him. Joe let him. It was

like he gave up everything to Mike, allowed him to take all the anxiety and relaxed for the first time since I'd seen him. And for a while Mike had the situation under control again. The whole time, Morgan made out with Joe and helped him get off. They were in it together. Kate..."

Alanso peeked up at Eli, who didn't try to shush him again.

"She played with me and Cobra. We did stuff. To each other."

A strangled groan left Sally's milky white throat. Whether it was approving or disgusted, he couldn't tell.

"And I liked it." Alanso gulped. "A lot."

Afraid to glance up, a weight lifted from his shoulders when Eli said, "I did too."

Kaige coughed around the slug of beer he'd taken to wet his throat. "Holy shit, guys. Well, I have to say of all the things we put in the pool as reasons for your bad mood...no one had *that*."

"I sort of did." Sally peeked at him from her spot against his chest. She laid her palm over his pounding heart. "I had lack of pussy. I know how you boys get when you hit a dry spell. And neither of you have been going out lately."

"You keeping track of us now?" Alanso couldn't say why it bothered him that she paid such close attention. Maybe it shamed him because he didn't care for any of the women he'd shared sheets with as much as he did for her.

Standing there, with her and Eli so close, sandwiching him between them, had him breaking out in a sweat.

"Excuse me, guys." Carver raised his hand, being ridiculous as always.

"What?" Eli growled.

"If *you* liked it...and *he* liked it...what the motherfuck is the problem here?" He scratched the stubble on his jaw.

"Good question." Alanso's spine straightened. "Apparently, Cobra only approves when he's hot. Afterward, he's horrified."

"Don't put words in my mouth." The corner of Eli's eye twitched, as it did when he got thermonuclear angry. It didn't happen very often, but when it did...

"I don't need fancy talk to explain when you avoid me like I gave you herpes or some shit. You fucking insisted I not tell them what happened and acted like I'd killed someone. Even tonight, you must have watched. You were on the scene a fucking second after I finished. But you didn't bother to join in or try to break their fingers for touching me. It's pretty obvious you don't give a shit."

Sally interjected, "I don't believe that, Alanso. I'm sorry he's made you feel unwanted. He's a dumbass, yes. But he loves you. We all do."

"You're our brother," Roman affirmed.

"And *that's* my problem." Eli latched on to the excuse. "How can I want him? Or more? Any of you? All of you. Because believe me, I do. I wish you all could have seen what we did. I think you might like it too. I remember those nights...when we were younger, undisciplined, dumber... There were some close calls."

He met each person's gaze for a moment or two before moving on to the next.

"What you saw affected you as much as it did Al." Bryce nodded, moving closer. "I can see where it would disturb you to blur the lines. You've always thought you had to look out for us."

"You realize we're plenty capable of holding our own, right?" Kaige chuckled. Hell, he'd single-handedly started and finished bar brawls regularly back when they were in their wilder days. "We're close, yes. Something more than family. And if this is what you two want, I'd be willing to dip a toe in and see where it goes. If it doesn't work for someone, or several people, we don't have to pursue it."

"I'd like to watch," Sally whispered. A few of the guys mumbled their agreement. When she lifted her face toward Alanso, he thought maybe for a second she would keep stretching onto her tiptoes and put that dark red mouth lined with something even darker too close to his. Tonight had left him with no self-control intact. He stepped out of her hold.

Unfortunately, that left him within Eli's reach.

Instead of making a grab for him, Cobra closed his eyes. He stood there, breathing hard for a moment or two before his lids fluttered open and he focused his brilliant blue laser stare on Alanso. "Get over here and kiss me."

Injustice triggered his stubborn streak. It didn't seem fair that he'd had to beg for months only to give in immediately to Eli's whims. "I'm not your bitch."

"Don't you wish you were?" Cobra canted his head. His high cheekbones were accentuated by the devilish smile Alanso knew so well. *Dios*, he'd missed that look. Homesickness roiled in his guts. He'd prayed for this man. And he didn't care if it made him a pussy, he caved.

"Sometimes." Alanso squared himself to his best friend, coming face-to-face. "But mostly I wonder what it would be like to make you forget about the world for one fucking moment. What if I could take away your obsession with the bills, worry about your dad's loneliness, the look you get on your face any time one of us doesn't feel well or, God forbid, has to go to the doctor? What would it be like to see you carefree? *That's* what I wish."

"Never gonna happen, Al." Roman sighed.

"Prove him wrong." The dare hung in the air. Eli knew damn well Alanso couldn't resist a challenge like that. "Go ahead."

Alanso didn't recall deciding to give in. One instant he was floundering, his whole life about to change—for better or worse he couldn't tell yet. The next, he'd stepped forward, grabbed Eli's head between his palms and tugged until the taller guy yielded.

Before their mouths could crush onto each other again, Eli murmured, "I'm sorry."

This time, when they met, something was different.

Sure, the urgency remained. A rough massage at the back of Eli's skull nudged him closer. Alanso practically climbed the garage owner despite their friends witnessing his undeniable craving for the guy he groped.

Yet their lips told another story. Eli didn't advance. He allowed Alanso to take charge of their exchange. Instead of powerful nips or the lashing of tongues, they traded swipes of soft, wet flesh against the same.

Eli fed a groan into Alanso's open mouth. He went still and calm. His movements turned fluid. The change spurred Alanso to escalate their encounter. The hard wall of Cobra's chest met his as they fused together full-length. And only when his hands roamed from that short, tousled hair past strong shoulders to a narrow waist and finally to Eli's gorgeous ass did he realize the shafts trapped between them were equally hard.

Hell, it felt as if Cobra really did have a massive trouser snake if the bulge poking Alanso's flexed abs was any indication. In the background, someone whistled.

Coming to his senses, Alanso opened his eyes. He imprinted the peace and desire in Eli's expression on his memory before he ripped away.

Cobra stumbled.

Carver appeared from beside them to brace the garage owner. It seemed he'd elected for a ringside seat to their little show. Sally clasped Eli's other arm, steadying him on his feet where he swayed.

"Great idea. It's time for bed." Their leader was back, and he had a mission.

"You think just because you rock at tonsil hockey, you're going to sleep with me tonight?" Alanso shoved away from Eli's chest. "Fuck off. I'm still pissed. It's going to take a hell of a lot more than one fucking tongue tango to convince me that you deserve a shot with me."

Eli grinned, wide and slow. "You think I'm a good kisser?"

"Kiss my ass, Cobra. *No me jodes*." He stalked toward his room, which shared a wall with Eli's, trying not to remember how Ronnie had done just that earlier, while Cobra observed from the shadows.

"Wow, Al. Maybe you really are a chick under all those

tattoos." Holden got smacked upside the head by Roman for his smartassery. Sally tossed in a defense for her kind too. She wasn't a head-game player like most women they'd run across.

A double salute from Alanso's middle fingers, without checking the rearview for reaction, marked his exit. The day had drained him. In more ways than one.

Maybe tomorrow he could process it all.

Until then, sleep sounded heavenly.

He locked his hallway door, stripped to bare-assed-naked and took a minute to brush his teeth in the bathroom he shared with Cobra. It didn't occur to him that his mind had stopped racing for the first time in months, making it easy to crash into his pillows and drift off.

Chapter Six

"Hey, that was the most interesting weeknight we've had in a few years." Holden clapped a hand on Carver's shoulder as the guys and Sally huddled around Eli. "We're getting old. Rusty."

Eli didn't even bother to level one of his shut-the-hell-up glares in Holden's direction. Suddenly, he felt weary. Unable to fight the tide that'd been dragging him out to sea.

"You gonna say something?" Kaige took up a spot near Bryce as they closed rank. "Eli, man, you all right?"

"I just want to make it clear that if any of you has an issue with what went down tonight, you bring it to me. Don't you dare shit on Alanso because of this." He bristled.

"I think the only guy here who's got a problem with it is you." Roman's stern tone didn't surprise anyone. As the oldest of their group, he had lived the hard life longer than most of them had, since Eli's family had given them sanctuary one by one as they'd wandered into the youth shelter Eli's mom had worked to build.

Roman had been a different matter. To this day, he worshipped Eli's father—Tom—for not calling the cops on him when he'd caught the young man trying to hotwire his truck. Instead, he'd offered a loan he never expected to be repaid and a job pumping gas at the garage and service station so Roman wouldn't have to stoop to petty theft ever again.

He'd busted his ass to fulfill his debt in record time, and he'd been there ever since.

The deep grooves around his mouth, his calculating eyes and the smell of hard liquor on his breath all combined to make him someone you didn't want to mess with in a dark alley.

"What are you planning to do now?" Sally patted Eli's chest, snapping his attention to the situation at hand. The fire in her eyes guaranteed he'd better answer this one right or risk her knee meeting his balls. She was quick and fierce. It'd hurt like hell.

"I—I have no idea."

Stunned silence echoed around the cavernous room, designed to hold them all comfortably.

"You've always got the roadmap." Carver's jaw hung open wider at Eli's indecision than it had at Alanso's dramatic declaration.

"Not for this." Eli scrubbed his knuckles over his eyes. "I don't have a fucking clue what to do. I know what I want, but I don't know what's right. Not for Al or for any of us. I realize this is all new to you guys, so I think you should take some time to really think about the implications."

Most of the Hot Rods nodded. Sally shook her head. "All I want to know is—do you plan to keep things between the two of you or expand like the crew did?"

"I can't say, Sally." He shrugged. Partly it depended on what the rest of the gang thought. He owed them time to process what they'd just witnessed. The lack of direction made him feel like his internal compass had crapped out. He'd always known where he was headed and marched toward his goals without pause. Now...he spun in circles. Changing his mind every five seconds.

Go to Alanso. That voice screamed loudest, but he resisted.

Back off.

Test the waters with the Hot Rods.

Leave them alone.

Show them how much you love them.

Don't fuck up what you have.

Indecision was driving him insane. Oscillating between two polar opposites, he felt like a piston moving back and forth at an ungodly RPM. He hadn't been this stuck since the time they'd attempted to drive one of their finds down the muddy, unpaved driveway leading from the estate sale they'd snagged the bargain at. It'd taken all of them pushing together to break free of that mire.

"Cobra, go talk to your dad," Bryce suggested.

"About this?" He backed up a step, then another. "No way. What am I going to tell him? That I think I'm into guys now? That I'm having some early midlife crisis? Jesus."

"You'll know what to say when you get there." Sally closed the gap between them and put her hand on his forearm. He studied her nails. She'd redone them again tonight. Now they were a hot pink color in two finishes—matte on the bed and glossy on the tip. Subtle yet not. Always interesting. Just like the paint jobs she designed and applied to the cars they restored. "He'll help you think it through."

Rather than argue those points, Eli picked something simpler. "It's after midnight. He's in bed by now, I'm sure."

"Nah," Kaige disagreed. "He stopped by for a few beers before. We told him something was up with you and Al. Actually, he kind of insisted that you come see him when you got home. Sorry, dude."

Holden jabbed his fingers into the mini-blinds and separated two of the slats to peer into the night. "The porch light is on. He's staying up for you. Better not keep him waiting any longer. Don't waste the chance to lean on what you've got. None of the rest of us are that lucky unless we borrow your dad."

"Crap!" For the first time since his curfew days, Eli suffered a moment of panic over walking through that door at this ungodly hour. "Fine. Fuck. I'm going. Who's opening with me tomorrow? Shit...today. Kaige? Carver? Get your asses to bed. Nobody should be dragging when we're working with the lifts and equipment. We'll talk about this more this weekend."

"Promise?" Sally looked up at him with wide eyes.

"Damn it, yes." With that he spun on his heel and jogged down the stairs, across the lawn and onto the porch of his father's home. He usually loved having the guy so close. But tonight, he wasn't sure their proximity played to his advantage.

Was he ready to share everything? Even if he didn't know what all that entailed yet?

He trusted his father above anyone else in the world. The death of Eli's mom had brought them closer. Almost more like friends than father and son. They'd been there for each other, then for the Hot Rods they'd discovered and inherited in the years following.

"In here, Eli," his dad called from the living room as if the flash of the TV, which probably aired some travel documentary, didn't highlight the way.

"Hi." Nothing else came to mind.

"So, you want to tell me what had you two kids peeling out of here like harebrains? Those damn engines are loud enough to have all our neighbors calling and complaining to me." Tom London didn't beat around the bush.

"Since when do you give a shit what Mrs. Shoff thinks of us anyway?"

"You're right, I don't give a damn." Tom clicked off the TV and angled toward Eli. "But *I've* had enough of this sulking. I want to know what's wrong."

Eli sank into a comfortably worn recliner, rested his elbows on his knees and put his head in his hands. "It's complicated, Dad."

"I'm not stupid. I'll follow." Tom crossed his arms.

"Are you pissed?" He narrowed his eyes at the rare irritation his father seemed to be barely containing. This wasn't good. Hell, was he screwing up with everyone he loved lately?

"Kind of. Disappointed, actually."

Eli hadn't heard that tone since a bunch of them had gotten busted racing for money on a dangerous road one night in his early twenties. He'd hoped never to earn that slimy feeling in his gut again. "Why?"

"I thought you trusted me." The statement rang with accusation.

"I do." Eli wasn't lying. His dad had always been there for him. Maybe he'd been stupid not to come here sooner for this talk. "It's just...my issue affects more than me. Not sure it's right to drag everyone else's skeletons out in the open."

"Is one of the Hot Rods in trouble?" Tom leaned forward in his seat. "You've got to tell me if they are. I can help."

"No. Nothing like that." He hated the relief that washed over his dad's face. His dad had really been worried. And without facts to go on, he'd probably assumed the worst. "It's kind of, maybe, good news. Things are changing. There's a relationship thing happening. But it could cause some issues in the gang. That's what's bothering me. I don't want to alienate anybody. I can't lose any of them over this."

"Are you trying to say a couple of you are pairing off?" A smile tipped the edges of Tom's mouth for an instant. Then his dad rubbed his temples as if he had a headache. "I've wondered for a while which of you was going to break up the band."

"What's that supposed to mean?"

"You know, which guy was going to fall for Sally first." He shrugged. "It was bound to happen sooner or later. She's gorgeous, funny, tough, mysterious, a little sad. A potent combination. You kids screw around plenty, but not one of you has ever found something meaningful in a partner. Why do you think that is, son?"

"Very few people get as lucky as you and Mom." The reminder of what they'd lost hurt them both. But it was the truth. The way his parents had looked at each other... Hell, his mom's heart monitor had soared every time his dad had showed up to take a shift by her bed at the hospital.

"Maybe." Even now Tom smiled when he thought of his wife. He still wore his wedding ring. Swore he'd go to his grave with the simple band hugging his finger. "Personally, I think you've been looking in all the wrong places. Or maybe refusing to admit what you already know. After all, Joe and the crew seem to have done pretty fine for themselves, haven't they?"

"Yeah." Eli cleared his throat. "About them..."

His dad didn't come to his rescue. He waited the pause out.

"Shit. Dad, did you know they're into group stuff?" He

winced as he considered the reaction he'd get or what the guys might do when they realized he'd spilled the beans on their complex relationship.

"It wasn't obvious?" Tom reclined in his chair, spreading his legs wider as he relaxed. "Hell, for a second there you had me worried. I thought you were going to tell me something awful."

"Wait, how could you tell?" *And doesn't it freak you out?* he wanted to add.

"It's obvious from the complete comfort they've always had around each other. Plus the way their wives folded right into that bond. Even if that weren't enough, it would have been impossible to ignore right about the time James and Neil blabbed everything to me. They were worried when all the other guys had found a woman that the crew wouldn't get together anymore." Tom waved a hand in the air. "Like the guys would be able to stay away after so many years together. I remember the days of being twisted up so tight you can't think straight, but seeing it from the outside… Yeah, a whole lot of drama over nothing. When it's right, it's right, and that's all that matters in the end."

"Oh. Well, fuck." Eli started to laugh. "I guess this might be easier than I thought to tell you, then. Maybe."

"Just spit it out already. Is it you or Alanso who's fooling around with Sally and making his best buddy jealous as hell?" Tom didn't usually gossip, but he scratched his head as he asked.

Eli closed his eyes, took a deep breath and borrowed a page out of Alanso's book. He'd fucking put it all right out there to the Hot Rods before. Eli admired him a little more after tonight. "Actually. It's Alanso and me who've kind of tangled it up a bit. Not as much as he wants, though. Not yet."

"Oh." Tom paused for a second. He blinked. "I see. I guess I don't quite understand why you boys are fighting then."

"That's all you're going to say about it?"

"I don't think I'm ready for details just yet." Tom chuckled. "Gotta give a guy a minute to work things out first. I'm not surprised you two love each other. Just not sure I figured you'd jump straight to that without easing your way in first. For so long I've wondered about Sally, I guess I didn't see it. Actually...something happened when you went out there to help the crew. After the accident. Didn't it?"

Eli swallowed hard and nodded.

"This is starting to make sense." Tom tapped his fingers on his knee slowly. "I've been trying to figure out what changed. I thought maybe seeing their close call reminded you of your mom. That maybe you'd realized you don't get all the time in the world to waste, so you'd decided to make a move."

"Actually, I think that's kind of what happened to Alanso. Yes." Eli sighed.

"But you're being stubborn, aren't you?" Tom grunted. "It's all coming clear now. You dumbass. You pushed him away?"

"You *want* me to be gay?" Eli jumped to his feet, flinging his hands in the air. "Is everyone losing their fucking minds around here?"

"I love you no matter who you decide to be with, Eli." Tom also stood. He might have been an inch or two shorter than his son, but there was no mistaking his ranking in their family. "I don't think things are as simple as terms make them out to be. You've got something with those kids. It's been there since the beginning. Who am I to say what's right or wrong? It is how it is."

"But it's never been like *that* before." Eli paced the modest living room. "Why now?"

"Maybe you weren't ready." Tom caged in his son, dropping his hand on Eli's shoulder. "You've done a hell of a lot of growing up over the past ten years. Built your business, your friendships. You played around enough to know what you like. And you've helped them all get to a somewhat normal place. That took a long time. A lot of healing had to be done. I think somewhere, deep down, you know the gang is ready to take this next step."

"You get that I don't just want Alanso, right?" Eli clenched the fireplace mantle so hard his knuckles turned white. "I have no idea what exactly this is going to look like when it's all said and done, but I think it's bigger than him and me. Yeah, you're right. I have a major thing for Sally. I'm pretty damn sure Alanso does too."

"Dream big, son." Tom grinned. "But maybe you'd better start with Alanso if things between you are spiraling out of control. No more of this fighting. I hate to see that. It bothers all of you kids. Sets everyone on edge. They've had too much misery already in their lives to borrow more from you. Hell, you two are practically an old married couple anyway. Just without the sex. Might as well add the benefits."

"And I think that's where I draw the line when talking to my father." Eli was attempting to be mature about this, but he hadn't even slammed a shot or two before coming over here to dull the awkwardness. What had he been thinking?

"Yeah, me too." Tom nodded. "But I did win that round of chicken."

Eli laughed. He went with his gut and turned to hug his dad. "Thank you for understanding. I do know how lucky I am, by the way."

"So do I." Tom clutched him hard enough to crack a rib. After all he'd been through it would have been easy to turn sour, angry at the world. Yet he never had. He'd held tight to the good times he'd had and the legacy his wife had left. Because of him, the Hot Rods all had a home. "Now get the hell out of here so I can go to bed."

Eli flung his arm away from where it'd been curled over his face. It was no use. He couldn't sleep. Hadn't managed to stop thinking about what he'd seen at Chestnut Grove for more than three milliseconds since he climbed into bed. Especially since he knew Alanso was right there on the other side of the wall that was bookended by the headboards of their beds.

Plus, by some miracle, not only his friends but also his father approved of the dangerous liaison he'd plotted and replotted during the endless hours of darkness. With the first rays of morning that beamed through his window, Eli saw clearly what he'd like to do.

Hell, it'd be impossible to miss the tent made by his sheets over his rock-solid erection.

He could slip through the adjoining bathroom he and Alanso shared, into the dusk-shrouded midst of the other guy's lair. After pulling back the black silk sheets, he'd tuck himself in to steal some of his friend's warmth.

Sleepy, Alanso wouldn't stand a chance at resisting. He adored morning sex.

Of all the Hot Rods, he was one of the few likely to invite a woman to stay overnight. Probably because he liked opening his eyes and seeing his date hadn't left.

Eli slapped the mattress a few times, gearing himself up to action. Just when he had committed and kicked off his blankets, the rush of water hitting the tile of their shower stopped him short.

What the hell? Alanso didn't open today. Or ever, really. The rest of the guys knew he preferred a lazy start to the morning and left him to the late shift most times. Eli generally stayed the whole day, opening and closing, no matter how often they told him to get the fuck out of his own business to enjoy some time off.

Truth was, when you loved what you did, and who you did it with, it hardly felt like a job at all. This—making things right with the guy who mattered most to him—was hard work. And he was prepared to do whatever it took to fix the damage he'd inflicted.

He staggered into the bathroom, surprised by how stiff he was. Christ, he'd had massive hangovers less painful. Had he lain there completely tense all night?

The running shower made wet noises as Alanso got clean. The splashes guaranteed Eli had to use the facilities before confronting his friend.

This was familiar ground. Ten years of sharing a bathroom meant someone often had to take care of business while the other was occupied in the shower. Usually it was the other way around. Eli preparing for the day while Alanso relieved himself of some of the beer they'd chugged the night before then stumbled back to bed for another nap.

"Hey." Eli tried not to startle Alanso as he made his way to the toilet. He wondered if Al was imagining his hand holding his dick when he didn't answer immediately.

"Look who it is... Asshole, party of one."

Eli didn't laugh along. The truth stung.

"Didn't hear your alarm go off. Thought you were still sleeping," Alanso finally responded. "Was it the shower that woke you? Sorry."

"Nah." Eli didn't bother with pajamas so it wasn't more than ten seconds before he tugged back the curtain and joined his partner in the shower, despite the sputters of outrage coming from the shorter man's luscious mouth. "I haven't really been to bed. Couldn't manage to doze off with the memory of your mouth on that dude's cock."

"Disgusted you that much, huh?" Alanso glanced away or he might have spotted Eli's hard-on. Even the chilly secondary splash from the shower spray didn't wilt the damn thing.

"Hardly." Eli had done so much harm. He knew one thing that would convince Alanso he was serious about changing the course he'd taken so far. "I think you should be on the lookout. My dad is likely to pay you a visit today."

"Why?" Alanso's breathing grew faster. He ignored the droplets forming on his mocha skin, streaming down his bald head, the powerful cords of his neck and onto his chest. The barbells in his pebbled nipples decorated his pecs, making Eli long to lean forward and lick them like Phil had done the day before.

They stared into each other's eyes. "I told him about us."

"You did *what*?" Alanso might have slipped and cracked his thick skull open if Eli hadn't lunged for him when he jerked. He banded his arm around Alanso's trim waist and tugged him close until they aligned, torso to torso. "Is he going to ask me to leave?"

"Jesus. Would you quit that? He's not your mom. He won't ever abandon you." Eli grabbed Alanso's chin with his free hand and angled the guy's face toward his. "No one thinks less of you for being honest about what you want. I should have done the same. A long time ago. My dad had it right. There's a reason I've never had a girlfriend. I couldn't stand the idea of anyone replacing you in my life. You were right last night when you said I didn't deserve you. But I'm asking you to give me a chance anyway."

"Cobra?" Alanso blinked up at him, crystal drops decorating his long, dark lashes.

"Yeah." He couldn't help but grind his cock on Alanso's hip. The guy was powerful. Stocky and tenacious. He reminded Eli of a pitbull. The possibility of that much strength focused on him…it had his engine revved in no time.

"As much as I'd kill for what you're offering—"

"What? You're still turning me down?" He drew away far enough to really scrutinize Alanso's expression as best he could in the dim light of the shower area.

"Maybe. I need to ask you something first." He plucked the shower gel from a rack in the corner of the enclosure and lathered up his palms. When he smeared bubbles all over his torso, Eli thought he might choke on his own tongue.

"Spit it out already." Eli couldn't wait much longer. Either to fuck or to know the offer was really off the table for good.

"Not to sound greedy, but…"

"Oh. That." Containing his grin would have been impossible. "Yeah, I plan to live it up, Alanso. I don't know who might be in or how the logistics will work, but, yes, I want what the crew has and I'm willing to do what it takes to sell our Hot Rods on the arrangement."

"*Come mierda!*" His head fell back, knocking into the tile hard enough to alarm Eli. "You're not fucking with me, are you? Please, don't do that to me. Be sure. I can't handle you changing your mind."

"Can't we take this one step at a time?" Eli shuffled closer, insinuating one of his thighs between Alanso's legs. The other trapped him in place. "We don't even know if I'm any good at this. What if you don't like it?"

"Don't think that's going to be a problem." Alanso slithered against him, spreading the soapy foam between their bodies. It felt so good. Hot, slick and soft on top of Alanso's hardness. "But I'm willing to test that theory."

"I hate fighting with you. No one's yelled at me for eating at the drive-thru for the past three days or photobombed my portfolio shots of the last two finished projects or changed the letters on the daily special sign into dirty offers when I wasn't looking. The last couple months have sucked." Eli closed his eyes as he said what he'd been thinking for quite a while. "I've missed you."

"Same goes. So let's make up." Alanso used some of his lady-killer Latin dance moves to undulate his abs and hips against Eli's wet body. Seems they were just as effective on guys. He almost came right then, shooting all over Alanso's thigh.

"Shouldn't that be *kiss* and make up?" Eli leaned in and nipped Alanso's lip before he could lose all semblance of control. But he couldn't stop at just one nibble. He sealed their lips together and devoured the full mouth that seldom stayed this quiet or this serious in his company.

He reached out with one hand, grabbing the bottle of gel. He flipped open the cap and squished a dollop into his palms, then retreated from the temptation of Alanso's kisses before he let the seduction steal all his rationality.

"Turn around."

Alanso obeyed instantly, showing him the array of artwork gracing the bunched muscles of his back, ass, thighs and calves.

"Good idea. I think I'd prefer *fuck* and make up." Alanso braced his hands on the tiles and shoved his ass in Eli's direction.

"Not so fast." Eli smacked that bubble butt hard enough to

leave a red imprint of his palm. The spank echoed through their bathroom, tempting him to do it again. And once more. Then he proceeded to massage the soap into Alanso's blushing cheeks before cleaning the rest of his skin.

"Come on, Cobra." He groaned. "I'm not a girl. I don't need that bullshit. I just need you to fuck me already."

"You might not need frills. Maybe I do." Eli squatted to clean Alanso's legs. He rested his cheek in the hollow of Alanso's lower back. He couldn't believe he'd nearly screwed this up. He wouldn't do it again. By the time they were through, Alanso would know he meant this to be about more than physical pleasure.

"Then why don't you let *me* take care of *you*?" Alanso spun around, rinsing himself off in the process. He lifted the gel from Eli and slathered it on his hands. Before Eli could think of some reason to stop him—other than the fact that he didn't intend for the other man to put himself in a one-down position—he'd begun to caress every part of Eli's body.

And all King Cobra could do was concentrate on not crashing to the floor and breaking his neck. Hell no, he planned to stay alive and alert for the fun ahead.

Alanso knelt on the floor and worked his way up from Eli's toes.

Eli held on to Alanso's bald head to keep his balance as he lifted first one leg then the other when instructed. He rubbed Alanso's scalp, enjoying the hell out of how smooth it was. How soft despite the hardness beneath.

"Shit, that feels good Cobra." He leaned into the touch, still cleansing Eli's ankles, then the rest of his legs. When his fist wrapped around Eli's cock, soaping him from root to tip then back again, Eli shivered.

As the water washed away suds, he imagined it also took the guilt and ugliness that had plagued him lately along with it. Alanso did that for him. Made him feel okay with all the blessings he'd been given. Even in the face of his friends' suffering and the total devastation they'd lived through. Sure, he'd lost his mom. But he'd always had his father. And the absolute conviction that his mother had loved him beyond belief.

He swore then and there he'd never let Alanso fear the people special to him could do any less. How could they not value this man? How could he doubt his own worth?

While he debated how to show Alanso what he meant, the man surprised him. The moist heat of his mouth sucking the tip of Eli's dick seemed a million times hotter than the steam billowing around them.

A groan tore from Eli's throat. His fingers curled in Alanso's shoulders, pressing deep into the muscles there. "Wait. Al, wait."

"I'm so fucking tired of delaying." He stopped only long enough to bitch before repeating the gesture, this time taking an extra inch or so of Eli's shaft into his mouth.

If they didn't stop this soon there wouldn't be any going back.

"Just another minute." Eli pressed on Alanso's forehead, moaning when his dick left the paradise it'd only begun to explore. "I have a better idea."

"Let me be the judge of that." Alanso swiped the back of his hand over his lips, making Eli wonder just how much precome had leaked from his cock already. "I thought it was a hell of a plan."

Eli slapped his hand over the shower handle, shutting off the water. He swiped his hands down his body, sluicing rain from his skin before stepping onto the mat and grabbing Alanso's towel. "Here."

He handed the well-used terrycloth to his friend before taking his own off the bar.

They raced to dry themselves.

Eli flipped the towel over his head to squeegee some of the excess wetness from the hair he kept short while Alanso buffed his baldness until it shined. Cobra couldn't help himself. He snapped his towel at Alanso's ass, laughing at his high-maintenance routines. "You know it always looks exactly the same, right?"

"*Come mierda.* So does yours. At least I've got some style." He stood with his legs wide apart, his bulging arms crossed and his cock jutting straight out. "So what the fuck was this great scheme of yours? So far I'm not seeing the perks."

"Last night when I watched you sucking Links' cock..." Eli headed for Alanso's bedroom. He wanted the man to be comfortable.

"Were you even a little jealous?" Alanso hesitated at the threshold. For the first time, he seemed uncertain.

"Hell yes." Eli whipped the plush comforter to the foot of the bed. "It took everything in me not to interrupt and insist you service me instead."

Alanso actually looked relieved. "So let me."

Eli held up his hand, palm out. "You didn't let me finish. Yes, I wondered what it would be like to have you working me over. But I also was curious about what it felt like to you. How did he taste? Did it feel good to have him in your mouth? I always thought women just put up with BJs for the sake of our pleasure, but...it seemed like you were really enjoying yourself."

"I told you. I sucked cock and I liked it. So what the fuck is the hold up?" Alanso stalked closer, staring at Eli's erection, which hung thick and ready against his thigh. "I want to try again. Just to be sure."

"I want to check it out too." Eli applauded himself silently when Alanso's jaw dropped open. "Let's sixty-nine. First guy to come lets the other guy fuck him as a reward."

Chapter Seven

"You're right. Your idea's better." Alanso took two giant strides and launched himself onto the mattress. His balls bounced as he settled into the comfort of his bed.

Eli grinned above him. Why did Cobra have to be so damn sexy? Tall, lean, tattooed discretely compared to some of the other guys in the shop. His mother's name perched over his heart and the Hot Rods logo arched across his lower belly.

"What're you looking at?" Cobra sank onto the bed, lying with his head toward Alanso's feet.

"Just thinking I'm glad your portrait of Tom is on your back. It'd freak me out to have him staring at me when I do this." Alanso didn't waste any time stuffing Eli's cock into his mouth. He wasn't about to give his friend the opportunity to run.

Coño, he tasted fine. Clean and fresh, without the fake minty flavor of the guy last night. Alanso couldn't have considered a condom with Eli. No more barriers. He knew the guy was clean. His jaw stretched and he psyched himself up to take the full length of Eli's shaft despite the fact that it was several inches longer than Links' or even Alanso's own cock.

Not quite as thick, he found as he measured the girth with his lips and tongue.

Eli groaned. He rolled, grabbing Alanso's ankles—one in each hand. As he rotated, he spread them far apart and pinned them in place. Alanso forgot to suck for a minute as he adjusted to the weight bearing down on him in addition to the wash of warm breath drying his cock and balls.

Sure, the gang hadn't been kidding last night. Catching women had never been difficult. He enjoyed flirting and playing up his accent when it seemed to suit a bar bunny's fantasy of taking a Latin lover. So he'd had a million blowjobs from women who knew their way around a guy's junk. But something about this was different. Whether because the mouth about to service him was male or because it belonged to his best friend, he couldn't say for sure.

He had a guess, though.

With his head tipped back onto his pillows, he let Eli's sac drag along his cheek. He flicked his tongue over the sensitive head of the Hot Rod's cock when he hesitated. His demand garbled around his mouthful of Eli. "Enough torture."

"Sorry, sorry." Eli came to life. He dropped lower, pressing them together chest to belly. Their height difference meant Eli had to hunch his back a bit, but he managed to get his mouth on Alanso's dick without pulling his own shaft out of Alanso's grasp.

"*Mámamela!*" The directive to suck would have been lost on Eli even if he'd known the term because his cock garbled Alanso's cries.

Still, the motion of Alanso's hips left no room for misinterpretation.

They both knew he was going to lose this battle of wills. He'd dreamed of this too long to keep from pouring his come down Eli's throat. Hell, this was bigger than he'd dared to let himself hope for. Yet he'd like to hold on long enough to qualify as something other than utterly pitiful in his attempt to keep up. In case he couldn't, he didn't want Eli wasting time. He wanted to feel the man's tongue laving him, his lips choking the base of his cock and the stronger suction a guy would impart, knowing just how damn good it felt.

"Is this what you want?" Eli grabbed Alanso's cock. "Feels weird and cool to touch you. It's like doing it to myself except not. I've wondered since that day with the crew if I imagined how hot you were. I didn't."

Eli prevented any coherent response from Alanso when he held the cock still in his grip and licked the head as if it were a lollipop. The smacking of his lips made Alanso sure he tested the taste of his best friend on his tongue.

He had to concentrate on the sequence of engine parts he needed to assemble later today to keep from letting that thought overpower his restraint. Eli hadn't even taken him totally in his mouth yet. Coming so quick wasn't an option. He'd waited too long to waste this opportunity, in case he never got another one like it.

The only way he knew to make Eli quit dallying was to fight fire with fire. He opened his jaw wider, letting Eli's cock embed more fully in his mouth. The angle and his length made his erection a choking hazard, but Alanso didn't let that stop him.

He tried to recall what Phil had done to him the night before and simulated that rippling finger thing with his mouth by hollowing his cheeks and wriggling his tongue all along Eli's length.

"Uhh." Eli grunted and flexed forward. His mouth surrounded Alanso with heat and temptation.

No way was he going to be the only one frantic with desire. He reached up and around Eli's hip to tease the balls threatening to cut off Alanso's air supply where they pressed near to his nose.

"Cheater!" Eli reared back long enough to shout. He shuddered and slurped Alanso's cock farther into his mouth on the return journey.

"Mmm." Alanso didn't have the luxury of retreating with Eli's pelvis trapping his upper body against the bed, but he wouldn't have done it if he could. The vibrations he sent along Eli's shaft seemed to aid his mission.

Then Eli retaliated. He bobbed his head over Alanso's erection, sliding up and down the length with lips and tongue and cheeks.

Alanso's thighs began to quiver as he curled his toes, attempting to stave off the eruption bubbling in his balls. *Just a few more minutes*, he begged himself. A little while longer to experience this bliss. *Please don't let it stop*, he prayed.

With the end near, Alanso took a chance. He let his

fingertip wander from the spot he'd discovered behind Eli's balls, which seemed to drive him wild, to the tight pucker of his asshole. The tongue-lashing Ronnie had given Alanso last night had sold him on the merits of playing around back there. He'd never imagined it could feel so fucking good.

But he'd sure as hell like to share that knowledge with Eli.

For two reasons. First being that he liked to please the guy. In bed and out. Second, because he hoped that Eli might be willing to treat Alanso to that riot of sensation from time to time in their future.

The thought that they might have a future at all nearly made Alanso shoot.

He howled as he clamped down on the urge to come. It was too soon to end this euphoria. Like an addict, he wanted to prolong the high.

When his finger nudged the clenched muscle at the opening to Eli's ass, it instinctively tightened. But when he continued to prod and massage, the muscle relaxed, opening to his exploration. Only the tiniest bit of his digit had poked through Eli's resistance when Cobra stiffened above Alanso.

They both froze in absolute amazement as Eli's balls contracted on Alanso's upper lip and Cobra's cock jerked. Eli ripped his mouth from Alanso's cock, probably to protect him as he spasmed. If Alanso didn't know better, he'd think the man was having a seizure.

Eli buried his face between the mattress and Alanso's leg. He growled, moaned and shouted Alanso's name before biting into his thigh. Not hard enough to hurt. Hell no, the pressure almost had Alanso joining the man on top of him in rapture. Almost, but he couldn't quite tip into climax without the escalating pressure of Eli's mouth on his dick.

And that was when he felt it. The first gush of come blasted from Eli's cock.

He prepared himself to drink it all, every last drop.

Stream after stream coated the back of his throat, making him choke a little as he swallowed reflexively. He offered up a silent apology to every woman he'd nearly drowned like this. *Carajo!*

As if Eli could sense his struggle, he attempted to lift up and steal Alanso's treat.

Alanso dug his fingers into Eli's fine ass and trapped him in place. Weak with ecstasy, Cobra couldn't escape and finished emptying those huge *cojones* into Alanso's open, waiting mouth. When he'd finished coming, he unclamped his jaw and kissed the ring he'd indented on Alanso's thigh. Secretly, Alanso hoped it would bruise so he'd have a reminder that this amazing wakeup call hadn't been some kind of dream.

Eli rolled to the side, collapsing on his back.

Alanso flipped around so that they were face to face, their feet propped on his pillows. He brushed the matted spikes of Eli's hair from his forehead. "You okay?"

"I'm pretty sure we can rule out high blood pressure. I'd have had a stroke if I wasn't in good shape there." Eli still gulped like a fish out of water.

A smug smile crept onto Alanso's face. He liked having this effect on his boss.

Then Eli's eyes cleared of the haze of his wicked orgasm. His throat flexed and his Adam's apple bobbed before he said, "Go easy on me."

Alanso flung out his arm, preventing Eli from rolling onto his stomach and presenting his ass. "Cobra. No. We both know I was supposed to lose that game."

"But you didn't." Eli sighed. "You deserve it. Earned a hell of a prize too. I've never felt like that before. Christ, Alanso."

He wrapped his hand around Alanso's neck and brought him close for a kiss. Another shock, as he didn't seem to give a shit that the mouth he tongue-fucked was dressed in his own release. Alanso found himself fighting against the pressure in his balls again.

"Just get me off. Somehow. I don't care. It'll take two strokes of your hand." Alanso grew desperate, writhing in Eli's hold. "Touch me. Please."

"No." Eli separated them. He smiled softly, then kissed Alanso's forehead. "Chicken? I'm about as relaxed as I'm ever going to be. Do it."

He did manage to roll over this time, presenting the full glory of his body to Alanso to do with as he pleased. A man could only argue so much. He didn't claim to be strong. That was what his Hot Rods were for.

Alanso lunged for his nightstand and took out the bottle of lube he used when he jerked off at night, sometimes to the sounds of Eli fucking a woman in the next room. Though, now that he thought about it, he couldn't remember the last time Cobra had brought someone home.

Definitely before the incident with the crew. Why hadn't he noticed that earlier?

"Here." He yanked a pillow from the head of the bed and slapped it against Eli's hip. "Lift up."

When Cobra obeyed, pride and something deeper rushed into Alanso. Eli wouldn't let just anyone do this. His trust and confidence in Alanso spoke volumes without a single word. Al swore to always deserve what Eli gave him.

After making sure Cobra was comfortable, with his limp cock and balls nestled on the pillow, Alanso spread his cheeks. He popped the lid on the lube and drizzled some in the valley of Eli's ass. The guy jumped, cursing under his breath because of the chilly goo.

"It'll warm up in a second." Alanso rubbed it around where it pooled in the dip of Eli's ass, making sure to get him good and slippery. With his other hand, he applied a generous amount to his own cock, working it in with several passes over his steely shaft.

"*Joder!* I've never been this hard." Alanso forced himself to let go. He didn't intend to shut down the party before it had really gotten started.

"Good. Should make this easier." Eli mumbled against the mattress. He'd rested his head on one bent arm. If it weren't for his shoulders betraying his elevated respiration, Alanso might have thought him ready to fall asleep.

"I don't know, Eli." Alanso hesitated. "I'm not sure you can take me. It's a lot just going right into this. You heard Links last night. He said I wasn't ready. That I should play with some toys first."

"He saw me," Eli confessed. "He knew you were mine. And that I'm yours. He told you that so no one would fuck you."

"Seriously?" Something in the neighborhood of Alanso's heart did back flips at the revelation.

"Yeah. There were lights in the bushes near me—"

"Not that part." Alanso rubbed his thumb over Eli's hole, pressing in the slightest bit.

Eli gasped. "Yes. We belong to each other. All of the Hot Rods do. But especially you and me. Always have. Don't you think so too?"

When he glanced over his shoulder, Eli shot him a look full of concern. Alanso couldn't bear to see the arrogant *pendejo* unsure of himself. It just didn't suit.

"Yeah. I do." Alanso leaned forward, blanketing his best friend. He covered the guy he would protect always. The proximity allowed him to lay a kiss, similar to the one he could still feel burning on his forehead, on Eli's cheek. This was so much more than sex to him.

But he was only human. And he needed relief. Badly.

His cock rode the furrow of Eli's ass. Every time the leaking head probed against Eli's entrance, they both groaned. "Last chance, Cobra. I'd gladly take the rest of that blowjob. You have a really talented mouth."

"Thanks, but no thanks. Fuck me, Alanso." Eli barked the command. He growled, "You had your finger in my ass a minute ago—I think that's enough warming up. Just get your cock in there before I do change my mind."

"If you're not sure..."

"That's not what I meant and you know it." Eli rolled his eyes, making Alanso laugh.

"Fine." He spanked the ass on display before him, not feeling the need to be gentle like when he played with a chick.

"But for the record, I barely touched you before you went off like a rocket. This is going to be a lot different, *cabrón*."

"Seriously? Your finger felt pretty enormous and deep to me." Eli looked over his shoulder, one eyebrow raised.

Alanso shook his head, giving him yet another chance to change his mind.

He didn't take it.

"Inside me. Now." And though Eli might be the one beneath Alanso, he had all the power. By submitting to this thing between them, he proved just how strong he was and how seriously he took their test. "You're not going to last anyway. I give you five strokes before you pump your load in my ass."

"Keep talking like that and it'll be three." Alanso wrapped his fist around his cock, aimed the tip at Eli's ass and splayed his free hand on his best friend's lower back. He let Eli brace his weight as he shifted forward.

At first he thought it wasn't going to work. No way could the tiny opening accommodate his epic hard-on. He started to retreat.

"Don't you dare," Eli panted. "Try again. Push harder."

"You've got to relax, Cobra." Alanso petted the boss's flank. Rock-hard muscles were drawn tight. At the soothing strokes, they began to loosen. He positioned himself at the gateway to Eli's body once more.

And this time he sank inside, bit by bit.

"*Hijo de puta!*" Alanso shouted. When he paused, Eli seemed to groan louder, so he forged on. Soon the pressure on the head of his cock abated a tiny bit and he plunged in several inches at once. He froze, rubbing Eli's back and mumbling all kinds of Spanish—endearments, curses and reassurances.

He tried desperately to focus on helping his friend accept him in his ass instead of ruminating on losing his male-on-male anal virginity. Otherwise he wouldn't be able to keep from rutting like an animal for the two and a half seconds it would take to explode.

"I'm good now." Eli's promise sounded strained. "Jesus,

you're fucking thick. What do you have, a tree trunk back there?"

Alanso laughed. They both moaned at the friction.

"Just little old me." He took the opportunity to smear more lube around the circumference of his erection, impressed at the chubbiness of his cock. It stretched Eli until the ring of muscle was thin and tight where it hugged Alanso.

"Fuck. You." Eli grunted. "No. Better. Fuck me. I don't know how long I can take it this time. Hurry."

"Damn. Sorry, Cobra." Alanso started to retreat. He didn't want to hurt this man. Ever.

"Don't you dare pull out. That'll be worse. Come on. At least let me feel what it's like when it gets good. I want you to come in me. I want to walk around with you inside me today and wonder if anyone else can tell. I hope they can." He sounded like he might be getting horny again.

And no way could Alanso resist that siren song.

He worked his way forward and back until the flat pad of muscle over his pelvis fit tight to Eli's ass. He couldn't stop staring at the juncture of their bodies, where he and Eli became one. Fusing them tighter, he bottomed out.

"That's right. I have all of you, don't I?" Eli already knew the answer to that question. They both did.

"Hell yes." Alanso nuzzled Eli's neck until the man tipped his head, making more room. Al applied his lips to the spot just below his friend's ear and began to suck in time to the rocking of his hips.

"Fuck yeah." Eli didn't try to run, not that he could have. "Leave a mark. Let them all know I'm yours."

Alanso couldn't help himself. He fucked Eli. Not delicately, but as he needed. He rode Cobra while running his hands over the other man's arms, down his sides and through his hair. Never once did he stop feasting on the slightly salty flesh of Cobra's neck. Not when he could feel Eli's heart pounding in the vein there and knew he loved every moment of this as much as Alanso did.

A lifetime of doubt and the fear of rejection flew from his soul. This man would take him, however he was. This friend would never shy away. He accepted Alanso and loved him enough to let him have this.

In fact, it was better than that.

It seemed Eli needed it too. His grunts turned from those of a guy enduring rough treatment to one who reveled in it. The muscles of his ass began to clench rhythmically as he fucked against the pillow beneath him.

When Alanso applied the barest hint of teeth to Eli's neck, he roared. "Oh shit. Al. You're going to make me come again. Fuck. Ahhh."

Alanso might not have believed it, but there was no faking how stiff Eli got beneath him or the way his ass nearly squeezed Alanso's cock in two. He had to ram his hips forward to penetrate the nearly impossible pressure.

Then it relented, becoming intermittent as Eli spilled what little his balls had left to give directly onto Alanso's pillow. The power of that surrender combined with the tailor-made caresses of Eli's body on his.

Alanso shoved up on straight-locked arms, his back arching impossibly as he roared into the quiet morning air. Come jettisoned from his cock, flying up from the very bottom of his balls. It launched inside Eli, splattering as far and deep inside the man as he was capable of sending it.

Still his orgasm continued, lingering until the clamping of his muscles became almost painful and he was sure he had not a drop left to deliver. He tried not to collapse and crush Eli in the process, but it was no use. Every atom in his body turned to jelly. He counted on his best friend to catch him, cradle him, while he recovered from the storm of passion they'd invoked together.

When his cock softened enough to slip from Eli's body, he shifted, snuggling beside the man who'd trusted him so completely. Sweat adhered their bodies, making him sad as they peeled apart once more. So much for that shower.

"Are you okay?" Alanso traced one of Eli's brows above his

closed eyes.

"Mmm." He sounded like more of a pussycat than a poisonous snake at the moment. "Think I'll just take a nap, if you don't mind."

Alanso chuckled. "I could go for one too. Do you need me to go get a cloth or something? Clean you up?"

"Nah. Just want to lay here for a minute. I'm pretty sure you're going to need a new pillow, though." Eli cracked open one eye. It glinted with mischief that was reflected in his crooked grin.

Alanso felt something shift in the space between them. The bond he thought was already indestructible grew and strengthened. From this moment on, he knew they'd never let anything come between them again.

"Thank you." He didn't bother to hide the sheen of tears in his eyes. How could he when Eli had ripped himself open and put his soul on display?

"Anytime." Eli shifted until he could engulf Alanso's hand in his. "Well, except next time. That's my turn to see what had you making all that racket back there."

Alanso coughed. Because he had a pretty good idea what had caused all the noise from beneath him. And he couldn't wait to experience it for himself.

They drifted in utter peace for several minutes.

"Cobra."

"Yeah? What do you need, Alanso?" It sounded as if even those few coherent words took a lot of effort to produce.

"Quit talking to me in your voicemail voice." Al swallowed hard. The sexy rumble made it hard to concentrate.

"What does that even mean?" Eli smiled. He loved it when Alanso made words up.

"You know, like when you recorded your message for the shop. Slow, clear, serious... I admit some of the hang-ups we got at first were me listening to it. It's sexy as hell, and—oh, shit... I just thought of something. It's Friday, right? Don't you have to be to work in..." He glanced at the clock. "...five minutes? Unless you talked someone else into accepting the tanker delivery this morning."

"Son of a bitch!" Eli slapped his palm on the bed. "You're right. I have to get down there. Unless…"

"I love you and all, but not enough to get out of this bed anytime soon, *cabrón*." When Eli slapped his ass—hard—Alanso full-out laughed for the first time since their trip to help the crew.

Eli leapt from bed and jogged to his room. Alanso rolled onto his side, braced on one arm so he could watch his *lover's* white ass in motion. Never in a million years would he have imagined Cobra would welcome him in there.

Or places even more well guarded.

Like his heart.

Chapter Eight

Eli kicked back in his office chair. It was the passenger seat of a Ferrari F360 Challenge the guys had salvaged and mounted on a swivel base. They'd surprised him with it for Christmas a few years back. Holden was a genius when it came to reupholstering and the interior work of their restorations. He'd done a great job on this and they used it as part of their portfolio when seducing upscale customers.

Sally had completed the masterpiece by imprinting the back of the headrest with a King Cobra logo and script with some fancy scrollwork he'd never get tired of looking at. In fact, it might have to be his next tattoo. Either that or Alanso's name.

Damn, one day into this crazy turn they'd taken and he was already dreaming like a thirteen-year-old girl. Might as well doodle some hearts on his classic car blotter.

Admitting to himself that detailed office work like the statement reconciliation he'd been attempting was futile, Eli reached for the mail overflowing his inbox.

Bryce handled customer service. He kept urging Eli to hire a business manager. Maybe he had a valid point.

Eli grimaced as the stack of envelopes spilled onto the industrial carpet.

He gathered them up, glancing at the return addresses, until one crisp letter caught his eye. The staid font declared it was from the *National Archives, Records of Immigration and Naturalization Service.*

Was it a coincidence he'd found this today? He'd mailed his inquiry months ago. Did he want to ruin the glow surrounding him and—hopefully—Alanso? He felt like they'd made some progress this morning. Maybe Alanso would finally believe he'd never shake Eli.

Unless something inside the envelope gave him reason to doubt again.

Eli cursed and ripped the letter open. He didn't *have* to share the contents, though he didn't believe in withholding info as a form of protection. Secrets always came back to bite you in the ass. Alanso had a right to know whatever was in this damn envelope. Maybe it was nothing. No news. Records were spotty at best in the government, right?

As he scanned the documents inside, his heart cracked.

It wasn't nothing. It was something.

He knuckled moisture from the corner of his eye. Too many times lately, he'd resorted to that gesture. This was going to suck.

Fortunately the gang had made a lunch run, all but him. He'd told them he'd watch the pumps and deal with any walk-ins while they were hitting the diner downtown. Alanso had offered to stay behind, but neither of them wanted to act differently around the Hot Rods.

Even Tom had joined his "kids". *Shit.* Eli could really use a sounding board right about now. Since it wasn't possible, he did the next best thing.

Abandoning his desk chair with a loving pat, he made his way toward the garage. He couldn't go for a drive, but he could sit in his car and devise a plan for how to break the news. In the garage, his fingers trailed over the high-gloss finish Sally had applied to his Cobra. The new product seemed almost like a thin coat of glass. The deep blue of his classic paint job shone even in the interior space and the contrast of the pearly white racing stripes made him sigh.

He loved this car.

Had since the moment he'd first seen one at a show his dad had taken him to as a kid. He'd sworn then and there he'd have one just like it someday. Once he made up his mind about what he wanted, he didn't change it very often.

This Hot Rod was his for life.

"Cobra?" Sally startled him when she knocked lightly on the passenger window, though he could hear her just fine considering the topless car. "Can I join you?"

"You didn't go with the guys?" He raised a brow at her.

"Nah. Wasn't feeling up to all that commotion. Thought I'd enjoy some peace and quiet for a bit." Her soft admission echoed in the emptiness of the usually bustling space.

Very unlike her to seek out solitude. She'd grown used to activity all around, being raised in a polygamous commune. Lack of company had never been an issue with untold brothers and sisters. When she'd first come to them, she'd often ended up sleeping at the foot of Alanso's bed or on the futon in Cobra's room because being alone frightened her.

Neither of them had minded.

The handle clicked as she pulled it and tucked inside, shutting the door carefully.

"You okay?" Eli scanned her from the Louis Vuitton bandana she tied her hair back with to the shit-kicker boots encasing her guaranteed-to-be-prettily-painted toes. She looked all right. Maybe a little flushed, but sexy as ever. Then again, the tough lady could be sitting there missing a limb and she wouldn't let her pain show. "Need me to take you to the doctor's this afternoon?"

"Oh. Nah." She smiled as she angled herself toward him. Only someone as petite as her would be able to manage folding their legs into that pretzel shape, while keeping her boots off the upholstery, in the tiny enclosure. "I'll live. I'm probably faring better than you, anyway. You only think in your car when you've got a big problem. This baby's for driving, not moping. Please tell me Alanso isn't the trouble. You're not going to dump him, are you?"

"What?" He shook his head. "Hell no. You know me better than that, Sally. Don't you?"

A ghost of sadness crossed her face, making him tilt his head when she answered, "I do. Yes. I'm betting you two are forever. You've been besties since the moment you met. Throw in good sex, and what more could you need? I'm happy for you."

"It doesn't seem like it." It was a statement, not an accusation.

"A little jealous, I guess." She shrugged and looked away. "I'm not getting any younger, Cobra. I want a guy that looks at me like you two drool over each other. Even if you were trying to deny it these past few months."

"I don't think that's going to be a problem, Sally." Eli wished Alanso were here now or that they'd had just a little more time to discuss their long-term game plan. Too many things swirled in his mind. Big things. Things he couldn't afford to fuck up by rushing.

One at a time, he cautioned himself. Slow and steady.

"Yeah. Right." She sniffled.

"You sure you're not coming down with a cold?" Eli lifted up to withdraw a rag from his pocket. He shivered when a slight ache reminded him of how he'd started his morning. "It's clean, I was just going to make sure I didn't get any bug guts on the car last night."

"Thanks." When she accepted the soft cloth, she noticed the paper in his fist. "What've you got there?"

"Bad news."

"Ah, shit. *That's* why you're out here." She wiped her nose daintily then held out her hand. "Well, let me see what's got you all knotted up again. I liked seeing you relaxed this morning. It's been a while."

He nodded, both permission and agreement, before handing her the letter.

Being smart, she read it faster than he had. Then she clutched the paper to her chest and raised the cloth to her face again. Dabbing her eyes, she managed to preserve most of her elaborate makeup. He loved seeing what creative work she did on the canvas of her already-gorgeous features each morning.

"His poor mom." She let out a tiny sob.

Eli reached over the gear shifter to hold her hand. He

considered dragging her into his seat but didn't want to risk tempting himself. She didn't need him mauling her now. Under the weather and heartbroken weren't conditions conducive to getting it on in a sports car.

Hell, not much was. But he'd make do, if he ever got the chance.

"I have to tell him, right?" He wished there was another option.

"Of course you do." Her wobbling lower lip firmed as she found her legendary determination. "If you don't, I will."

"Will what?"

Eli jumped at the sound of Alanso approaching. The guys must have dropped him off outside so he could walk his bike into the shelter. He'd been upset enough last night to ditch the glowing neon motorcycle at the bottom of the staircase to their apartment.

Not far behind him, the rest of the men marched toward the shop.

In his rearview mirror, Eli spotted them joking around. Bryce punched Holden in the shoulder as wisecracks were doled out like candy at Halloween. Staggered in an uneven line, their forms were impressive. And reassuring. Together they could survive this like so many other devastations before.

He looked to Sally and nodded.

They both climbed from his beloved hot rod to greet the gang.

"Hey, guys. Come in here, would you?" Eli waved them forward and motioned for them to gather around. He was glad to see his dad bringing up the rear. Tom would make sure they didn't go haywire.

"Oh shit. This must be serious. Let me guess...Alanso is horrible at sucking cock and you've decided to go back to women?"

"Kaige!" Sally glared at him.

Tom pretended to plug his ears. But he grinned while he did it.

"Just kidding, *Salome*." The bastard knew she hated her full name. "Everyone in the fucking apartment knows how good Al is. They weren't exactly quiet. Jesus. Could you guys at least have the decency to wait until a respectable hour to make that ruckus? Some of us need our beauty sleep."

"Clearly." Carver looked down his nose at Kaige and plucked one of his dreads from the bunch. "What you're getting ain't working, buddy."

Kaige took a half-hearted swipe at Carver. The bickering could easily have deteriorated into a scuffle if Roman hadn't stepped in and separated them.

"Thanks." Eli swallowed hard. "I'm glad we're all together because what I have to say is going to be difficult. Especially for one of us."

Alanso went white as a sheet, impressive given his darker skin, when Eli looked in his direction.

"Careful, son." Tom put his hand between Alanso's shoulder blades and leveled a serious stare in Eli's direction. "You sure you want an audience for whatever bomb you're about to drop?"

"Yeah. This isn't...personal...about me and Alanso, I mean." He cleared his throat.

"Anything you have to say to me you can say in front of them." Al looked up and down the line of mechanics. "It's not like I won't tell them right after anyway."

Despite Eli's reassurance, the gang seemed on edge as they positioned themselves between Cobra and Alanso.

"I wish you'd all give me a little fucking credit. I'm not going to ditch him. Not today and not ever. Who could walk away from a guy who's your best friend? And more?"

Alanso swallowed hard and nodded. "*Loco,* but I believe you."

"Truth is, Al. No one could leave you."

"Tell that to my mom," he sneered.

"I would." Eli handed Alanso the letter. "I tried, actually. But I'm sorry, Alanso...she passed away."

"What?" He might have stumbled back if Tom hadn't been there to catch him or the rest of the Hot Rods didn't crowd in closer to lend their support.

Mumbles raced through the team as Alanso read the paper, which wobbled like a wheel at the end of a bent axle in his grasp.

"It says she never made it to Cuba." Sally couldn't restrain her tears as she related the official history in much nicer phrasing than the version Alanso digested. Those clinical descriptions would probably be branded into his brain for life.

Eli crossed to him, putting his hands on Alanso's shoulders as he finished discovering the details of an event that was ancient history.

"I guess they didn't believe her when she said she had a child. That she'd left her son at daycare in the morning so she could work. They thought it was an excuse because she couldn't produce any proof. No papers or pictures. How stupid!" Sally swiped the back of her hand under her nose and sidled closer, laying her cheek on Alanso's knotted biceps.

"They took her by van to Florida to deport her." Eli took up when the rest of the Hot Rods looked to him for more information. "Along the way the car broke down. In the middle of the night. They said she was distraught, hysterical, about her baby. The guards didn't listen. And when they took everyone from the vehicle on the side of the road, she ran. In the dark."

"She fled into the highway," Alanso finished reading in a monotone that scared Eli. He crumpled the letter in his fist, then finished on his own. "Was struck and killed instantly by a passing car. Not a drunk driver. Just some poor bastard on his way to third shift. The judge ruled no fault. None but her own."

"Oh God." Tom squeezed Alanso's shoulder from behind. "I'm so sorry, kid."

"Al." Carver reached over and put his palm on their friend's bald head. He rubbed it before stepping aside and letting the other Hot Rods near.

The rest of the guys followed suit, instilling what comfort they could.

Eli stared straight into unfocused eyes. "She never left you, Alanso. Not because she wanted to. All those times, you weren't wrong. She loved you very much. Maybe now you can honor those memories, preserve and cherish them, instead of doubting."

"Don't tell me what to do, *cabrón*. Just because we fucked doesn't mean you know how this feels." He wrenched away from the helping hands on him and punted an oilcan across the garage. It clattered as it rolled before skidding to a stop.

"Fuck you." Eli got right in his face, to hell with the guys attempting to hold him back. "How dare you tell me I don't know what it's like to lose your mother?"

"Eli! Alanso!" Tom cut through their rage in a second. His censure was like a hot knife through butter. "Shut the hell up. Both of you. Neither of your moms would condone this. Haven't you suffered enough?"

"You're right, Tom." Alanso hung his head. "*Lo siento*. I think…I'm going to go for a ride. I'll be back when I can think straight. I promise."

He wandered toward the exit in a crooked line.

Tom murmured, "Don't let him go. He needs you."

Doubt, confusion, hurt, fear and anger all melted away. Only one thing was important right now. Comforting his mate.

"Alanso, wait," Eli commanded.

And his lover obeyed.

Alanso turned around slowly. A mixture of fury, pain and anxiety radiated from his chocolate eyes, but he returned step by step until he lingered by Eli's side.

"Not alone." Eli opened the door of the Cobra and ushered Alanso inside. "I'll take you anywhere you want. Stay as long as you need. You don't have to grieve by yourself. Trust me, I *do* get it. How bad it hurts. I don't even mind if you need to swipe at me. Anybody. Whatever it takes, I'll have your back. I would never leave you to sort through this on your own. I'd never leave you period. Understand?"

"I think so." Alanso leaned forward, grasping his knees and

curling into himself. "Thanks, Cobra. Just motor. I don't care where."

"You got it." He jogged around to the driver's side. Holden shut the passenger door carefully, patting Al's shoulder as Eli tossed his garage keys to Roman. "Lock up tonight, please?"

"Of course." The slap he landed on Eli's ass stung a little, but the pressure was welcome. It gave him something other than the agony in his heart to concentrate on while he buckled his seatbelt.

"We'll see you guys later. Don't worry. Everything will be all right," Roman assured them.

"Come on, Cobra." Alanso rocked now. "Fucking go."

Tom nodded when Eli glanced at his father.

Salome blew them a kiss as they rolled from the garage and weaved down the winding road into the countryside.

Chapter Nine

Alanso nearly crashed off his teetering barstool as he leaned forward to flag down the bartender, Ward.

"Don't break your neck, Hot Rod." The guy ambled over as Eli set Alanso to rights on the precarious perch. Swaying himself, it was a tricky operation. "I see you. I'm just not serving you another drink."

"Ah, come on. Plenty of time 'fore last call." He concentrated on not slurring.

"Right. But no way in hell am I risking your girl Sally kicking my ass for poisoning you." He shook his head while running a cloth over beer glasses. "She scares the piss outta me."

"Hey now," Eli chimed in. "Watch yourself."

"I know, I know." Ward grinned. "Nobody messes with your gang."

"Damn straight." His assertion was somewhat less threatening when he belched loud enough to crack Alanso up.

"I'm so glad I'm not going to be you guys tomorrow." Ward smiled as he shook his head. "So what's the occasion, anyway?"

"My mom's dead." Alanso raised his glass, unsure if he would laugh or cry at the dry toast. Didn't matter when the vessel slipped from his fingers and clattered to the bar where it lay rolling in an uneven circle. Luckily, unbroken.

Ward paused. He looked to Cobra, who nodded from where he sat shoulder-to-shoulder with Alanso. "Happened a long time ago. Found out today."

"Shit, man." The apology didn't stop Ward from collecting the empty and refusing to replace it. "I'm sorry to hear that."

"'S okay. Means she didn't walk out on me."

A big, warm hand rested on his shoulder. Eli. "Maybe we'd better text somebody to come get us. A couple somebodies so my car gets home too."

"Sure, Cobra." Alanso patted his pocket. "Don't think I got my phone."

"Here." It took several tries for Eli to jam his hand in his jeans and retrieve his smartphone. "Fuck. Dead battery."

"I could call for you." Ward reached for the bar phone.

"Did I hear that right?" A sultry voice snaked between Cobra and Alanso, followed by the woman who'd spoken. It might have been beer goggles talking, but she looked pretty fine to Alanso. She sported a low-cut bedazzled T-shirt, skintight jeans and a pair of sexy cowgirl boots. "Two Hot Rods looking for a ride?"

"Fawn." Eli groaned softly. "Imagine seeing you here."

"The Psycho Ward *is* one of my favorite bars. Maybe yours too after the last time we ran into each other, huh?" She rubbed herself on Alanso's man like she owned him. He would have staked a claim—with a big juicy kiss or maybe a public blowjob—if he'd been able to coordinate his limbs well enough to reach around her fake, balloon-sized tatas.

Well, they were sort of pretty, anyway. He'd like to motorboat them.

"I suppose I have some fond memories here." Eli glanced to Alanso. "But not tonight so much."

"Aww, having a bad day, honey?" She practically climbed into Eli's lap.

Alanso wished he'd thought of that himself. Well, maybe they should go home. It could comfort him to curl up on their enormous sectional couch with Cobra and the rest of the gang.

"More Alanso than me. But yeah." Eli tried to evade her wandering hands and edge toward Alanso.

"Oh boy, that's no good." Her overdramatic pout emphasized her full lips. She wormed her way between them and nestled her rounded booty against Alanso's thigh. "I bet I can help turn things around for you guys."

"Which one of us?" Alanso couldn't believe she'd be as bold as she sounded.

"Well, your boss here can vouch for my skills." She snagged a cherry out of her froufrou drink and twisted the stem into a knot with her tongue. A few chews and she swallowed the fruit, depositing the stem into his empty glass. "Wouldn't mind trying you both on for size."

Ward seemed to have vanished, retreating into the shadows to attend to patrons on the other side of the polished hardwood.

"More than anything, I need to take a whiz right about now." Eli stood and brushed her clinging limbs from his body. She was like a grabby octopus. "You've had more than me, Alanso. Come on."

"We'll be right back." Al grinned at the woman and her sparkly boobies.

"Then maybe you'll give me a few dances before we hit the road?" She gyrated against him. He was only human. She felt good and smelled pretty. Club music acted like kryptonite on his better sense. It worked him up every time.

"Sounds good, Bambi."

"It's *Fawn*, baby." She patted his bald head. "Don't worry, I'll make sure you don't forget after tonight."

Batting her lashes hard enough to start a windstorm in Kansas, she turned and sashayed toward the juke box in the corner.

"Are you crazy?" Eli grabbed Alanso's ear and dragged him to the men's room.

"Nope. But I'm pretty hammered." He laughed as he began to forget about why he'd been so damn depressed. "And I'm about to piss on your sneakers, *maricón*."

"Fucker." Eli shoved him through the swinging door, a begrudging chuckle edging around his disapproval. "Don't you dare."

They adopted their stances, whipping their cocks out without any awkwardness. Hell, they'd done this about a million times before. Except tonight Alanso remembered what it was like to taste Cobra's cobra. What it was like to touch him, hear him, feel him.

"*Mierda!* I can't go with a hard-on." He concentrated on the business at hand.

"How the fuck do you have a boner?" Eli looked at him as if he were a freak of nature. "I'm pretty sure we broke some records tonight."

"Eh. Good genes, I guess." He sobered for an instant. "Look, Eli. What's the deal with this girl? Was she hot? Do you like her? Can we...try something?"

"Like what?" Eli tried to stuff his penis in his pants, but the truth was he sported some wood himself, making it difficult to repackage his junk. "Today's been wild enough, hasn't it? Maybe we should call it quits before we do something stupid."

"I'm asking you to do her. With me. I want to know if we can. I didn't like seeing her touch you. But...I still like pussy, Cobra. I'm not, like, completely not wanting chicks anymore." He washed his hands off, then scrubbed some cold water over his face. "*Joder!* This is hard."

"I hear what you're saying." Eli took his time drying his hands. "I agree. I don't know how to say what I want. But, yeah, like the crew. Like the guys. I want both."

"So we're bi, I guess is what I mean." Alanso swallowed hard and looked up at Eli. "Right?"

"Uh, sure." Eli shrugged. "Why do we have to call it something?"

"No reason." He turned to leave.

"Wait." A restraining arm wrapped around his shoulders from behind, tugging him toward the solid warmth of his best friend. "I want you, Alanso. That's not going to change. And yeah, I still feel like messing around with other people. Women. Maybe the Hot Rods if they're into it. Only if you're with me. But...I'm not sure Fawn should be on that list. I'm kind of over sex for the sake of quick relief. It's so much better when it means something. Like this morning."

"I know who I'd like to have most." Sally flashed through

Alanso's mind.

"Yeah, me too." Eli rested his forehead on Alanso's baldness.

"But I don't want to fuck that up. This is like starting over. Nothing I knew about dating and how stuff works is true anymore." Alanso hated the tightness in his throat. "I don't have any swag when it comes to this. I need training wheels. Or…whatever Fawn's packing in that skimpy shirt."

Eli chuckled against him. The heat of his breath and the dampness of his lips weren't helping the situation in Alanso's pants.

"Okay, what you're saying makes sense. Kind of." Eli shook his head. "But I don't think tonight's the night. It's not smart. We're wasted. Let's consider this when our brains dry out."

"Mmm-hmm," Alanso agreed. "Fine. Right, as usual. But can we at least dance some of this off so I'm not dying tomorrow?"

"I'm not so great at that. Not like you with those damn hips." A groan fell from Eli's throat.

"You weren't complaining 'bout my hip action this morning, *amigo*." He trotted toward the door before Eli could retaliate. "Come on. You're drunk enough not to care what you look like."

"Great. Real comforting. Asshole," Eli grumbled, but followed.

"Maybe later you can play with it. If you practice the motion of the ocean." Alanso didn't wait for a response. He strode over to the dance floor, undid a few buttons on his shirt, and showed off his chest and abs as he undulated to the beat of Don Omar's "Taboo".

When he curled his fingers to beckon Fawn or maybe Eli, who stood behind her, they both answered his call.

A couple hours later, Eli believed he was much more grounded. The loopy daze and comforting numbness had worn off. In fact, some of him felt like he'd gotten internal road rash. He couldn't wait to faceplant into his bed. Or maybe Alanso's.

Those damn sheets had been as luxurious as they looked.

"You boys going to invite me in for a drink?" Their courtesy cab driver licked her red lips and tossed her hair as she parked in front of Hot Rods.

"I don't think we're up for that tonight, Fawn." Eli climbed from the car. "Sorry we dragged you out of your way, if that's what you expected. Go ahead and pull up to the pump. I'll fill your tank for your trouble."

"I'd rather a tour of your shop instead." She winked at him. "I have a thing for big engines, you know?"

Alanso caught his gaze and shrugged. What was five more minutes before getting upstairs to the rest of the guys, Sally and bed? Ugh. It seemed like a lot, but what could he say? She *had* carted their lame asses home.

"Sure." He opened her door and handed her out. Mostly so she wouldn't bust her ass in those crazy cowgirl boots. Last thing they needed was a lawsuit.

Of course she took the opportunity to falter, snugging up tight to his side and encircling his waist. Though he knew it was just his hormones talking, Eli couldn't deny she felt nice. Toned, yet soft in all the right places.

Maybe he was being too rash. He'd had her once before. At least, he'd come in her mouth after a behind-the-bar blowjob. When he'd offered to return the favor, she giggled and said she'd take a rain check. He'd assumed she just liked the power of reducing a guy to begging. Now he wondered if she expected him to make good on his debt.

Alanso glanced over at him and mouthed, *Please?*

The uncertainty mirrored in his friend's warm gaze stabbed Eli hard in the gut. If this would ease his worry and erase some of the stress of the day, instead of adding more, who was he to make that call for them both?

"Shit." Eli remembered too late that he'd tossed his keys to Roman. Double shit when he grabbed the handle, tested it and the heavy metal swung open. "It's impossible to find good help these days."

He made a mental note to follow up on security measures in the morning, then held the door for their guest. When Alanso passed, Eli whispered, "You're on. Let's see what we can do. Together. Practice for when it actually counts."

Alanso winked and trailed his hand over the bulge in the crotch of Eli's jeans. "My turn."

Chapter Ten

Salome twirled her paintbrush, then dabbed it in the purple oils she'd mixed up to exactly the right hue on her palette. She swirled the bristles through the paint then began to stroke it onto her canvas. Which wasn't actually a canvas at all. Nor was it a car for once.

The memorial rock she decorated mimicked the one that held a place of honor in Tom's memory garden. Surrounded by wildflowers, it had become a spot for all of them to go to contemplate what they'd lost and the home they'd found.

Alanso should have a marker for his mother. Something to remind him of the adoration his heart had harbored since he was a little boy. He'd loved the woman who hadn't abandoned him by choice. Now maybe he could give himself permission to admit it. At least Sally hoped he'd work up to that stage eventually.

Art was the only thing that could calm her when her mind raced along dangerous curves. She couldn't put the brakes on imagining all the horrible reasons the pair of Hot Rods hadn't answered her calls. Or Tom's, for that matter.

Where had they gone? Were they safe? Was Alanso okay?

She switched brushes and added an elaborate swirl of contrasting green behind his mother's name.

And then she heard it. The roar of an engine. It didn't sound like Eli's Cobra, but no one else would pull up at this hour. Maybe they'd taken a taxi.

"Oh thank God." She finished the section she worked on, unwilling to risk a color mismatch in the morning when it'd cost her just a few minutes to complete the design. She was nothing if not a perfectionist.

Besides, it'd take a bit for the guys to pay the driver and collect themselves. Especially if at least one of them had been drinking. Still, why hadn't they called her for a ride?

Her nerves got the better of her.

Cans rattled as she slopped thinner into them then dumped in her brushes. A few more details and she'd be set to advance. Ready to open her arms to Alanso, she covered the switch with her fingers. About to shut the light to her workspace off, she prepared to welcome him home. Gently, with warmth and empathetic kindness. In some ways, she'd lost her entire family too.

And that's when she heard a gasp.

"I knew you boys would change your minds." Obnoxious fake giggling followed.

They didn't! They wouldn't!

Sally cracked open the door to her studio and saw... Yes, they surely would.

Artificial platinum blonde hair whipped around as the object of their combined attention squirmed onto the hood of the Fisher restoration they'd just finished today.

Sally couldn't believe they'd brought some skank to the garage. Even worse, Eli let that bitch make an ass print on the perfect paint job she'd slaved over for a full day. Those fucking pricks!

She tried to drum up more anger. But the truth was, it hurt.

Watching them together last night had bruised her heart. She wanted so badly for them to reach out and enclose her in their circle of desire, trust and love. But they hadn't. The only thing that had kept her spirits lifted was the stupid idea that maybe they were taking things slow. Finding their way.

But, it looked more like despite their constant flattery, she just wasn't their type.

Her boobs couldn't compare to that fake rack. For Christ's sake, those things didn't even budge when Eli yanked up his guest's shirt, rocking their toy several inches higher on the hood of the candy apple red '57 Thunderbird.

Even worse, Sally was trapped.

If she broke from her hiding spot behind the cracked open door to the painting booth, they'd spot her instantly. Enduring the awkwardness of that encounter was not something she wanted to add to the list of horrible experiences she'd been subjected to in the past twenty-four hours.

Crying was not an option. She'd done too much of that over these jerks already. Couldn't they see how much she loved them? Didn't it matter that she'd worship them and only them—well, just the Hot Rods, at least—instead of half of Middletown? And she wouldn't be stingy with her affection as soon she got off.

Apparently it didn't bother them to drive a model with sky-high mileage.

Not if the way they unwrapped the woman's tits was any indication.

Hell, it might as well have been Christmas. The lacey bra, which Sally begrudgingly admitted was very pretty and ultra feminine, was like some fancy paper removed with delicate swipes by the pair of dirt bags.

She liked her own style, but it blended in enough edge that it intimidated some guys.

Somehow, she'd thought her Hot Rods were different.

Guess not.

Each man took up residence on one side of the airhead. Alanso moaned, *Fawn*, before he latched on to the hardened tip of her nipple. Seriously? Big, dumb prey? She did have doe eyes that were rolling back as the guys got her up to speed.

Yet Sally couldn't back away, close her eyes or even blink. Because she'd imagined a similar scenario so many times, she couldn't believe that what she saw was real and not a figment of her envious imagination.

Eli reached up to knead the mound Alanso suckled. He plumped it for his best friend and helped the gorgeous bald man feast until he got his fill. Hungry, he licked, nipped and sucked some more.

While the engine man concentrated on laving Fawn's breast, Eli turned his attention to Alanso.

He stroked one hand up the guy's back, inspiring a shiver so intense Sally caught it from her station. When Cobra reached chest height, he snaked around and began to undo the buttons of Alanso's shirt. Some must have already hung loose as it didn't take long before Eli peeled the soft chambray from his best friend.

He paused when Alanso's wrists became entangled in the fabric. Pinned behind him, the shorter of the two didn't struggle to get free. In fact, he seemed to linger in the confines of his soft prison, implicitly trusting Eli to drive.

Shaping the result of their actions into pleasure greater than the two of them could have experienced alone seemed effortless for their boss. He used his thumb beneath Alanso's jaw to tip his head back. Then Eli took advantage of his friend's prone position to swoop in and seal his lips over the parted mouth of the panting engine master.

Instead of enjoying the show, as Sally would—hell, as she *did*—good ol' Fawn began to whine. "I thought you two were into me. Not each other."

"Why can't it be both?" Alanso hesitated.

If that bitch hurt him or made him timid about expressing his desire for Eli, nothing could hold Sally inside her bay. She'd jab a paintbrush in the woman's eye and beat her with her own boot.

"I like to be the center of attention." She pouted.

"Sorry," Alanso nuzzled her breasts, insinuating his face into her cleavage. "Got carried away there. Good point. Eli, we have to always remember to not let our girl feel left out."

The endearment from him nearly made Sally sick.

Her knees trembled and her stomach flipped.

Why couldn't she have been the one to satisfy them?

Fawn made a grab for Alanso, but he resisted kissing her on the lips. "Sorry, I'm not big into that."

Eli looked at him like he was full of shit. Hell, hadn't they just been about to suck face for a solid half-hour at least? It'd sure seemed like it from here. Sally could have watched that all day, never mind for a few minutes.

This girl was dumber than she looked. And that was saying something.

"Fine then." She huffed. "Let's jump right in. Somebody take their damn pants off. Mine too."

Eli didn't hesitate or bother to argue. He reached down and unbuttoned her jeans, then peeled them over her hips. She shed the denim like a snakeskin, making Sally realize how unappealing her own baggy work cargos and paint-slathered coveralls were compared to something like...that.

Once Fawn's pants drooped to her ankles, she kicked them off with a dainty flick, leaving her boots in place. Sally cringed when the bitch propped those clunky heels on the bumper. Apparently Alanso had his limits too. He removed the shoes with a swipe of his hand over each foot and tossed them a safe distance from the polished automobile.

Seduction had no place here. The guys operated in sync, with efficient yet brusque movements. They had a goal. It was right there between Fawn's thin, spray-tanned-to-the-point-of-oompa-loompa-orange thighs.

She must have decided not to wait any longer and wriggled out of her skimpy ass-floss, flinging the loop of lace into a toolbox nearby. Without wasting any time, she dipped her fingers onto the heart-shaped landing strip of trimmed hair above her pussy and played boldly with herself.

Sally had to give the girl props on that at least. She would have been a lot more shy. *Note to self: Maybe guys like confidence in bed.* Holding her own in the shop was easy. In sexual situations, less simple. Sometimes she still panicked at that look in a guy's eyes. The one that proclaimed he was about to take away her control...

Swallowing hard cleared the knot from her throat.

The guys helped too.

They got naked in a hurry.

Salome drooled. For a moment she erased Fawn and the ghosts of her past from her mental scenery. Actually, more like all she could see were the two Hot Rods. Sure, she'd drank in the sight of them shirtless a bazillion times as they strutted around the garage covered in grease and sweat. Or spied them in their shorts, grazing the snack cabinet of their shared apartment in the middle of the night.

She couldn't even count how often she'd spotted their bare assess when they'd gone through that mooning phase in their early twenties. Oh, those were the good old days. But it'd been a while and the guys had filled out some. More of the artwork she'd approved, and even drafted in some cases, decorated their skin.

To her, they were masterpieces.

The scar on Eli's elbow where he'd thrown his arm in front of a falling piece of sheet metal to protect Holden made her want to kiss it.

"You first." Eli graciously gestured toward the willing woman laid out for their enjoyment. He took himself in hand. It surprised her to see he wasn't entirely hard. Didn't he want to fuck this bar babe? Or maybe they'd drunk too much to perform up to their usual standards.

They'd been gone forever. And she had no doubt of their prowess. None of them were especially discreet, either with accounts of licentious nights or with the vocalizations of their pleasure when they brought women home. She thought she'd gotten used to it.

Clearly not.

Especially when they'd finally explained what had happened with the crew and how all her dearest fantasies could actually be within grasp. Right before they'd shattered her hopes.

Alanso looked to Cobra, then shook his head. "Be right back."

Sally gasped when he turned toward her hiding spot. He

jogged in her direction, his erection swaying in time to the fluid grace of his strides. *Oh shit!*

He tipped his head at the light streaming from her studio. Then shrugged and veered to the right. Into the supply closet.

What the fuck?

Several rapid heartbeats later, he emerged with something shiny in his fist. Condoms. The guys kept an emergency ration on the shelf by the first-aid kit. She had often tried not to notice how quickly the level dropped.

Was it because of her upbringing that she got horned-up by the community of sexy men surrounding her each day? That secret fear had kept her from expressing her misplaced curiosity for years.

Alanso handed the packets to Eli, who ripped one open.

Wetness gathered in her decidedly not ass-floss panties when Cobra grasped his mechanic's hips, rotated the guy toward him, then sheathed his cock with expert handling. He gave Alanso's hard-on a few test pulls before slapping his partner's ass and encouraging him to, "Go get her."

Fawn wrinkled her nose at the display that warmed Sally's heart, along with regions slightly farther south.

Alanso stepped between the woman's knees and tugged her low enough to align her pussy with the tip of his cock. His jerky motions and the way he kept glancing at Eli emphasized the impact of today's revelations on the man. He was never less than smooth.

"Do it," Cobra encouraged him. "You wanted to know what it would be like."

"It's not the same as I thought," he murmured.

Eli stepped behind Alanso, blocking some of Sally's fantastic view. Well, replacing it with a different manscape. He wrapped his lover in his arms and held on for a moment before sliding his hands lower to the still-firm cock and heavy balls at the apex of Alanso's thighs.

The way he touched his friend, with authority and a sense of how much pressure was enough, awed her. So different than the care she'd taken with the men she'd tried on for size.

Cobra positioned Alanso's cock so that the tip insinuated itself in Fawn's pussy.

When the woman's eyelids fluttered closed and she mewled, Eli swooped in close. He whispered things intended for Alanso's ears only. If the woman a dick's length away couldn't interpret the swish of sound, Sally certainly had no chance. But whatever coaching Eli did seemed to slam Alanso into gear.

Spanish began to flow from his lips. She loved to hear him speak it. He'd taught her enough that they could piss off the rest of the Hot Rods by having coded conversations. But now it was too fast, too broken for her to catch more than a lot of curses.

Ones he meant in a good way, apparently.

He tipped forward and began to fuck. His powerful thighs flexed as he bent then straightened. The quasi-squat drove him deeper into Fawn with each thrust. Sally was surprised to see he'd closed his eyes when the bounty of their catch's chest loomed so near.

Instead, he seemed more infatuated with the pressure of Eli's now-stiff cock riding the crack of his ass.

"Are you going to do me, Cobra?" He glanced over his shoulder.

"What?" Fawn roused from the hood. She levered up onto her elbows. "Are you guys gay or what? I never heard any rumors about that. Lots of other crazy stuff, but never that."

Holy shit. Was she enjoying the lavish attention of these two dream guys or not?

Sally wanted to march out there and slap the cunt. Her voice didn't even hold a hint of smoke. She'd snapped from her artificial moans the instant the guys didn't grant her their full interest. Fawn might have even bigger issues than Salome.

Huh.

Anger crept up inside her, burning her chest, neck and cheeks. The Hot Rods were wasting their effort on this ungrateful cow. Sally would have taken their affection and magnified it. She would have reflected it back, brighter and more focused than they shined it on her.

"Do you want him to fuck you or not?" Eli growled.

"Yeah, yeah." Fawn collapsed onto the hood again, her hair billowing out from beneath her shoulders. "Harder. Give it to me."

Sally rolled her eyes.

With Fawn's attention diverted, Eli continued his subtle flexing. His ass cheeks bunched then relaxed, gliding his cock through the valley of Alanso's crack as the man began to pick up steam. At the end of the day, it was a physical reaction, especially with Eli triggering illicit pleasure from behind.

Had they done it yet? Had they tried fucking?

It sure had sounded like it this morning. But she knew the guys well enough to know their voices. Even when they turned into guttural shouts and groans.

It had been Eli making the most noise.

What if he'd let Alanso take him?

Sally couldn't help it. She slipped her fingers into the waistband of her pants, rubbing the knot of her engorged clit. Ignoring Fawn, she concentrated on the intersection of Eli's and Alanso's bodies. If Eli hadn't taken him yet…did that mean…

Was Alanso still an anal virgin?

Was Cobra teasing him mercilessly?

It sure would explain the way Al threw his head back, so it rested on Eli's shoulder and the cording of his neck as he pumped his cock deeper, harder, faster into Fawn.

"Now we're talking." She scratched her fire-engine-nails down Alanso's chest, probably leaving a mark. When she made like she'd repeat the gesture, Eli removed her hands.

Clearly, no one had the right to claim Alanso. No one other than him.

Sally wished she could be appended to that list.

She rubbed circles over her pussy as Eli shuffled closer, nestling his dick against Alanso's ass tighter so the man had to be imagining what it would feel like to be stretched wide and welcoming his boss deep.

Hell, Sally was. Wondering both what it would be like to see Alanso taken and to experience the rush herself as a third in their exchange. A gasp left her lips when the idea alone triggered a clenching of her internal muscles. No one seemed to notice.

She bit the inside of her cheek to keep quiet.

Alanso made no such effort.

He grunted so loud the guys upstairs probably heard. Except they'd assume he was fucking Eli down here, not some cheap date.

Okay, so part of her knew she was being unfair to Fawn. The woman wasn't doing anything wrong. But it wasn't like they even cared for her. Not like the girls they sometimes laughed with or found interesting for a week or two. Yet she didn't seem to care.

If Sally were to be offered the chance to switch places with the woman right now, she wasn't sure she'd do it. She had to have both. Their carnal hunger *and* their affection. Neither of which seemed likely.

So instead she focused on what real caring she could see.

Eli continued to love Alanso from behind. Gentle, steady and thorough—he combined his subtle rocking with the counterpoint of Alanso's thrusting hips. Together they worked the system to deliver what they both needed.

In fact, Eli began to flush. His cheeks grew ruddy, like they were when he came in from a long run. His respiration emulated those early-morning post-workouts too. His chest met Alanso's back on each ragged inhalation. The contact seemed to rev them both higher.

Fawn began to chant, "I'm close."

The men let her derive whatever pleasure she could from their presence, but they seemed intent on each other too. More so, if Sally was being honest. Poor Fawn. Eli's hands migrated to Alanso's waist and gripped him tight. The white-knuckled clasp proclaimed his desperation and shot sparkles of arousal through Sally's veins as if champagne bubbled there instead of blood.

She wanted to witness Cobra surrender his legendary control.

Just this once.

Please.

Alanso held on with Herculean effort. His jaw clenched as he kept fucking and fucking—both Fawn when he drove forward and Eli when he put it in reverse. She would have sworn he did it for Cobra. If it weren't for his best friend, he'd have come already and gotten his quick relief. At least his misery seemed to have morphed into something easier to handle for the moment.

A few more passes of Alanso's toned ass over the full-length of Eli's impressive hard-on and Sally couldn't believe her eyes. Cobra stiffened. He dipped his head enough to bite into the nape of Alanso's neck like a dog securing its mate.

The mouthful of muscle also kept him from shouting and alerting Fawn to their game. With her eyes closed, absorbing the impact of Alanso's ramming hips, the woman on the car missed everything special about the encounter.

From this angle, Sally had all the good stuff to herself.

She beamed. Her fingers moved faster, tracing her slit and playing with her clit. She knew what was coming and she had to share it with them. For tonight only. And every night after in her dreams. Because she would never be able to wipe this from her memory.

Recalling the bond between the two men would be enough to fill her fantasies forever.

Her eyes dried out as she refused to blink, afraid to skip a millisecond of the impromptu peep show lest her arousal stop building along with theirs. She didn't want to miss her chance.

No need to worry.

The instant Eli erupted, splattering Alanso's lower back with a puddle of come, she mimicked him. Her body launched into an epic orgasm that seemed to match his in intensity.

Every time he spasmed, launching another shot of cream across Alanso's glistening skin, she clenched too.

Orgasm exploded through her, making her see stars. She leaned against the doorjamb to stay upright and covered her mouth with her free hand to keep from alerting them to her presence. Eli's pleasure seemed to go on as long as hers did.

The amount of semen he painted across Alanso impressed her.

Until she began to float down from the high and realized she'd crashed their party.

Horror infiltrated her relief. Guilt ate at her consciousness. Fully engrossed in their play, they wouldn't notice her if she stuck to the shadows she bet. Hell, they hadn't spotted her as more than a friend in the decade they'd lived together. She might as well be invisible.

Sally withdrew her hand, her body still humming. She took a deep breath, then snuck from her hideout, clinging close to the wall as she fled the scene of her crimes. It would have been impossible to stand there and watch them finish. To witness them give everything she wanted to some animal who didn't adore them for anything more than the size of their cocks or their handsome faces or the attention they'd give in exchange for basic relief.

Cool night air splashed her face and doused some of the flames they'd inspired. Ice froze her heart. The door might have made some noise as it shut behind her but she figured they wouldn't notice just now. When she raced upstairs, she didn't stop to answer the guys who called to her from the couch, where they watched some action flick.

The sound of explosions covered her sobs.

It also masked the echoes of her name on Alanso's lips as he overflowed the garage with his cries of completion, royally pissing off Fawn.

Even if it weren't for the sound effects of the Hot Rods entertainment, the shattering of Sally's heart deafened her.

Chapter Eleven

"I'm so glad your kids get you up at the asscrack of dawn." Alanso smiled and waved to the babies Joe and Mike held. "Plus the time difference between us helps."

"Why aren't you guys in bed yet?" Morgan wanted to know. She sat between the men and alternated entertaining each of their children. "Rough night?"

"You could say that. We fucked up." Eli let his head fall back and thump into the dark wood of Alanso's bed.

"No kidding." Joe laughed. "You should have done this months ago."

"Well, yeah, there's that. Mistake *número uno*." Alanso shook his head. They sat shoulder to shoulder in his room, videochatting with various members of the crew.

This was pretty cool. To see them and talk to them. It made Eli feel less far away from his distant family and the guys who'd become extended members by default.

No wonder Alanso had been addicted to this thing lately. He always had been the smarter of them when it came to people. Emotions.

Hopefully he could figure out a way to go forward. They needed direction.

"Don't let them bully you." Kate popped onto the screen as she snuggled into her husband's grasp. Mike sat with Joe, not unlike Alanso and Eli. Except their warmth and happiness was undeniable. The two little babies the muscular guys held attested to the strength of their love and its ability to grow.

Nathan and Abby cooed at each other, their miniature hands seeking their pal with clumsy swipes. Alanso noticed too. "Damn, they're BFFs already, aren't they?"

Kate giggled as she finger-combed Abby's hair. "Yeah. If we take one out of the room the other will bawl until we bring them back together."

"It's not pretty." The wry grin on Joe's face declared he didn't mind so much. "They're assuming control over here. Not even a year old and they have every last one of their aunts and uncles wrapped around their fingers."

Eli wiggled his own fingers when Nathan glanced his way. He smiled at the wide-eyed fascination in the little guy's gaze. "This one included."

"Then maybe you'll come see him in person sometime soon?" Morgan fit just right in the gap between her husband and Mike.

"If I can find the time. Business is doing great. Lots of work." Pride filled him. Even in tough times for luxuries, their clientele never slimmed. They did good work and people knew it. Customers came from several counties away to have Hot Rods attend to their babies.

Only the best.

"I was kind of wondering." Mike hesitated. As the foreman of the crew, he and Eli had always had plenty in common. "Wasn't sure about that since you could spare Mustang Sally for a few weeks."

"What?" Eli cocked his head.

"Uh-oh." Joe poked his crewmate in the side. "I don't think she's told him about her vacation yet."

"Look, King Cobra." Morgan always loved to use their nicknames. "She said she had time coming and she never gets to hang out with other women. Please don't harass her. Let us take her shopping and spoil her and...talk to her."

"What's all this about?" Alanso leaned in closer, scrutinizing their expressions. "When did she tell you she was coming?"

"Honestly, *we* told *her*." Kate sat up straighter, daring them to say one word. "Something's wrong. It's obvious. Just when we've got you two straightened out. Now Sally."

"What the hell are you talking about?" Eli didn't like the unease infiltrating his gut.

"She called earlier." Morgan looked at something off screen so she didn't have to meet their horrified stares. "It was obvious she was upset. She didn't say why, but I can guess."

"It's our fault." Alanso sagged. "Do you think she's grossed out by me and Eli? Will it bother her to live with us now?"

"I think you're *still* fucking this up," Mike barked. He didn't often lose his temper. The babies fussed a little and he melted immediately. He kissed Abby on the forehead and hugged her tight to his chest.

"Stop talking in code." Eli couldn't take much more of this.

"I don't think Sally's offended by your relationship. I think she's crushed you left her out." Kate spoke softer, "I know you didn't do it on purpose but something…somehow…"

"It was very obvious," Morgan confirmed her best friend's observation. "She's had her heart broken."

"Then let's go find her. Talk to her. Cobra, we can't let her leave. Not after tonight—"

"Fuck!"

"*Joder!*"

They cursed simultaneously, if in two different languages.

"It didn't take long for you to start thinking in each other's brains." Mike laughed. "But maybe you want to clue us in."

"We sort of hooked up with a chick in the garage earlier." Alanso scrubbed his hand over his face.

"Do you think…could she have seen us?" Eli had never felt so sick—or so embarrassed—in his life.

"*Come mierda.* I saw the light on in her studio, but I thought she'd just forgotten to turn it off again like usual." Alanso froze.

"Yep, I'd say there's a pretty good chance." Joe grimaced. "You idiots. Why? Why did you waste your time when you knew what you really needed?"

"Because I was afraid of fucking it up." Alanso didn't sound like he felt any better than Eli did. "I wanted to be sure before we approached her."

"And I'm still working my way through this." Eli waved his finger between Alanso and himself. "My dad said something about breaking up the band. Wondered which one of us would fuck up Hot Rods first. Not in so many words, but... Yeah, it made me worry."

"I understand the responsibility you feel." Mike didn't try to bullshit them about everything at risk. "But you aren't helping anyone by putting off the inevitable. You're only causing a lot of drama and delaying the outcome. Man up, Eli. Take your Hot Rods to the next level."

He closed his eyes.

When he opened them again, he nodded. Alanso smiled and knocked his shoulder into Eli's chest, causing the garage owner to show his hand. "Okay, then I guess we'd better go find our girl. Alanso took some notes while we were...busy...earlier. Maybe we could put them to good use."

"Uhhh." Kate looked to her husband, who nodded. "Sally's not home. She's sort of on her way here."

"What?" Right now?" Eli bounded from bed, uncaring that the camera now only caught him pacing. "When she's upset? In the dark? Jesus. It's a five-hour drive!"

Alanso buried his head in his hands, leaving his bald scalp to reflect the soft lamplight. He murmured, "She left?"

"I'm not happy about her hasty retreat either." Mike grimaced. "I tried to convince her to wait until morning—well, later morning—but she wouldn't hear of it. Honestly, though, she's got her hands-free unit hooked up and Kayla's in the other room keeping her company on the road."

"Thank God for Kaige and those new additions he's been testing out." Eli unwound just a tiny bit. "I don't like it, but I guess there's nothing I can do."

"You could get your plan together. Talk to Alanso. Talk to the rest of the guys. Figure out what you need so that when she comes home, you're ready." Mike's direct tone convinced Eli he'd thought about the solution for a while. "Don't chase her,

Cobra. She'll be safe here. Let our women talk to her. Convince her of the benefits so you can plead your case once she's cooled off and calmed down. It might do you some good to be without her for a bit. Maybe then you'll get your priorities straight. These people are not going to hang around forever. Not even for you. If you don't love them back—"

"I do!" Eli pounded his fist into his palm.

"All right, then." Mike held his hand out. "Take the time you wanted. You've got it now. Do this right. I'm afraid it's going to be your last shot."

"You text me the moment she walks her pretty ass through that door," Eli snarled.

"Want me to spank her for you?" Joe wiggled his eyebrows.

"Hey!" Morgan slapped her husband lightly on the shoulder. "Isn't it enough that you have four guys and four women of your own to play with?"

"Just offering a public service." He bussed his wife's cheek. "I can't handle anymore anyway. I pity the Hot Rods. That's a tall order."

The crewmembers laughed.

"I want to be you when I grow up," Alanso said softly.

"You're going to get there, honey. It's complicated." Morgan blew him a kiss. "Just keep your King Cobra in line and you'll be on your way."

"Promise?" He couldn't help but smile at the pretty woman who'd tamed Eli's cousin.

"Cross my heart." She did.

"Take care of Sally." Alanso rubbed his head. "I love her."

"We know." Kate smiled back at him. "And she's obviously got feelings for you. Strong ones. Or she wouldn't be running so hard."

"I hope we haven't destroyed that." Eli groaned. "Not when we were so close."

"Don't get ahead of yourselves." The voice of reason, in the form of a construction foreman, warned them. "In fact, it seems like you've had one hell of a day. Why not hit the hay? If

Mustang Sally isn't here in the next three hours and forty-two minutes or she gets disconnected from Kayla, I'll call you back. I swear."

Alanso seemed to melt into the pile of pillows on his bed. "You might have another great idea there."

"Please, don't make his head any bigger." Kate rolled her eyes. "Sleep well, guys. And Alanso, I'm so sorry to hear about your mother."

He let his lids sink and nodded. Eli climbed under the blankets beside him and gathered him to his chest. "You're right, it has been a long one. Thank you. For everything."

"Anytime. Goodnight boys," Morgan said with a smile.

Joe, Mike and Kate waved just before the screen went black.

Eli closed the laptop and set it on the nightstand before curling up behind Alanso. "We'll make this right. I'll fix it for us, Alanso."

"We'll do it together, Cobra."

"Even better." Eli smiled and laid his head beside his best friend's on their shared pillow. The rumble from the living room entertainment center soothed him as he thought of the rest of the Hot Rods nearby.

All but one.

Chapter Twelve

"Eli." The soft call rang through the darkness. Though the barest hint of salmon had begun to brighten the window, the man in Eli's arms was still draped in shadows.

"Yeah." He wrapped Alanso tighter, drawing him flush to his chest. They'd ended up lying on their sides, Eli behind his head engine tuner. Holding on to the other man helped ease his anxiety over Sally's safety just a little. More than two hours remained on the countdown clock to full-out panic.

"I can't sleep, Cobra."

"Me either." He sighed. "I keep thinking of Salome and how unworth it tonight was."

"*Lo siento.* This is all my fault. I pressured you. And I have to be honest." Alanso held his breath, then let it out slowly. "That sucked donkey dick."

"Mmm. Yep." A snort caused Eli's head to bounce on Alanso's shoulder as he tucked around the shorter man. He rubbed up and down Alanso's calf with his foot. The hair and hardness there felt so different from the women he'd slept with, it fascinated him. "It did. The worst sex I've had since my first time with Mary Beth Cole. I swear, I thought she was going to bleed to death after I popped her cherry. Tonight was so awful—you've ruined me for flings. But I'm responsible too. I've been in denial for months. You wouldn't have looked for a surrogate if I'd just given in to what we really lusted for in the first place."

"I guess." Alanso was too polite to admit the truth.

"I was trying to keep us from jacking up our relationship with the Hot Rods, yet in the end, that's exactly what I forced us into doing. Damn it." Eli deliberately relaxed each grouping of muscles in his body when Alanso began to caress his forearm, alerting him to how tense he'd become.

"Plus, I'm still horny." Alanso picked his head up just to thump it onto the pillow again. His bald skull left a dent in the feathers. "That bullshit screw didn't help at all. Especially when I can't stop thinking of Mustang Sally watching us. I know it's messed up but that kind of turns me on. A helluva lot more than *Bambi* ever could have."

"Oh thank God." Eli grabbed him and rolled. "I'm dying over here."

"You want to fuck me?" Alanso squirmed on his belly. Though the pillow obscured half of his face, the other half darkened. With need, embarrassment, or both, Eli couldn't quite tell.

Never again would he leave someone he cared for to wonder about their standing in his life or his heart. "So damn bad. I love you. I want you in every sense of the phrase."

"I want to be yours," Alanso whispered. "*Te amo, querido.*"

And though Eli had worried about the softer side of their affections, it didn't weird him out at all to drop a light kiss on Alanso's cheek. Maybe he deserved to take this man after all. He promised both of them he'd always respect and honor this bond, whatever they called it.

Stretched out over Al, Eli reached for the lube in the nightstand. He sat on his heels, with his thighs bracketing Alanso's. From there he was able to insert his fingers beneath the waistband of the briefs that hugged his boyfriend's sculpted ass, framing it to even greater perfection.

Thinking of Alanso like that sent shivers racing up and down Eli's spine and pumped his cock even fuller than it'd already been.

"I think I can feel traces of my come on you from before. Good boy for not washing it off. You liked it when I staked my claim, didn't you?" Eli rubbed his knuckles over the small of Alanso's back. Slightly sticky, they both moaned at the memory of how close they'd come to living their dream.

"*Mierda, sí!* No more almosts, Cobra." Alanso turned steely.

"This time for real. All the way."

"I'm glad you agree." He smacked the ass laid out before him, slightly paler than the rest of Alanso's tan skin. After another spank he kneaded the quivering muscles, separating the cheeks just a little. "Because no chance in hell am I stopping now."

He retrieved the lube from the sheets and snapped open the cap. In the brightening space he still had some trouble seeing the transparent liquid. Alanso's hiss let him know when the cool gel hit bull's eye.

"You'll appreciate that in a minute." Eli grunted. "Trust me, I can still feel how deep your cock was in me when I move. Thick fucker too."

Alanso stilled. "Did I hurt you?"

"Not in a bad way." Eli grinned. "Behave and I might even let you do it again soon."

"I'm about to come just thinking about it." A groan tore from his parted lips.

"Oh no." Eli slicked his fingers then his cock before tossing the lube onto the bed. "I want you good and fired up when I slide my cock into that tight ass."

"Not a problem." Alanso wedged his hand beneath his body to cup his hard-on. Even if he couldn't jerk himself in that position, he could apply some pressure. Maybe to squeeze the base of his shaft and prevent himself from tipping over the edge far too soon.

The angle of his hips presented his ass even more fully to Eli's roving hand. Cobra tucked his finger between those rock-hard cheeks and followed the valley between them to Alanso's hole.

They both shouted something unintelligible at the initial contact.

Eli sank inside his best friend, rubbing in tiny circles as he penetrated the rings of muscle protecting his rear. "Don't worry, *amigo*. I've done this before with chicks. If they can take me, you can."

"Just wish you'd hurry. All talk and no action, *pendejo*." Alanso grunted when Eli pushed harder, spearing deeper on each pump of his hand. "I'm no girl. Don't treat me like one."

"I don't doubt you can handle anything I have to dish out." Eli withdrew to shuck his own briefs. He groaned at the weight of his erection flopping free and the room temperature air on his hand, which felt downright icy after Alanso's core. He planted his knees on either side of Alanso's once again and tipped forward, shoving his hands beneath the guy's shoulders, cupping them in his palms to anchor his head mechanic while he roughly aligned their bodies. "But this is more to me than sex. Understand that or I stop right now."

Alanso gasped when Eli nuzzled him. "Wouldn't let you fuck me if it wasn't."

"You gave those guys in the woods a chance to touch what's mine." Eli had never experienced the burn of jealousy before. Never wanted to again.

"Practicing for you." Alanso rocked his ass backward. When the tip of Eli's cock wedged in perfect position for penetration, they both cursed.

"Do it. Do me." Alanso practically begged.

Eli hugged him and said, "My pleasure."

He began to forge inside Alanso, using steady pressure on the opening to his body.

At first he met with so much resistance, he wasn't sure he'd ever make it through. When he whispered, "Let me in. Please," Alanso relented.

Eli breached him.

Alanso's eyes flew open in the new dawn.

A beam of sunlight streaked through the window, illuminating his chocolate eyes as they widened. Eli advanced, joining them more fully. As Alanso's ass hugged inch after inch of Cobra's cock, he blanketed his lover with his body, hoping Al realized that Eli intended to have his back for life.

That hadn't changed, at least.

When he'd buried a significant portion of his shaft, he

paused.

"No." Alanso bucked beneath him. "You'll give me everything or nothing at all."

"Jesus. Crazy Cuban. I'm just letting you adjust." Eli gritted his teeth to keep from riding like he yearned to.

"Ever notice patience is not my strong suit?" Alanso shoved against the bed. He thrust himself up over Eli's cock until they met abdomen to ass. Not a single molecule of air separated them.

Eli prayed he wouldn't embarrass himself by shooting before he'd even begun to really fuck. He thought about the model number of the new spark plugs he had to order tomorrow, and tried to figure up the total cost to distract himself from the pulsing of Alanso's fist-tight flesh.

The tang of iron made him realize he'd bitten his tongue again too.

Under control, barely, he reprimanded Alanso for nearly stealing his thunder. "If you do that again, I'll make you wait a year before I fuck you next. I'd like to give you a proper ride, if you don't mind. Don't fucking sabotage me."

"Fancy shit later." Alanso moaned when Eli withdrew then slammed deep.

"You're that close, are you?" Eli grinned when he recognized the burn of impending orgasm in his friend's tone, the set of his jaw and the dazed quality to his stare.

"*Estoy en el borde. Date prisa.*"

"No fucking idea what you're saying, but you sound sexy as hell." Eli dropped down to nip Alanso's lip.

Al turned his head and whimpered when Eli began to ply his mouth with tender kisses, even as his hips alternated liquid glides with pounding strokes. He tried to make it good, but primal instinct led him to mix a claim with his promises.

"I'm not coming without you, Alanso." Eli spoke low and firm. "We're in this together."

"Can't, Cobra." He pounded the mattress. "Hurts so good. Need more."

"I said let go." Eli refused to relent.

Alanso shivered beneath him now, in ecstasy and maybe some pain from the intensity of their sharing. Refusing to be denied, Eli rolled to his side. He tipped Alanso with him, still joined. His hand roamed down the solid slab of his friend's chest, pausing to tug on the piercings that decorated his nipples.

Alanso shouted Eli's name.

"What do you want, *amigo*?" He walked his hand lower, all the while still plowing into Alanso from behind. The flex of his abs began to burn at the awkward angle and he knew he couldn't keep it up forever. Luckily, neither of them would need very long. "This?"

His fingers closed around Alanso's cock. The moment they did, the smaller man howled. He fucked forward into Eli's fist. His ass grew tighter, practically strangling Eli's cock.

"Yes. Yes," Eli chanted. "Come for me. Let me watch you shoot while I'm fucking buried in you. Deep as I can get."

He aimed the head of Alanso's cock at the man's tattoo-covered chest. He wanted proof that his lover enjoyed their fucking as much, or more, than he did. And Al didn't disappoint.

Alanso roared Eli's name.

He stiffened in Cobra's arms until he might have shattered.

And then he did. His ass locked over Eli's erection and the first jet of come launched from his cock. Instead of the target Eli had intended—his pecs—he overshot the landing pad, spraying Eli on the chin and across his smile.

Alanso stared at him with wide eyes as he spasmed, adding to the mess on Eli's lips.

Making sure neither of them would ever forget this moment or how fully he pledged himself to the man coming apart in his arms, Eli opened his mouth. He swiped a droplet from the corner of his lips with his tongue and ingested the silky substance.

The taste of Alanso, and the utter devotion in the man's

stare, combined to trigger his own orgasm. He crushed his mouth over Alanso's as best he could given the angle. Somehow they made it work. They were meant to fit together.

Their tongues parried as Eli filled Alanso's ass with gush after gush of come.

And still Alanso's cock jerked, as if the pleasure Eli pumped into him enhanced his lingering climax. He shook and cursed until fluid dribbled from his sated cock, as though it wished it had more to pump out.

Insatiable, Eli speared into the steaming, now sloppy paradise he claimed a few more times, until all of his strength leeched away along with doubt, fear and delays.

This is what he'd been made for.

"Cobra," Alanso whispered.

"Yeah?" He shivered when their positions and his softening cock meant he slipped free of Alanso's body sooner than he would have liked.

"That was...everything." His respiration remained uneven and labored.

"For me too." Eli traced the streaks of come on Alanso's ripped abdomen. He smeared them over the ridges and valleys of muscle there before lifting his fingers to his friend's lips. The smaller man didn't hesitate before taking them into his mouth and suckling them like a pacifier.

"This is the beginning, Alanso. Another start," Eli whispered against his lover's neck, just below the small spacer in his earlobe. "I promise you, no matter where the road leads from here, we'll drive it together. *I* will never leave you."

"Hot Rods for life." Alanso nodded and smiled, a little shy and a lot hopeful.

"Hell yeah," Eli agreed.

Just then Pitbull's "Secret Admirer" warred with AC/DC's "Dirty Deeds" as Cobra and Alanso got synchronized texts.

"Sally!" Alanso cried out. "Not bad news. Not now."

"No." Eli refused to believe that. Especially when he knew her so well. "She's really fucking early. She had to have set a speeding record in at least one of those states. Driving like a bat out of hell."

He reached across Alanso to retrieve his phone and punch in a response to Joe's note telling them to stand down and wait. The crew had Eli and Alanso's girl. It was going to be a long two weeks before they gave her back.

At least Cobra had Alanso to help him relax.

"Tell Joe to go ahead and spank her after all." Alanso's eyes drifted shut as relief mingled with exhaustion.

It'd been one hell of a day for them all.

As sunlight spilled into their nest, Eli smiled and burrowed close to his right-hand man. "I'll save that for us. All of us. *When* she comes home. We'll be ready and waiting."

"I do love you, *cabrón*." Alanso smirked without opening his eyes.

"Then shut up and let me sleep." Eli didn't have to wait more than ten seconds before light snores lulled him into dreamland. When Alanso snuffled and snugged closer, he knew the other man understood, if not heard, his drowsy whisper, "I love you too. I always have."

Mustang Sally

Dedication

For everyone who contributed to bringing the Hot Rods to life in the amazing artwork on the covers of these books.

Of course to cover artist superhero Angie Waters, as always, for your vision and Photoshop skillz.

To Dawn Martin for going out of your way to procure the images I fell in love with.

For my editor, Amy Sherwood, who didn't kill me when I sent in a twenty-one page cover art request form.

And to Sophia Renee (plus her sexy models!) of Unique Portrait Services—last but definitely not least—for taking the pictures that sparked my imagination.

Thank you all as well as any others that had a hand in the process behind the scenes!

Chapter One

"What's it like to have sex with five guys at once?" Salome Rider couldn't believe the question had finally popped out. Her curiosity had overridden politeness. Then again, it was after sunrise and she'd been awake for twenty-four painful hours straight. Not that she'd have been able to sleep after the horror she'd witnessed.

The miles had droned on for the span of three different states, through which she'd forced a break from the men and place she loved so dearly. Staying had seemed impossible once she'd realized her Hot Rods didn't return the sentiment.

Fleeing also triggered flashbacks of the last time she'd abandoned her home, when she was fifteen and escaped from the religious zealots who'd *raised* her. Who could have guessed she'd find sanctuary with a motley gang of mechanics? Truly, back then they'd only been boys who'd wandered into the youth shelter shortly before her.

Together, they'd forged more.

Their fuel station and restoration business thrived. Their camaraderie had grown into something like brotherhood. Still, part of her had shriveled as she hid her true feelings—day after day, year after year—for the men she lived and worked with.

And the only refuge she could imagine, a shelter where like-minded people would understand her dilemma, was hundreds of miles away. Or it had been before she'd started this mad journey in her beloved pink '69 Mustang convertible. Now, the crew's mountain retreat grew nearer with every heartbeat that separated her from Hot Rods.

As if afraid Sally would doze off at the wheel, her friend Kayla had chatted over the open line of Sally's hands-free phone while she ate up the distance between them. Kaige, her fellow mechanic at Hot Rods, had installed the device not too long ago. The proof-of-concept had shown that opting for a classic car didn't have to mean forsaking modern conveniences. The mechanics she ran with were skilled enough to hide technoperks while preserving the original detailing of an antique. No problem-o.

Genius. They'd earn the garage a mint with some of these doodads.

Plus, the communicator gave her the opportunity to pry into her friend's alternative lifestyle before they were face to face. Time was running out. As was Sally's stockpile of bravery. It'd been a hell of a day already. The dashed center line blinked rapidly enough to guarantee she'd have to finish this conversation in person. But at least she'd have the answers she'd wondered about the whole drive.

Hell, more like forever.

As long as she could remember, she'd had fantasies about the gang of misfit mechanics who'd taken her in, though she'd been terrified to admit it, even to herself. Was it because of her childhood that she believed multiple partner relationships were no big deal? Living on a commune in Utah, she'd seen every possible combination by the time she turned ten or so. Well, at least when it came to a man possessing several wives. She'd often dreamed of flipping the paradigm. Of loving more than one husband.

Did that make her open-minded and evolved or plain old fucked-up?

She hoped to find out soon. Spending a couple weeks with the crew's women should help her separate non-traditional love from the not-so-nice elements of the extremist religion she'd been exposed to in her youth. Complicating factors incorporated into an already complex situation had muddied the playing field. Forced marriages, sex with minors and brainwashing certainly had no place on her list of turn-ons.

Her GPS said there was less than three minutes to go in her should-have-been five-hour drive. So what if she'd made it in record time?

King Cobra—Eli London, owner of Hot Rods—wasn't there to disapprove or punish her for her gross speed infractions. Too damn bad.

By now he was probably well into round six or seven with that slut he and Alanso had picked up from the bar last night. *Fawn.* What the fuck kind of name was that anyway?

At least the guys called her Mustang Sally. Horses were strong. Free. Not helpless like some freaking deer. And certainly not innocent. No, it'd been a hell of a long time since she'd been classified as that. Maybe that was why the mechanics weren't interested despite the fact that she could offer them a hell of a lot more than a sloppy fuck on the hood of someone else's car.

And Kayla still hadn't answered the million-dollar question, despite the meandering path of Sally's thoughts, which was almost as convoluted as the road she now hauled ass along. Gaining altitude, she flexed her jaw to pop her ears and continued the climb, loving the purr of her engine. Alanso had worked miracles on it.

"Kay? Still there?" Sally paused, hoping her friend stayed with her just a little while longer. She truly didn't wish to be alone with her thoughts just yet. Crying while driving was not recommended, no matter the skill of the driver. "Sorry if that was too personal."

"Hmm?" Kayla sounded farther away, not closer. "Oh, no! You're fine. I was just thinking of how to describe it to you. It's beyond words."

The other woman's dreamy sigh was like a punch to the gut for Sally. Maybe she was better off not knowing what she was missing. Because having a taste of that delicacy then going on an eternal diet would be far more painful than simply never having sampled such a fine treat.

"You know, it might be better to show you. Devon, Neil and James came over a few minutes ago. The guys are supposed to be working on a project at Bare Natural for me today. I'm sure they wouldn't mind a long lunch."

Oh. Wow. Sally pictured the muscled construction workers. They were nearly as hot as her grease monkeys. Almost.

"Part of me wants to scream 'hell yes', but part of me is afraid." She slowed to ease the Mustang onto the twisty mountain road that led to Kayla's naturist retreat. Maybe a few weeks of getting in touch with her sexy side and roaming the woods naked would do her some good.

If the Hot Rods weren't meant to be hers, it was about time for her to look elsewhere for a life partner. Or a half dozen. But the mere thought of seceding from their group broke her heart all over again. Shards dissembled into smaller fragments, splintering her soul.

"What about the part of you that's curious?" Kayla prodded gently. "The part that needs to be loved for who you are? Your Hot Rods know you. They love you already. They're being dumbasses."

"Maybe we can figure that out after I have a nap under my belt?" She yawned.

"If you're getting sleepy, pull over, sweetheart." The anxious rumble of Kayla's husband Dave's bass rained from her speakers. "It's not worth getting in an accident. Trust me."

"Am I on speaker?" Sally would have knocked her forehead on her white steering wheel if she didn't need to focus all her attention on the route and the thick underbrush, which lined the shoulder and could be hiding an army of deer. Stupid Fawns.

"Well, not technically." A giggle escaped Kayla. "But Dave is cuddling right next to me."

"Hey, don't be pulling any pervy stuff with your wife while we're chatting you big lug."

"Don't worry. He's mostly behaving. The guys offered to drive out and meet you on the side of the road. Just stay where you are and they'll come get you. Promise they'll go gentle on your baby."

"Just let's hurry this up." Dave grunted. "I drew the short straw and I don't want the whole city seeing me driving that girly Pepto-mobile."

"I'll have you know she's the perfect shade of pink with a

hint of metallic flake in the top coat. I tried fifty-seven before I decided on this one." Sally wasn't joking. "And no worries, I'm pulling in your driveway right now."

"Holy shit." Dave sounded like he was on the move, muffled and fading. "How fast were you driving?"

"Nothing could have gotten me away from there soon enough." A sob hitched her breathing now that the peak of her friends' A-frame came into view.

"It's going to work out. You'll see." Kayla's reassurance barely cut through Sally's bone-deep exhaustion.

By the time she rolled to a stop at the edge of the expansive yard, the porch overflowed with welcoming friends. The five-guys-and-one-girl crew plus their wives and two babies. With Sally, they'd make an even dozen.

Neil and James approached in synch. Neil opened her door and drew her from the car. He didn't hesitate to wrap her in a big bear hug. "We've got you, Mustang Sally."

James checked the empty backseat. "Is your suitcase in the trunk? Let me get it for you."

She shook her head against the warm strength of Neil's chest, closing her eyes as she leaned on him. "I'm stupid. I didn't even grab a bag. This is all I brought."

"We've got you covered." Devon, who belonged to both James and Neil—or maybe she owned the pair—joined the gathering.

"Yeah, you're tiny enough to fit in Dev's stuff." James ruffled her hair a little. "Or you could always feel free to join in with the naturist guests."

"Right now I just want to crash." She hid a sniffle against Neil's soft cotton shirt. It smelled of sawdust, not oil or rubber. Though it was nice, it wasn't right. It wasn't home. The difference had her cringing.

"You got it." James cut in on his mate and swung her into his arms. She normally would have protested mightily. This time she let him sweep her into their midst.

"Hi." Sheepish, she peeked up at the crew as they passed.

"Glad to see you again, kid." Joe stepped forward to kiss her cheek. The resemblance to King Cobra soothed her a little, even as it riled her again. He held up his phone. "Just texted my dumbass cousin to let him know you arrived safe and sound."

She angled her face into James's body once again, embarrassed by the pain she couldn't hide.

"Eli was horrified when he realized what had happened, you know?" Joe rubbed her shoulder. "Maybe you should give him a quick call? Sort some of this out? Could it be a misunderstanding?"

"I didn't mistake Alanso's cock pounding that ungrateful bitch while Eli cheered him on. Nope. No confusion about that. I'm not ready. I don't know what to say—what I want—since I can't have what I'd hoped for." Opening her lids became more and more difficult. The peaks and valleys of the past couple days weighed on her.

Not only her own aches and devastation.

Whether they accepted her care or not, it had broken her heart when Alanso had charged into the common area of their apartment above the garage and declared he was bisexual, as if they'd think less of him for his orientation. Or when Eli had received the letter detailing the death of Alanso's mother. New news, though ancient history. She'd wept as he informed his best friend and lover, wishing they'd take her along to comfort them instead of drowning their sorrows in cheap liquor and picking up some stray prey.

"No. Not talking to them," she mumbled, not caring how petulant she sounded.

Sleep encroached on her consciousness, lulling her into the oblivion of dreams where all she desired could still come true.

"Okay, honey." Joe backed off. "I'm not sure what that means, but you can tell us later. Maybe right after we give you the spanking Eli and Alanso told us to administer. They're none too happy about your land-speed record."

"Fuck them." She slumped beneath the weight of the tiredness plaguing her.

"I think we'll leave that to you." Mike took his turn squeezing one of her ankles, which dangled near him. "But Joe's right. Let's set you up in the living room. We'll leave you alone so you can sleep this off. Things will look better when you're rested. I promise."

She tried to argue. It was too much effort.

Instead, she surrendered to their care. Safe, surrounded by allies, she drifted away from the agony radiating from the ragged hole in her chest where her heart used to pump. She'd left that worthless organ splattered on the floor of the garage when she'd bolted from the men she loved. They hadn't noticed or cared. Not while they slaked their lust on a barfly who didn't give a shit about them or their love for each other.

Stupid bastards.

"Basking in the sunshine again, huh? You've come a hell of a long way in two weeks. What a pretty sight you make, Mustang Sally." Buck-ass naked, Neil sauntered over to Sally's chaise on the deck.

The crew had built the grand platform to harness the raw beauty of the panoramic view. The mountainside, with its lush greenery and the lake at its feet, was laid out for Bare Natural's guests. Not to mention the resort's owner and her friends.

They were the first to enjoy the new addition, during the maintenance and renovation window. Guests would return in a couple days. Spruced up and ready for another prosperous season, the place looked great. No wonder Kayla had carved out a niche in the specialty destination market.

Sally took a sip of the fruity mixed drink Neil—one of Devon's pair of husbands—handed her before she set it on the fragrant cedar beside her chair. She flipped over onto her stomach.

"It's still kind of weird to be flashing my ass all over these woods." She hoped the color creeping up her neck into her face looked like a product of the rays they soaked up instead of her mild embarrassment.

"We'll miss your cute behind around here." James smacked it lightly as he joined Neil and Devon. The trio beamed at each other like the lovesick fools they were. "Want me to rub some more tanning lotion on you? You're getting a decent base built up, but you were white as snow to start. Don't think you want to chance a burn at this point. Five hours, even in your sweet ride, won't be comfy if your tush is crispy."

He waited for her nod before he reached out. They'd been so damn careful with her, as if she was made of glass. Eli and Alanso would never handle her with kid gloves. She sighed.

A steady massage from James's skilled hands proved Kayla had been sharing her trade secrets. The pressure protected and soothed Sally simultaneously.

That must have accounted for why she murmured her thoughts aloud. "Do I *have* to go home tomorrow?"

Joe's baritone, so similar to Eli's, caused her to jerk. James scrubbed the tension from her shoulders. "You're always welcome here. Indefinitely. But I'm afraid my cousin will go berserk if you postpone your reunion. At this rate, he'll be as bald as Alanso when you turn up."

"Yeah, right." The indignant huff she tried for sounded more like a pout. "Why would he care that I'm gone?"

Crying was not an option. Not after fourteen days of shoring up her weakness with fun, cookouts, movie nights, shopping, laughter and girl talk. These past two weeks had strengthened her friendships with the crew and their ladies. Plus, she'd remembered what it was like to be independent. Something more than one of Eli's gang.

For the first time, she wished there were other women at Hot Rods. Someone who could relate like Kate, Kayla, Morgan and Devon did when she needed to indulge in a men suck moment.

As if he could sense her mounting despair, James brushed a kiss over the crown of her head, then left her alone.

"I realize the toolbox hasn't done a great job of showing you yet, but your guys adore you as much as we do our girls," Joe continued. "I'm sure of it."

She couldn't deny that. Her gang cared for her. Like a little sister or another one of their buddies. The appreciation she'd had for that equality suddenly soured, transforming into something bitter.

It just wasn't enough anymore.

Watching the four new families and the greater crew they comprised had ratcheted Sally's aspirations to pretty astronomic levels. "I'm afraid I'm going to have to leave the gang."

She rolled over and drew her knees to her chest, crossing her arms on top of them.

Resting her chin on her stacked wrists, she sighed.

Half the crew surrounded her now. Morgan had accompanied her sexy-as-sin husband. They'd probably left baby Nathan with Mike, Kate, Kayla and Dave. The big guy still had to rest fairly often after working his leg too hard. His limp grew more pronounced when fatigue set in. Luckily, his wife *was* a massage therapist. She'd do her best to unwind any lingering knots. Seeing all the crew had overcome made Sally feel guilty for her disappointment.

There were so many things she had to be grateful for. Why couldn't she ignore the one thing she couldn't have?

Morgan and Joe claimed seats on Sally's right, balancing out the trio on her left when James and Neil raided Devon's oversized lounger. She didn't seem to mind being squished between the two handsome men. Her husbands.

Their bronzed skin glowed in the heat of the afternoon.

"I may not have known you all that long—or as well as I do now—when you bailed." Devon slid her sunglasses to the top of her head, pinning her short hair out of her eyes, to peer at Sally. "But I'm positive you're not a coward. So what's with all this running away bullshit? Haven't you had enough hiding yet?"

"Who says I'm—"

"Don't bother arguing that one, cutie." Joe shook his head. "Last night you sold yourself out. I haven't seen you haul ass in two weeks like you did when Eli and Alanso's Skype request popped onto my laptop. You practically dove over the couch like an extra in *Saving Private Ryan* to dodge those idiots. Nothing's going to be resolved until you talk. All three of you. Hell, the entire gang of crazy mechanics. You're just prolonging this torture for everyone."

"Because once we discuss it, it'll be final." She thanked her lucky stars for the dark-tinted glasses that hid the tears stinging her eyes. "I'll be homeless *and* out of a job. And lonely."

"You think they were calling to fire you?" James snorted, yet he still managed to look adorable.

Devon pinched his exposed nipple. "I remember a certain guy nearly walking out when he convinced himself he was going to lose the love of his life. Even though it was obvious to everyone else that Neil will love you until the day he dies."

"And even after." The taller guy laid one hand on his husband and the other on his wife. "Both of you. Forever."

Their dedication almost derailed Sally. "Wait. You guys fought? Really?"

"Oh, hell yeah," Joe interrupted. "They were annoying little fuckers as they tried to figure out how to be together. Like it's that complicated. When you know who you want—the person or people you fit with—you stick with them. That's all there is to it."

Sally didn't contradict him. Her heart ached as she considered that might be true, *if* she weren't keeping a monumental secret. One Eli's noble nature would never let him ignore. They were fucked on every level, even if her would-be guys didn't know it yet.

"Sure." Deflated, she realized her confidence leeched away. "Like it doesn't matter what they think of you. Or if there are other...*circumstances*. Idealistic crap only works if you're lucky enough to be someone else's everything and there are no other roadblocks."

"I think you'd be surprised how King Cobra and his

sidekick feel about you." Neil shrugged. "If you'd give them a chance to tell you."

"There's so much to gain." Morgan leaned forward. Her wide eyes urged Salome to listen. Really listen to what they were saying. The promise of something so sweet scared her. Could all her fantasies come true?

"And everything to lose." She bit her lip.

"Haven't you already lost it all?" Neil ignored the simultaneous slaps both James and Devon delivered. "No, really, if you don't do something to change the situation, it's over anyway, right?"

"I guess." Sally sniffled. "Maybe I should just have Kaige box up my stuff. I could rent one of the guest cabins from Kayla for a bit until I found a place. If there's any vacancy."

"Or you could go the hell home and fight for them." Neil tried to fire her up. "Isn't even the smallest chance at this worth it?"

The guy drew his partners close to his side as if they were his lifelines.

Morgan surprised Sally by crossing to sit beside her. The woman's hug didn't bother her despite their nudity. It felt nice to have someone hold her. The shelter the crew had provided when she'd needed it most would never be forgotten.

Joe joined them, squatting beside the lounge chair. "I realize you had a lot to sort through. We don't mean to be harsh. Sometimes you just need a kick in the pants...or bare ass. It's terrifying and risky, but the rewards outweigh any potential harm. And we've watched you suffering this whole time. Whether you admit it or not, you're already mourning your Hot Rods. Maybe you don't have to."

"Trust me, Mustang Sally, it's a no-brainer." James stared at her for a solid ten seconds before he cleared his throat and declared, "I think you're ready. To see. I know we've behaved ourselves around you since you got here. But maybe you need a taste, to know what you're battling for?"

"Are you suggesting..." She gulped. "What exactly are you

proposing?"

"Watch me love Devon and James." Neil stared directly at her as though he could see through her shades. "I dare you. Bet you'll make it home in three hours flat this time."

"I appreciate the offer, but I've already witnessed a threesome." Bile rose in her throat. "I checked out Eli and Alanso working over that babe from the bar, remember? *Fawn*? No, thanks."

"Guarantee the two experiences would be nothing alike." Joe reached out and encircled her ankle in his warm grasp. "You're not looking for a meaningless bang. What these guys have is so much more. It's powerful."

"Beautiful," Morgan added.

"Perfect." Devon smiled, sure and content. "I believe you're destined for your own amazing things, Sally. It wouldn't hurt this much if it wasn't meant to be. Alanso took one peek and it changed his outlook forever. Didn't it?"

Sally swallowed hard then nodded. He'd talked so passionately that night he'd burst through their door and declared he was gay. No, bisexual. Describing what he'd seen here. With the crew. Alanso had painted a picture so very different from what she'd observed in the garage. Maybe part of her was terrified that she might get what she'd always craved only to find out it was nothing like what she'd imagined.

Where was the romance? The tenderness? The true love?

Her inherent belief in those values and the existence of something more than sex for procreation had been a huge part of her decision to abandon her family at the ridiculously young age of fifteen. And if Eli and Alanso, two of the most generous and kindhearted men she knew, couldn't drum up some of those emotions, then who could?

The trio in front of her offered to validate every last one of her fantasies. Right here. Right now.

Salome took a deep breath, angled herself toward them more fully then whispered, "Show me. Please."

Chapter Two

"My pleasure." Neil speared his fingers into the short hair sported by his husband and his wife. He closed his eyes and sat straighter, as if touching them gave him strength. They leaned into his hold, relinquishing all control to the man at the core of their group.

Responsibility for his mates appeared to mix with genuine desire to give. Neil kissed first James, then Devon. Slowly, with lingering swipes of his moist lips over theirs. When he finished, he let the pair enjoy each other while he examined the bond between them. His radiant smile reflected the bliss their connection generated. Each of them amplified their combined happiness.

Without clothes to block the view, it was easy to see the effect Neil had on them and the greater impact they had on the man binding them together. Both of the guys had impressive hard-ons in record time. Devon reached over to encase their erections in the softness of her fingers. Well, she probably had a few calluses mixed in, but they didn't seem to mind any roughness in the female construction worker's grasp.

Unlike the debacle with Fawn, chatter had no place in their union aside from whispered praise. They didn't need to verbalize their desires. Criticizing someone else's needs wouldn't have been tolerated. The three members of the performance crew—who delighted Sally with their open, honest affection—fed off the reactions of their counterparts.

Like a perfectly built transmission, each gear ticked and fell into place with another. Balanced, they pivoted and swung around, one person acting then accepting the advances bestowed by another.

Tears dripped off Sally's cheeks. One splashed onto

Morgan's hand, which held her own.

"It's going to work out." The other woman and her husband bracketed Sally. They rubbed her back in platonic circles and surrounded her in a bubble of confidence she couldn't seem to muster. "What you guys have is this beautiful too. It's just covered in grime right now. You have to polish it. Let this shine through."

Devon moaned when Neil placed his hand over her heart, cupping the left side of her chest in his palm. The woman was petite and proportional, but her guys seemed to enjoy her high, firm breasts. James mirrored his lover, covering the opposite half of their wife's torso. They teased her, ramping up her desire until she seemed to forget about their audience.

Her eyelids drooped closed.

Joe picked up his wife's train of thought. "It's true, Mustang Sally. You've let your relationship rust. It's broken down. Stuck somewhere juvenile, in a spot you needed it to be for a while. Then I'd guess that companionship became habit. A safe rut. Maybe because none of you were ready to take the wheel of something this powerful. Time to dissect your bond and restore it just like one of your projects. The potential for an end product better than the original is under all this bullshit. What you make of it is up to you. All of you."

Neil devoured James's lips while they manipulated an obviously erogenous zone for Devon—her heart. When she whimpered and writhed between them, Neil broke away. His chest heaved as he struggled to draw a lungful of air. Eyes burning bright, he stared at James.

"I love you," he whispered, then used his free hand to nudge the smaller man's shoulder.

James grinned as he slid his fingers down Devon's torso. He gripped her hips, lifting her easily as he reclined in the chair. When he'd finished his maneuver, he stretched out on his back and cradled his woman on his lap. The not-so-subtle rocking of his hips broadcast his intentions.

Neil glanced over his shoulder from his position between the two pairs of legs spread around him. His wide-eyed gaze met Sally's for an instant and he spared her a sad smile. "I know how it feels, when everything is fractured inside you. You'll get it together right. When the pieces lock, it's smooth as glass."

Though he spoke to her, he curled his fingers toward his upward-facing palm.

Joe leaned over just long enough to rummage through the cabinet built into the bottom of the side table, which sat beside her chaise. He tossed out several toys—bullet vibrators, a butt plug, furry handcuffs and a few other things she didn't recognize—before he grunted his approval.

A small bottle of clear gel flew across the space separating the loungers. Neil caught the lube out of the air with one hand. James groaned as he lifted Devon away from his body, stealing the friction of her skin from his cock. Reaching between them, Neil did something to Devon's ass that made her yelp, likely coating her with the cool gel. Her back arched. Then she shivered, relaxing.

James hissed next when Neil slathered more lube on his palm before pumping his fist up and down his partner's modest yet ultra-stiff shaft. Ensuring they were ready, he aligned James's cock and Devon's ass before sinking between their thighs. The slight weight of the crew's smallest member pressed her downward until she and James were united completely.

Both of them moaned in unison.

Their cries escalated when Neil applied his mouth to their exposed genitalia. He alternated licks across Devon's pussy with kisses and sucking on James's balls. Yet the man being tortured by the sight of his lovers fucking didn't move.

Instead, Neil stewed in the pleasure surrounding him.

Devon tipped her head to the side and he rose to trace a finger along her jaw. He murmured something to her that Sally couldn't hear, but she understood the complete adoration in his tone. The kiss they exchanged was the most romantic, beautiful, sweet expression she'd ever witnessed. Following it, Neil turned her back over to James, who continued the gentle melding of mouths.

Despite the fact that James was buried in his wife's ass while their husband made a meal of every electrified nerve ending he could find, neither Devon nor the man she rode were in a hurry. They enhanced the glide of their lips with tiny grinds and flexes of their abdomens. The passion in their eyes seemed to prod their mounting ecstasy more than their physical interactions.

Long minutes passed, filled with endless pleasure and pure love. Neil caved first. He monitored his lovers with hungry eyes as he continued to eat Devon in earnest. His clever fingers sought James's sac and rolled his partner's testicles in an apparently maddening pattern.

Devon gasped. Her hand flew to Neil's hair, stroking. She didn't force him closer. Didn't have to. He chased her when she rocked backward into James. Wherever she went, he followed.

"I'm on the edge," James growled. "Make her come. Quick."

Neil didn't hesitate. He swirled his tongue around Devon's clit with amazing accuracy and dexterity. Clearly the man had practiced this a few times. As he pushed his long fingers into his wife's pussy, the wetness overflowing her was obvious.

Sally squirmed in her chair. What would it be like to have Alanso hold her while Eli subjected them to such sweet torture? She'd have gone off like a rocket the instant they touched her with such respect and awe. Picturing the warm, smooth skin of Alanso's bald head or Eli's tousled crop of spikes beneath her palm nearly had her embarrassing herself in front of her new friends.

"Feel free to take care of yourself." Joe lifted a brow as he glanced in her direction. "Unless you'd like Morgan and me to help. It's only fair, you know. Katiebug did the same for your guys. They nearly put her eye out when they shot. So hard. And I guarantee they were thinking of you."

"I'm g-good." Sally had to wet her lips three times before she could utter the lie. As tempting as the offer was, she only wanted one man to touch her these days. Well, two. Okay, fine, seven. But those garage guys were a couple states away when she really needed a hand. Or a cock. *Damn it.*

Morgan laughed, not unkindly. "You're not fooling anyone. But you *will* be okay. Soon."

Devon drew their attention to the show once more when she froze, then screamed. James held her steady while she came apart. Secure in his hold, she kept nothing back. The uninhibited release impressed Sally, who guaranteed she'd never had an orgasm as thorough or satisfying as the one pulsing through the woman in front of her.

So it shocked her when Devon's eyes sprang open and she demanded, "More. Both of you. In me. Now."

"You didn't really think I was going to lounge around all day without fucking you, did you?" Neil's wicked grin proved impossible for his spouses to resist. They reached out as one to draw him up higher on their pile of limbs.

"In that position, she'll be able to feel both of their cocks rubbing against each other through her. When they trap that thin barrier between them, it's like nothing you've ever imagined." Morgan sounded breathless. How many times had she experienced a similar sensation?

"We'll see if Mike or Dave wants to play when we get back to the house, cupcake." Joe reached around Sally to stroke his wife's long hair.

Morgan shivered despite the sun.

When Sally's attention shifted to the trio once more, Neil had levered himself over his pair of soul mates. He kissed each of them before rubbing his nose against Devon's. As they smiled into each other's eyes, he advanced. Linked together, they all groaned.

Devon called out her undying love for the entire mountain to bear witness.

Neil and James echoed the sentiment.

Again, they didn't hurry or fuck in rushed lunges that would threaten to snap their poor chair into kindling. Subtle motion and focus on the full connection of their bodies and souls was all it took to gratify them.

The three people undulated, their torsos moving sinuously

against each other. Each of them reached out, touching both of their partners. James had one hand on Neil's ass, encouraging his penetration of Devon, while he linked fingers with her.

Sally wondered if they could keep this up for eternity. No one seemed eager to end their session or complete the ultimate joining they were part of. She couldn't say she blamed them.

Every second became a testament to their love. Selflessness allowed them to hold on and prolong the gift they gave each other. It reminded her of what she didn't have.

The part of her that reared its jealous head ashamed her.

Looking away would have been impossible, though.

Like a solar eclipse, the rare phenomenon in front of her tempted her to stare despite the danger to her retinas or her tender parts buried deep inside.

"I can't," Devon gasped.

"No need." Neil smiled as he rested his forehead on his wife's.

"We're with you," James promised.

"Always." All three of them swore the oath before Devon's spine arched impossibly. She clung to her men, counting on them to ground her when she shattered. If their grunts, curses, pledges and moans were any indication, they depended on her for the same.

Sally cried as they shuddered then went still in each other's arms.

It was the most striking thing she'd ever seen.

Envy clawed at her throat.

She didn't realize she was trembling until Joe and Morgan put their arms around her. The contrast of their rock-solid embrace and her mushy guts left her reeling. Inside, she expected to hear rattling from the broken bits clanging around in her core.

As much as she appreciated the comfort they intended to bestow, Sally craved the touch of two different people. Homesick, she couldn't stop the rising urge to return to Hot Rods.

The garage and her men.

Shit. What had she done by staying away? Why hadn't they come after her? So what if she'd thought she wanted space? Couldn't they tell she needed them more? Or didn't they care? Worse, did they suspect—? No, they couldn't. No one knew about that.

Even if she could drum up some miracle to fix things with Eli and Alanso, how the hell was she going to tell them she dreamed of even more? The whole gang.

"Now you see?" James's rasp broke her from her cycle of thoughts.

Making a sound without sobbing would have proved impossible. So she nodded instead.

"We could show you again if you need another demonstration." Devon stretched, then snuggled into James's chest. She looked like the broadest mechanic—Bryce, AKA Rebel—after Thanksgiving dinner. Stuffed and like she might not move for a century.

"Speak for yourself, Dev." Neil kissed the exposed line of her neck. "I'm gonna need a minute."

"That's what you always say." She winked at him.

Sally glanced away from their casual intimacy. It hurt too much to see what she was missing out on. With her eyes averted, she accidentally scoped out Joe's crotch. How had he stayed so calm when he was that hard?

"Holy crap," she muttered.

"Ah, yeah." Morgan chuckled. "I'm a lucky lady."

"Am I in the way?" Sally started to rise.

Joe held her in place with two fingers on her shoulder. "A boner never killed me before. Hell, it's kind of a constant thing around here."

And that had her thinking. Alanso had recounted stories of all the crew together, not just the couples she'd come to know and adore. "How—?"

A lump in her throat kept her from probing about what she was dying to know.

"Go ahead," Joe knocked his knee into hers when she stalled out. "You've come this far. Finish it. Ask your questions."

"I can see they have something…special. But then I feel this sense of belonging to your whole group. How is it different? When you play with the rest of the crew, how does that work?" He was right. Why stop now? She might as well go for broke.

"Sometimes we stay in our pairs or trio and just share the energy of our attachment with each other," Morgan considered carefully as she replied. "Other times it's more than that. A bonding. It started with the guys. They needed something beyond what we could give. When they take each other, it's…mesmerizing to watch. The way they touch is so different."

"I bet." Salome recalled the intensity on Eli's face as he guided his cock through the valley of Alanso's ass. And they'd only been simulating the real deal. What would it be like to see him bury himself in his best friend?

Linking them in pleasure.

"And after a while, we kind of branched out. Things evolved. It seemed silly to all be there and sharing but then to keep to ourselves. So we didn't. If it feels good to the person doing it and the person receiving it, any action is acceptable." She sounded smug.

"Don't forget about the birthday special." Joe hummed. "Birthdays are the best. Not just because of Morgan's cakes, either. There are two hundred and seventy-three days left until my next one. Damn it."

Sally tilted her head and scanned the five people lounging around her.

Morgan came to the rescue again. "Well. See. Kate had the crew all to herself at first. And once I came into the picture, before we'd worked things out, I would play with the four guys beside Mike sometimes. Kay got three when Dave found her and poor Devon settled for just her pair. After a bit, we decided that wasn't exactly fair. And the guys had only ever had one of us at a time so they were at a serious disadvantage."

"Holy shit. Are you saying that the birthday boy or girl gets everyone?" Sally couldn't imagine the logistics needed to pull that off. But she sure would like to give it a whirl.

"Mmm-hmm." Morgan practically drooled.

"Put your tongue back in your face, bitch." Sally nudged the other woman's foot with her pink-painted toes. She'd crafted elaborate designs on her own as well as the crew ladies' to distract herself from the ache of missing her artwork. Her studio. Her muses.

"Well, if you'd quit screwing around here and go home, you could have a chance at *seven* guys to yourself. We've only ever had five. Well...Devon's had five guys and a girl on occasion." Morgan giggled.

"Who's the smart one around these parts?" Devon buffed her nails on her collarbone, then pointed at herself.

"Seven. Jesus." Sally croaked, "Where do you put them all?"

The crew members cracked up.

"Uh. No. Seriously." She couldn't bear the heat flooding her cheeks.

"Damn, you're pretty when you're shy." James smiled at her kindly. "We take turns. Plus, you'd never guess the number of places a guy can rub himself if he's motivated enough. It's more about the attention, though. When it's all heaped on you..."

He shivered.

"It's addictive," Joe finished for his friend.

"Don't be intimidated, Mustang Sally." Neil offered his advice. "Start slow. You have two guys who want to make things right. You might have left the room each time they called, but we had to listen to them whine about missing you. Wanting to know every detail about your day and if you'd mentioned them at all. Put them out of their misery. Start with them. If you trust them enough to want this with them, they'll help you figure out the rest."

"Wow. Way to make me feel like a threesome is a piece of cake." Sally laughed. "Okay. Okay. You're right. *This* is what I want. And…I'm willing to fight for it."

"Now we're talking." Joe ruffled her hair. "Look, I know he doesn't talk about it a lot, but I was there when Eli's mom died. It almost destroyed him to lose her. I don't know if he could handle it if you walked. He loves you. Don't allow him to get away with letting you think otherwise simply because he's too scared to admit how he feels."

"He loves *Alanso.*" Hesitating, she wondered if she was about to make a big mistake.

"He loves you both. All of you, really." Joe hugged her. "Put him on the spot. Ask him pointblank. I can't imagine he'd lie about his emotions even if he's freaked out. He'd never hurt you like that. Not when he knows, deep down, that everything you say to someone could be the last words they hear from you."

"I might do just that." She had to be sure once and for all. Even if the answer to *do you love me* was *no*. Then she could move on. Or maybe move East a few states. Somehow, though, she knew the crew was complete. Their unit didn't have room for an outcast.

Her place was with the misfit mechanics.

"My poor cousin won't know what hit him when you barrel into that driveway in the morning." The crew members around her chuckled and nodded.

"Maybe I shouldn't wait another minute. I'm ready now." She stood and kissed each of her friends on the cheek. "I don't want to lose my nerve. Again. Thank you. For everything."

"You can name your first kid after us or something." Neil kept her from bawling with his wiseass routine. "Wonder if he'll be bald like your Cuban dude or ugly like this guy over here and his cousin."

Just the thought made her stomach flip.

"Don't get overwhelmed." Morgan hugged Sally. "Take it step by step and you'll be surprised where you end up. I know I was. And I couldn't be happier."

"If those garage rats fuck this up, you come back to us." Neil winked at her. "We'll be more than glad to give you a wild ride."

"You're not going to need that option." Devon finally managed to pry her eyelids fully open. Replete, she offered up a slow smile. "Go get 'em, Mustang Sally."

"Can I at least make them squirm a little first?" Excitement began to course through her veins for the first time since she'd realized that Eli and Alanso getting together didn't mean she'd be invited into their circle.

"We wouldn't love you so much if you didn't." Joe smacked her ass. "Now get the hell outta here. I'll give you a head start then let Eli know you're on your way. He can have one of the Hot Rods call us when you get there. I have a feeling you're going to be tied up for a while."

"If King Cobra's anything like you, that might not be an exaggeration." James grinned.

Sally crossed her arms over her chest, then started jogging toward the house, her clothes and her keys. It was time to attempt to clean up the oil slick she'd left behind without falling on her ass.

Chapter Three

Eli London strode into the garage a few hours after noon. He'd spent the morning in bed with Alanso. Fresh, new, exciting and too damn good to sacrifice, the alone time had suckered him into loosening up a bit on his duties for the first time. Ever.

It felt fucking weird not to have been there for opening, but Kaige seemed to have done just fine on his own. The check sheets hanging by the door were completed, the day's schedule was in order and the gas pumps outside had several cars in mid-fill.

The guy had more business sense in that dread-covered dome than Cobra, his technical-boss, did anyway. He was always coming up with new strategies and initiatives to grow their classic car restoration outfit. Because of him, they'd started offering records research on the history of specific cars, show preparation services and storage for winterization products like snow tires that customers might not have room for at home. All excellent moneymakers that had increased the standard of living for the Hot Rods, who shared equally in the garage's profits.

Kaige had proven he was invaluable in the office in addition to knowing his way around a toolbox. Maybe Eli should let the Hot Rod take more responsibility. It might be time for all of them to grow a little. Especially if he was going to be spending long, sleepless nights with his lover, Alanso.

No, his *lovers*.

Mustang Sally would be home tomorrow. She had to come back to them. He kicked a tire as he passed, wishing he could stuff his boot up his own ass instead. How had he been so stupid? Risking his relationship with one of his closest friends, and potential mate, over some sloppy ass that hadn't even done it for him? Insanity.

Not being able to make it up to her for two weeks had him on edge. Beyond reasoning.

Eli had tried to sleep in as long as possible to make the time pass more quickly. Another day without Salome in the shop would likely kill him. If it didn't, the lack of her laughter in their apartment above the garage might. The missing colors of her nail art, auto art or just plain *art* art had bleached his world drab.

And didn't he feel like an asshole for thinking that when he finally had the man he'd been lusting after for months? Hell, years. How fucking many blessings did he need to count before he'd be satisfied? Maybe just a couple more.

His best friend had been the only thing keeping him sane during Sally's exile.

Then again, Alanso was worse off than Eli. Every time an engine came near, Al perked up despite the fact that he could tell Sally's Mustang from any other '69 in a thousand-square-mile radius with his eyes closed and while asleep. He was the best tuner around. And he'd practically rebuilt the damn thing from scratch to make it perfect for their girl.

Pathetic. Both of them.

They'd moped like naughty puppies who'd been smacked with the world's largest newspaper.

The absence of someone important to him was cruel punishment. Sally knew how it would impact him to lose someone he cared about, even temporarily. Shit, they hadn't been apart more than a few nights in the past decade. And then only when the crew had needed him during Dave's emergency. The void she left behind was like a gaping wound in his chest.

Worse, he deserved every bit of the pain.

Eli couldn't deny they'd screwed up big time. He'd known fucking Fawn in a three-way with Alanso was a mistake and yet he'd done it anyway. A perfect example of why he never intended to let either of them touch the alcohol bearing his nickname again anytime soon.

Nothing good ever came of that frat house level of intoxication.

Still, blaming the substance—or the emotional upheaval caused by the horrible news they'd received that afternoon—was an excuse. At the end of the day, he'd let his insecurities bend them over and fuck them up the ass. And not in the delicious way Alanso and he had been practicing every chance they got for the past couple of weeks. That sharing alone had made the purgatory bearable.

More than anything, Eli wished he could flog himself for hurting Sally.

The way they'd made the tough-as-nails woman run. From their family. Their home. Everything she loved and possessed in the world. She hadn't even grabbed her sketchbook. Jesus. They had to have ripped her deep.

And as shitty a man as it made him, part of him hoped that meant she loved them too.

Or had.

If she would just come the fuck home, they could try to convince her that they'd been absolute morons. Well, she already had some clue about that. Maybe they could explain that they never intended to be that stupid again.

The office phone rang. Its shrill cry, designed to be heard above power tools, reverberated in the echo-friendly garage. Which happened to be empty. Where the fuck were all his mechanics? Did he pay them to sit around and take breaks all day?

As if he cared about that bullshit. He closed his eyes and deliberately reached for the new leaf he planned to turn over. The one about not masking his true feelings anymore. His dad was right, time was precious and wasting it with false pretenses had only earned him regrets.

Truth was, he needed a friend or six and couldn't believe that not a single soul wandered the premises during business hours.

"Someone answer that!" he bellowed as he ripped open the

office door.

Bryce lifted the receiver as Eli was halfway through shouting. The man raised a brow along with the phone and supplied the garage's name in his best customer-service voice. Sometimes the well-spoken, well-mannered side of their garagemate surprised Eli. There was a reason they used him to talk nutjobs off the ledge and handle any disputes that might arise.

"Yes, that is Mr. London you heard yelling." He barely suppressed a smile when Eli stomped closer, glaring at the other men—including Alanso—who ringed the huge, dark-haired dude.

What was this?

Some kind of staff meeting? Without him? Had he destroyed their faith in him as a leader? *Fuck.*

"Okay. Yes. I understand. I'll pass along your message. Thank you."

When Eli gave him a what-the-hell shrug, Bryce's poise cracked a little.

"No, seriously, Mike. We appreciate the crew and your ladies being there to catch Sally when she needed a place to think. Your support means a lot. And we won't forget it anytime soon."

He paused.

"Yeah. I get how the Dave thing might have made you feel that way. But you don't owe us anything. We'd do it again in a second. We've got your backs and we appreciate you having ours."

The urge to strangle Bryce for teasing him—not to mention whatever powwow they'd been holding sans King Cobra—warred with the need to hug the guy for saying what Eli couldn't find words for. He slumped a little as the fight went out of him.

"You got it. He's right here. I'll let him know now. See you soon I hope. Say hello to Kate and everyone from us." Bryce returned the receiver to its cradle.

Eli thought he did really well by counting to ten before

snarling, "Don't screw with my head. What did he say?"

"Mustang Sally is coming home. Early. Today. Mike estimated her arrival in two and a half hours. I'd say we've got about ninety minutes, if I know our girl." The entire Hot Rods gang seemed to relax. Until he continued. "And we need to talk to you. You're not going to fuck this up for all of us."

"What?" Eli's hackles rose despite his recent convictions.

"We love her. If we were still young and dumb, we'd have beat the two of you up by now." Roman, the oldest and toughest of them all, pointed at Alanso and Eli. "I get that shit is going crazy. But it's not cool to take that out on her. I can't believe you chased her away, and I won't let you do it again. None of us will. She has a place here. Same as we all do. If you're going to drive her off you might as well kiss us all goodbye."

Alanso got to his feet, his bald head turning a darker shade as he defended his friend, boss and mate. "Hang on. This is *my* fault. Don't blame Cobra. It's me you should be pissed at."

"Don't make excuses for me. They're right to be angry." Eli waved his partner off, though he appreciated the loyalty. He deserved the censure of the rest of the guys. "What happened that night was the culmination of months of terrible decisions. Sure, you talked me into Fawn. Drunk and horny, both of us made a bad call on that one. It made sense at the time. Practicing a threesome before the main event. But if I'd manned up a hell of a lot sooner, none of that would have happened. We both know that. They're right. I fucked up. Big time."

Eli could have heard crickets chirping in the office. It wasn't everyday he admitted fault for a major transgression. He tried to live so that such apologies were unnecessary. This time he'd let them all down. Hard.

Carver and Holden nodded. The two most easygoing of their group were quick to forgive and forget. Roman crossed his arms over his defined chest. Now that Eli understood the contrasts between a man's ripped body and a woman's lushness, thanks to caressing every inch of Alanso, he wondered what all those muscles would feel like beneath his palms.

Jesus. Focus.

"It doesn't matter who got us here," Bryce interjected with that political air of his. "We just need to figure out where we're headed now. And we don't have a hell of a lot of time to do it. Mustang Sally is incoming."

"Remember how much she loved that surprise party we threw for her birthday a few years ago?" Kaige supplied the perfect solution as usual. "Let's *show* her how much we missed her instead of chatting about it like a bunch of old ladies. Tom's around—he can help us cook something quick. Or we can order pizzas. And I think there are some balloons and shit left from the President's Day sale we had. Plus, we just stocked up on beer yesterday. We can slap together one hell of a welcome-home celebration."

"Genius. She'll get a kick out that." Alanso hugged Kaige and they all pretended not to see the sheen of tears in his eyes. "But what about the rest...?"

"Are you referring to the fact that every man in this room has a crush on our roommate?" Bryce spoke up again as his gaze flitted from Hot Rod to Hot Rod. Alanso perched on Eli's desk, which Kaige sat behind in the Ferrari chair they'd crafted for their boss. Roman stood beside the spot Carver had taken on the floor, his back to the wall, his elbows propped on his knees. Holden leaned against a file cabinet with his ankles crossed, relaxed. "Or the possibility that you and Eli are going to convince her to sleep with you two bastards tonight or another time soon while we all listen in from our rooms or the shared space? If she's half as loud as Alanso, nobody will be sleeping without earplugs then."

"*Coño.* Both." Alanso bit his lip. The nervous habit made Eli's hand itch to reach across the space separating them. Maybe to brush his thumb over the abused spot. Better yet, to tug his guy close for a reassuring kiss. He'd never get over how it felt to lock lips with a man. Especially that one. It was so much more than physical, though that awed him too.

"I could be way off base here." Eli appreciated that they all stopped talking instantly, giving him their attention. "But I don't think it's just Alanso and I she might be curious about.

It's hard for me to believe, but I talked to Joe about it last night. He swears she isn't freaked out by the crew. More like he thinks she's studying them. Watching. Wondering."

"Mike mentioned there was an incident today." Bryce cleared his throat then adjusted his package. A dark five o'clock shadow flexed when his jaw clenched. "He didn't give me details. Said to ask her if we need to know. But he thinks her eyes are wide open and that she's coming home ready to rumble."

"So I guess what I'm asking..." Eli took a deep breath. "...is who in here is interested in Sally. Sexually. Long term. Hands up."

Alanso's tan fist flew into the air before Eli had even finished his question. *No shit.*

Right behind him was Holden, which surprised Cobra a bit. Sure, he joked with Sally plenty, but he had never seemed especially passionate around her. Then again, maybe they'd all learned early to shutter their emotions. Even Salome had mastered the skill. Otherwise, they'd have been getting it on for years, he was sure.

Damn, how much time had they wasted?

No more.

Cobra blinked. Every guy reached for the sky. Even Carver, though the least sexually active garagemate's hand was last to wave. They stared at each other as if the similar gesture were a pact they swore. After all the tough times they'd endured separately and healed from together, this seemed like an advancement. Why not use that bond for pleasure instead of simply surviving pain?

"Okay." He swallowed hard, trying to determine if it was excitement or jealousy that would win out. Exhilaration by a mile. If Sally had witnessed the connection he and Alanso had been lucky enough to see between the crew, she wasn't going to settle for less.

She shouldn't have to.

But would the rest of the Hot Rods be able to handle what

their King Cobra had in mind?

"What if Alanso and I claim her? We're not just talking about sex, guys. We want her. Forever. Like Mike and Kate. Or Joe and Morgan. Or Dave with Kayla. Well, actually, I guess mostly like Neil, James and Devon. If there's anyone that can't handle that, maybe we should have a going away party. Because you're right about one thing—we caused enough collateral damage. I won't stand for anyone to repeat my mistake. And believe me, if I could take it back, I would. God, I *would*."

Carver rose and eliminated the gap between them. His hand landed on Eli's shoulder and squeezed. The guy usually stuck close to Roman's side, his humor a counterweight to Barracuda's darkness. Today, he acted as insulation between them, dampening the hostility still radiating from the older guy. "We know it wasn't on purpose, Cobra. And I don't have a problem with the three of you getting it on. Permanently. I don't know what the hell you call it or how the rest of Middletown is going to treat you guys, but in my opinion, the more the merrier. At least when it comes to positive energy. We've all had too much shit in our life to begrudge someone finding happiness wherever they can. However they can."

Joining them, Holden added his palm to Eli's back. "And if some of that spills over to us, we're willing and ready to fill in. If not, we'll respect Sally's decision."

Bryce strolled over to lend his support. His huge fingers wrapped around Eli's biceps. Meanwhile, he stared at Alanso as he spoke. "Either way, we're here for you guys. Damn proud that you've come this far. Your moms would be happy tonight."

Eli didn't realize he'd squeezed his eyes shut until Roman slapped his cheek a bit. "I'm still claiming the right to kick your ass if you fuck this up. But yeah, I agree. Give Mustang what she wants. It's pretty obvious that's the two of you pricks for some fucking reason. I thought she had better taste."

Spinning out of the executive seat, Kaige wandered closer, his dreads bobbing. "Just don't make me wear a fucking tux for the wedding. I look ridiculous in those things."

When his hand slapped Eli's ass, they all laughed.

Alanso hopped down and came closer until they stood toe to toe. He placed his palms on Eli's chest. Cobra wondered if the engine tuner could detect the ticking of his heart. When he rested his forehead on Eli's sternum, nothing could have kept him from bracing the guy's shoulders in return.

Locked together, they made an unbreakable unit.

For the first time in a while, hope and pure adrenaline raced through Eli's veins.

"Let's do this, Cobra," Alanso whispered as he lifted his head to stare directly into Eli's eyes with his melted-chocolate gaze.

"Then it's settled." Eli started to grin as a crushing weight lifted from his guts. "Alanso and I will fix what we've done. We'll tell Mustang Sally how we feel and that we mean for it to be a forever thing. If she doesn't rip our balls off and stuff 'em down our throats by the time we get that far, we'll work on rebuilding her trust. When the time is right, we'll bring you guys into the mix. If she's ready, we'll let her make the call. Slow. We're not going to blow a gasket. We'll keep this whole thing in first gear. Agreed?"

"We're counting on you, Cobra." Roman nodded his head. "I don't know if you're the right guy for this job. I'm not trying to start anything. It's just, we all know how you are. The more you care, the more freaked out you get. So Alanso, don't let him ruin this for us all."

The bald man angled his body until he stood shoulder to shoulder with Eli. Them against the world. "Together we've got this. We won't let you down again."

"I'm more worried about Salome." Kaige tied his dreadlocks in a bunch. "So I'm going to do what I can for now. I'm going to raid the snacks in the service station 'cause we don't have time for a cake and she always hides a box under her bed for when she's watching chick flicks. Can the rest of you start on the balloons?"

"I'll go tell my dad." Eli nodded. "He'll want to be here. Hell, I think he missed her more than we did."

"He loves her." Carver looked up. "We all do."

"Enough to hang back and wait until the time is right to show her," Holden added. "*If* it ever is."

"Hell, it's been ten fucking years already." Roman sighed. "What's another one to wait for you kids to find your assholes? Don't fuck this up."

"We won't." Alanso and Eli answered together.

Chapter Four

Where the hell was everybody?

Maybe the crew had it all wrong. Her Hot Rods hadn't called her directly or even texted in two whole weeks. Sure, she'd asked for space. But when had those jerks ever listened to a request before if it wasn't what they wanted too?

On top of their radio silence, they didn't come down to meet her or help her carry her nonexistent suitcase upstairs as they usually would have. In fact, there wasn't a single light on to warm the windows of their massive apartment, even though she knew Mike would have ratted her out during her return trip.

What the hell made her bold enough to assume they'd be onboard to fuck her when they wouldn't even say hello? Instead of waiting to see her, they probably had gone out to some trashy bar to scout women despite having been apart from her for two whole weeks. All her insides went numb. Maybe they were angry at her for taking off? Even that would be preferable to...nothing.

Because she certainly felt *something*.

The time away had eaten at her. She hated being separated from the Hot Rods.

Dreams of warm male shouts and warmer hugs as she burst through the door evaporated. She considered getting right back in the car and driving with the top down and the wind in her hair until the fresh air made it easier to breathe again. And dried her endless tears.

Shit, she hated crying. Somehow she figured she should have bought the double pack of tissues this time. But she'd had enough of running. It wasn't her style anymore. She'd done it once, abandoning the life she'd known her entire childhood.

Reinventing herself again would be impossible.

Instead, she forced herself to evacuate the white leather interior of her baby. When she leaned against the door, psyching herself up for the eventual confrontation that would either make or break her future, she noticed even the main house was dark. Eli's dad still lived on the same property as the Hot Rods garage and the mechanics' apartment above it.

Tom. She gulped. What would he think of what she intended?

Would he still love her like the daughter he'd never had?

It was a lot to risk.

Everything important.

The stainless steel skeletal butterfly on her fob rattled against her car and house keys as she ascended the open-backed stairs at the rear of the industrial building. The two slivers of metal reminded her of all the stakes. Her home. Her car. Her Hot Rods, who'd given her the trinket, binding them together on the first Christmas she'd spent with them a decade ago.

The badass butterfly had been her signature logo ever since, painted on each piece she created. That included her own Mustang and every other vehicle the Hot Rods obsessed over. Why did they mean so much to her if she didn't matter a bit to them? Their sexy bodies and friendship had obviously warped her judgment.

When she went to fit her key in the lock, the door at the top of the stairs swung open. Had they forgotten to pull it closed? A bunch of them had grown up on the streets or in places a hell of a lot less protected. Security wasn't something they slacked off on despite the relative safety of Middletown.

"Um, hello?" A shiver ran down her spine. Something wasn't right. When a skitter of motion flickered through her unadjusted peripheral vision, she didn't hesitate.

Using the self-defense instruction Roman had often given her, she balled her fist and swung at the shadow rapidly encroaching on her. Her knuckles connected with flesh. *Holy fuck.*

It hurt, but not enough to keep her from landing a second punch to someplace softer. Who the hell was in their house? In the dark? Had they hurt her Hot Rods?

She'd rip them apart with her bare hands if they had.

"*Oompf.*" The grunt sounded somewhat familiar. But Sally wasn't sure the person she'd decked was Eli until he hollered, "Guys! Turn the lights on."

Brightness flashed into existence, blinding Sally.

"Welcome home!" a chorus of male voices shouted, mostly together.

She nearly toppled onto her ass when fight or flight instincts propelled her headlong into the bizarre scene in front of her. Eli bent in half, clutching his abdomen with one hand and his face with the other. Alanso stood slightly behind him, eyes wide and mouth hanging open.

After them, a mass of guys milled around with beers, ridiculous party hats, oversized balloons from the shop and an impressive assortment of snack cakes that looked like they might have come from the convenience section of the gas station.

"Uh-oh." She dropped her keys.

Holden cracked up first. He adored mischief. This one might go down in the history books as the most awkward greeting of all time. "Well, he had it coming."

"Somebody hand me some paper towels." Alanso rushed to Eli's side. A trickle of blood spattered onto the floor.

"I'm fine. It's fine." Eli tried to shake it off. He lifted his head and ignored any discomfort he might be in. Peeking at her from the slivers of his eyes not scrunched in pain, he said, "Hey, there."

"Oh my God." Sally's shoulders drooped. "I'm so sorry. I thought... It was dark. I didn't think you were home. The door was unlocked."

"And you still came inside. By yourself?" Roman practically growled at her.

"She can hold her own." Eli surprised her by taking her side. He pressed the napkin, which Carver had offered, to his face and tipped his head back as he pinched the bridge of his nose.

And just like that, Sally couldn't handle any more. She didn't give a fuck if they thought less of her. She'd always made a point of showing no weakness around the gang of mechanics. Or at least she'd tried. But tonight there was no stopping the flood of tears that swept over her.

"Shh." Alanso was there in an instant. He smelled nice, like grease and the cinnamon gum he liked. Breathing deep, she didn't resist as he wrapped her in his stocky arms and fitted her to his chest. "It'll take a hell of a lot more than a bop on the nose to put King Cobra in his place. It's okay. We shouldn't have startled you like that. *Hijo de puta*, why do we keep screwing things up?"

"No, no." She squirmed in his hold, wanting to peek over his shoulder to verify she hadn't imagined the effort they'd gone to. They cared. They'd missed her. Maybe even a fraction as much as she'd pined for them. "It's perfect. Amazing. I ruined things. Again."

"I wouldn't say that, Sally." Kaige raised his beer in her direction. "I'm having a wicked good time. Nice hook, by the way."

A weak smile began to turn her frown upside down. Her eyes skipped over his bold tattoos and his golden dreads to the older man standing quietly at the rear of the gang.

King Cobra's dad, Tom, nodded in her direction, then held his hands up so that his curled fingers made the top of a heart and his thumbs pointed together, completing the shape. The gesture alone brought fresh tears to her eyes.

Damn, this wasn't going to be pretty.

She let go of Alanso just long enough to flash the sign in return.

Together she and the engine tuner faced Eli.

"It's stopping. All cool. No worries." He crumpled the paper towel and jammed it in the back pocket of his jeans. "I missed you, Sally."

"I missed you too." She held out her arms. Both Eli and Alanso stepped into them. She hugged each of them with one arm and they mimicked her until the triangle was complete.

With the three of them bonded in their own private assembly, Eli whispered into her ear, "We have a lot to talk about. After the party. You. Me. Alanso. Please let me explain?"

She froze. The plan had been to charge in and hit them with her demands, both barrels. Would she still have the nerve to be so bold after an hour or two of hanging out, pretending all was normal when everything inside her had disintegrated and rearranged? And what about her unfinished business? She wouldn't have time to dive into it before the three of them hashed things out. *Crap!*

Is this how Alanso had felt when he'd returned from the guys' visit to the crew after Dave's accident? If so, she had no clue how he'd held it all together so long. His strength awed her. Just like it had when he'd burst inside that night a few weeks ago and announced he wanted to experiment with guys. She had to take a page from his book and be brave enough to share her desires. Otherwise, there was no hope of getting what she needed.

Sally kissed the bald guy's cheek as she rubbed his head. He nearly purred when she found the spot he loved so much. Then she turned to Eli to bestow the same peace offering on him. Though she'd kissed his cheek a million times in their lives, this time was different.

At the last instant, he turned his head.

They met lips on lips for the first time.

Sally's heart sputtered in her chest like the engine on one of their fresh finds. To finally touch him, like this, with *intent* to do more—it amazed her. He was gentle, more than she would have expected. His thumbs brushed her cheeks as his fingers buried in the long strands of her hair.

When her knees turned to motor oil, Alanso held her up, tucked tight to his frame.

He lifted her toward his best friend, allowed the man to feast at her mouth.

Eli's tongue traced her smile. He nibbled on her bottom lip while she tried to shake herself from the stunned trance his touch induced. She purred, then kissed him back, clutching both him and Alanso as they made out in front of all the witnesses that mattered.

With a moan, Cobra reversed a tiny bit. Just enough to angle her face toward Alanso.

His fingers held her in place for his best friend.

"Ah, *mami chula.*" The engineman's endearment healed some of the wounds on her heart in an instant. Two weeks away had barely staunched the bleeding, but his hungry lips acted like a balm as they caressed hers. She rose up on her tiptoes to knit them more fully.

Freedom raged through her. To finally be able to show them how she felt unlocked a whole fleet of emotions. Her nails dug into their powerful shoulders, impressing them with her mark. She could have continued their exchange indefinitely if it weren't for the commotion infringing on her concentration.

"Uh, kids? Remember, I'm still in the room." Tom cleared his throat.

The three of them jerked apart as if someone had flipped the poles on their magnetic attraction. Eli sucked in a huge breath while Alanso shook his head as if to clear it. She could relate. What they had was potent.

Whistles and catcalls winged through their spacious living-dining-kitchen area with its high, exposed metal-beam ceiling and textured concrete floor. Area rugs and furnishings they'd pretty much let her pick out on her own dampened some of the cacophony of testosterone-induced cheers. The canvases hanging on the wall helped some too.

The portrait of Eli behind the wheel of his Cobra was probably her favorite. Short hair, dark glasses and tattoos highlighting his muscles caught her eye as she averted her face long enough to wipe the tears from her cheek.

"Wow. I don't think I've ever seen Mustang Sally blush before." Bryce seemed impressed. "You know, it's your party if you want to blow us off."

"Would you mind if we didn't?" She could hardly believe she had enough self-control to keep from dragging them to her room and ripping their clothes off so she could prove once and for all who Eli and Alanso belonged too. But she'd missed them all and wanted to ground herself before they did anything that might jeopardize the assurances they'd granted each other with one simple kiss.

Maybe things didn't have to be complicated after all.

"We'll do whatever you want." Alanso lifted her hand to his mouth and dusted his lips over her knuckles.

"No need to rush. We're not changing our minds," Eli promised. When King Cobra gave his word, nothing else needed to be said. "We owe you an apology whether now or later. A big one."

"I wouldn't pass on a beer or two first." Alanso shuffled from foot to foot. His thick socks skidded on the smooth floor.

"How'd getting trashed work for you last time, son?" Tom interjected from where he leaned against the bar.

"Right." Alanso cursed under his breath. "*Una.*"

"Go say hello to the gang. They missed you." The light pressure of Eli's hand in the small of her back had her shivering. So she appreciated the heat from each of the Hot Rods that hugged her as she threw herself into their arms.

"Next time you go to play with the crew, take us with you," Holden murmured against the top of her head.

Carver stole her away from his friend. "You have no idea how glad I am to see you."

"No kidding," Roman cut in. "These two are even more of a pain in my ass when they're grumpy about their fuck-ups. Go easy on them, Mustang Sally."

"Nice to have you back, squirt." Bryce patted her back with his big hands.

"It was kind of quiet without your ridiculous music

pumping in the garage all day." Kaige tempered his jab with a chocolate cupcake, which he extended to her. "I needed a vacation from Katy Perry."

She paid him back by putting her hand up and mushing the treat into his smug face.

The rest of the Hot Rods rioted with laughter.

Kaige swiped the cake and cream filling into his mouth, not too upset by the force-feeding. In five seconds or less, the last crumb had vanished without a trace. "Mmm. Haven't had one of those in forever. I forgot why you love them so much."

"If you two are finished with your shenanigans..." Tom interjected. The whole room went quiet when he approached. "Welcome home, Sally. I sure did miss your face. With just these guys to look at it was a hell of a lot less pretty around here."

She banded her arms around the man who'd acted as her father long enough to claim the title in every way but the genetic one. "You're okay with this?"

"All I've ever wanted is for you kids to be happy." He kissed her forehead. "Looks like I'm about to get my wish."

"I'll do my best to take care of them." She hugged him.

"Good luck." He ruffled her hair. About the only person in the universe who could get away with it, he reached around her for a strawberry pie and tore into the package. He raised the treat and toasted her return.

A few hours later, Eli's dad had gone home and most of the guys had fallen in front of the TV to watch a mixed martial arts tournament. Beer bottles, snack wrappers and pizza boxes littered the coffee table. Sally reclined near the end of the sectional with her head on Eli's thigh and her feet propped in Alanso's lap. Nothing too out of the ordinary there. She'd spent plenty of Sunday afternoons exactly like this.

Except now she was ultra-aware of every twitch of Cobra's fingers on her shoulder and the stiff length of Alanso's cock against her calf as her toes fidgeted. Despite her original plan, she was glad things had settled down a bit from her emotional high. The familiar routine reminded her that they'd had disagreements in the group before.

A fight didn't mean the end of the world. Good thing too, because she was still pissed off and hurt by what her guys had done. Only difference was now she believed they could work things out. As long as they all had the same goals.

"I think it's time." Eli's gruff declaration had her springing to her feet. Alanso followed right behind. They marched toward the guys' adjoining rooms by tacit agreement as Eli peeled himself from the leather.

"Sweet dreams, boys and girl." Kaige gave them a finger wave and a smirk.

The rest of the Hot Rods pretended not to notice the trio's exit.

Roman turned the volume way, way up. Carver, Holden and Bryce shouted over the din in support of their favorites. Hopefully the only people coming to blows would be the ones onscreen. Unless it were special blows…

Sally appreciated the sound buffer as she couldn't promise herself she wouldn't shriek at the guys trailing her into their lair. Maybe she should have gone to her turf, but their rooms were bigger. And so were their beds. Alanso even had those silky sheets she loved to finger when they came out of the drier—hot and smooth.

She'd rubbed them on her arms before, wondering what they'd feel like to lounge on naked. Hopefully she'd find out soon. *If* they convinced her to go with the half of her in love with them versus the half that kind of hated them at the moment.

Pausing at the threshold, she waited for Cobra to pass by her with an oddly blank expression. Once he had, she slammed the metal door. Digging deep, she latched on to the outrage and indignation their fling had inspired instead of the pain.

"Why the hell are you two so stupid?" She clenched her hands at her sides.

"Uh, I sort of thought we were all good, *chica.*" Alanso shrugged. "Did I miss something?"

"I should have known that was too easy." Eli shuffled between them, as if shielding the engine tuner from her wrath. "Gonna deck me again?"

She promised herself she wouldn't crack a smile. Not until they'd heard everything. Glossing over their issues was no way to apply a basecoat for a relationship. "No. Unlike you two, I would never intentionally hurt you."

"Totally got it." Alanso held his hands up as if surrendering to her ire. "For the record, it was my idea. You know, to fuck Bambi. I didn't think about how it would make you feel. I gotta get better at that. It's just—"

He didn't finish.

"What?" She crossed her arms over her breasts, trying to hold herself together. He hadn't considered the effect his actions might have on her? That seemed worse than whatever else she might have concocted.

"*Lo siento,* Salome." When her real name rolled off his tongue, the thrill it gave her lit up her whole being. He never called her that. This was serious shit. "I don't want to make excuses. My mom, everything with Cobra, the drinking—none of it matters. I'm ashamed of what I did. What I dragged Cobra into. The real problem was that I was a pussy."

Eli reached out, wrapping one arm around his best friend's waist and tugging the guy until they stood shoulder to shoulder, bracing each other.

"Oh yeah, you looked terrified while you plowed that bitch all over the hood of the Fisher job." She huffed. "Not only were you slumming it with trash who treated you like shit, but you screwed up my paint job too. Asshole."

"For the record, he fixed the hood himself the next morning." Eli understood the pride she took in her work. "And he's not lying. We were both afraid because we've never done this before. You know, it's a lot. Deciding to try being with a guy for the first time. It's amazing. And fucking terrifying."

The guys stared into each other's eyes for a moment, making her a tiny bit jealous of the bond they'd formed. In the short time she'd been gone, their friendship had morphed into so much more. It moved her to see them completely integrated.

"It was fresh. Neither of us has had to find our way in the bedroom in a long time," Eli continued. "For a guy, that's...unsettling."

"Didn't seem to be having any trouble from my perspective." She rolled her eyes.

"Really?" He drew up taller. "Because I don't remember touching Fawn. Not that night. I didn't have it in me. Not when all I could think of was Alanso. And you."

Sally couldn't argue with him there. The memory of him humping Alanso to get off was etched into her brain. She'd woken up sweaty, having come in her sleep, several nights of her stay at Kayla's cabin. Thankfully her hosts had been too gracious to mention any nocturnal cries. No way would she have been quiet.

"What he's saying is that I begged him for a practice run with someone who didn't matter. Didn't need more than some quick relief from us." Alanso stared at his socked feet. "I didn't have the *cajones* to make a play for what I really wanted. Not feeling like that."

"Like what?" Sally couldn't help herself, she inched closer. The sight of his anguish impacted her, even if she would rather hang on to her self-righteous anger.

"It took all the courage I had to lay things on the line with Eli. I didn't know if he would accept me. And I didn't know if it would change how I was with women. With you. I wanted to be sure I could do it. That we could make it work before I messed with our relationship." He swallowed hard. "I can't lose you, Salome. Not as a friend. If that means we walk from this right now and forget it all, I will. I need you. I'll take whatever you can give and do my best to deserve something so fine."

"But Alanso." She tried hard to believe. One thing kept tripping her up. "I heard you call her your 'girl'. You told Eli you wanted to remember to keep the focus on *our girl* so she didn't feel left out."

"That?" Eli gingerly rubbed his eye. "*That's* what you singled out? He was referring to you, Sally. Or did you wipe out the part where Fawn smacked him for screaming out your name when he finally busted in her?"

"What?" She craned her neck.

"How could you have missed that?" Alanso grimaced. "Gentler breed, my ass. We've been taking a beating lately. I'm glad it was Cobra's turn tonight. I swear my jaw has been clicking every time I chew for the past two weeks. Not that I've been able to eat much with you missing."

Now that he mentioned it, he did look a little gaunt. Slimmer.

Sally bent over, bracing her palms on her knees. A deep breath filled her lungs, then another. Could she have had it all wrong? Well, other than the part about Alanso's cock in Fawn's pussy. That hadn't been a mistake.

"You okay?" Eli knelt at her feet. He held her shoulders, supporting her as she reeled.

"Can't stay." She could barely force out the words, remembering the lance that had pierced her heart that night.

Cobra's ashen face and Alanso's feral cry made her rewind. "*Couldn't.* Couldn't stay. I ran out of there after you came on his ass. It was fucking hot. I felt so alone. Left out. I didn't think I ever had a chance at what you were giving that ungrateful slut. She was incredibly selfish, only wanted you for herself. I can't believe you let her keep you from loving each other. *That's* what hurt the most. That you still weren't being honest. That you might never be ready to admit the truth."

"*Hijo de puta.* You really didn't hear what happened after that? See it?" Alanso scrubbed his hands over his bald head. "No fucking wonder you're pissed. I don't blame you. I made you hate us."

"I don't—"

"You have every right to," Eli admitted softly. "In my heart I knew it was wrong. I feel like I cheated on you. I know we haven't exchanged any promises, but when it comes to lovers, there's only room for Alanso and you in my soul."

"If that's true, then why didn't you text me or anything? Didn't you want to talk?" A sniffle snuck past her guard.

"*Chica,* you left us." Alanso canted his head as if he simply couldn't understand her. "And when we Skyped the crew we'd always catch your sweet ass running from us in the background. You made it clear you wanted nothing to do with us. We were giving you what you asked for. Weren't we?"

"I don't know anymore." Part of her, a weak fragment, had wished they'd chase her down so she'd be confident they cared. At least a little.

"Me either. All I'm sure about is that I didn't want to jack up our chance with you by being awkward. I mean, Eli hadn't even fucked *me* yet. What if it was awful? What if we started something we couldn't finish?" Alanso turned and kicked the chest at the foot of his bed. "And it looks like I ruined it anyway. I'm sorry, Cobra. I should have listened."

"Enough." Eli stood. He reached out and gathered both Alanso and Sally to his chest. "We all hurt each other in some way. I'd do anything to score a do-over on this. Life doesn't work like that. So all I can offer are my apologies. To you both. For not protecting you. And swear that I'll do better in the future. I can also promise that I won't be touching Fawn or anyone but you two either. I can't lose you. Either of you."

Sally gulped. No use in stopping short now. "What about the rest of the Hot Rods?"

"What about them?" He stepped carefully.

"What if I want something like the crew has?" She peeked at Alanso from where she rested on Eli's T-shirt-draped pectoral. From here, they stared directly into each other's eyes.

The delicious chocolate of his gaze warmed at her question. Was he with her on this too? Was it fair for her to ask when she'd ripped them new ones for fucking someone else?

"I'll try my best to give you anything you'd like." Eli's response came slowly, as if he weighed every word. "It's still a ton to process. Don't you think? Why don't we focus on here and now without getting ahead of ourselves?"

She nodded. After all, hadn't she bargained identically with herself? Talk to the guys first, clear up her past as soon as possible after. One step at a time. "It's just hard not to visualize the big picture. I don't want to sign up for something then realize later I wasn't clear."

"How about this for clarification?" Eli held his partners out at arm's length. He gazed first at Alanso then at Sally. "I, Eli London, am madly in love with both you and you. The kind of magic thing that my parents had. The kind that lasts forever. I know what that looks like and I feel it for you. For so long it's worried me. I couldn't figure out how to show you without pushing one or the other of you away. Until Joe and the crew proved to us how crazy shit *can* work with the right people. And Alanso seemed onboard. I just...I can't believe it's like this. That you guys need what I do too."

"It's true, *cabrón*. And if you would have listened to me months ago we could have worked this from our systems by now." Al licked his lips. "Gotten all the kinks out."

"I admit I fucked up too. Worst of all. But I highly doubt we're going to ever get this out of our systems. And the kinkier the better." Eli broke. He swooped Sally into his arms, making her squeal as he tossed her onto the bed.

Chapter Five

Before she'd finished bouncing, the two guys descended on her like dogs fighting for a bone. Eli. Alanso. Both. They drooled over her. Thank God.

Their intensity impressed her when they crawled above her and dropped down low, each working some article of clothing free of her body. When Eli whipped her shirt over her head, her arms got stuck.

For a split second, she lost her breath. She couldn't get away now even if she wanted to.

"Hang on," Eli ordered Alanso, noticing her plight immediately. "Slow up."

Sally shook her head, wriggling until he divested her of the entrapping top. "Sorry. Not ready for bondage yet. Actually, that one might be on my never list."

She laughed, but Cobra didn't mimic her smile.

"If it's too much, you tell us." He paused both his speech and his advances. "We've had a while to get used to how powerful this is. And I can already tell it's going to be better with you. But it's extreme. We know it is."

"It's not that." She sighed. Their pity wasn't what she craved. "For a second there I remembered stories I heard growing up. You know, of girls being forced on their wedding nights while their husband's friends got to watch or helped brainwash them into accepting the polygamous culture."

"*Mierda.*" Alanso drew up so fast he nearly flew off the edge of the bed.

Eli grabbed him by the biceps and kept him on their oasis. "Is that how we're making you feel? Forced? Persuaded?"

"No." She scrunched her eyes closed.

"How can this be what you want?" Alanso sighed.

"It's different with you. And the crew too." She shrugged. "That wasn't what spooked me. After weeks of sadness, I went from furious to horny in a snap. Well, maybe that was there all along in layers. But you turned it around on me. I can't blame you for the decisions you made. And I need you. So badly. It frightened me for a second, that's all. You're both so…big…and strong."

"You've had boyfriends before." Eli stalled, as if he struggled to understand. He froze, schooling his features into a serene mask. "Please tell me you're not a virgin."

She snorted. "Hell no. I'm skittish, not a saint."

"Her dates *were* a bunch of real weenies." Alanso shrugged at Eli.

King Cobra nodded. "It's starting to make sense, though. I can see where they would have been completely non-threatening to our Mustang. You could have kicked their asses with one hand behind your back. Especially that last guy. Blake?"

"I mean, who the fuck wears a sweater vest anyway?" Alanso shook his head.

"Bryce has a couple in his closet." Sally didn't deny her taste in men had been…tame. "Even Kaige has one."

"Uh, yeah, no. His is badass. It has skulls and flames on it. Plus, it lets all his tattoos show. Not the same at all as those diamondy kind." The bald guy had her chuckling, the last of her instinctive flinch receding.

"The pattern is called argyle." She couldn't help but fill him in.

"Whatever." He sank forward again. "They're butt-ugly. And lame. Not anything like the girl I know."

"She's cool enough to score a Hot Rod or two." Eli grinned as he returned, giving her more space but proceeding to slither his hands beneath her body and unhook her bra. "Forget being one of many unloved possessions, like her moms. Our girl can have as many men as she wants to wrap around her little finger."

Seven, her mind cheered.

"Two sounds like plenty tonight." She smiled as she contorted her shoulders, dropping the straps of her bra from them. Then she shrugged, brushing Eli's hands away to ensure the scrap of lace draped over her chest didn't reveal the goods just yet.

In the meantime, Alanso unfastened her jeans and drew down the zipper. She shivered when Eli pressed open-mouthed kisses low on her belly, across the V of skin his friend exposed for their enjoyment. As Cobra distracted her from any potential shyness, with flicks of his tongue that made her think he'd been aptly named, Alanso walked tight denim over her hips then down her thighs and finally off her completely.

His groan surprised her. When she peeked up, the Cuban hottie rubbed himself through his own ripped and grease-stained pants. "You're perfect, *mi corazón.*"

"Does he always let this much Spanish slip out when you're getting it on?" She shifted her attention to Eli.

"Hell yeah. Sexy, isn't it?" Cobra rubbed his thumb back and forth across her lips. "And don't try to change the subject. He's right. You're gorgeous."

She laughed. "I'm hardly a starlet. Same ol' Mustang."

For the first time in her life, she wished she were a little more feminine. Softer. But the bold slashes of color in her tattoos and her obsession with piercings were part of who she was. Apparently the guys appreciated her style.

Eli touched the heated metal decorating her skin. The spike below her lower lip was the first he traced reverently. Then the hoop in her brow and the tiny diamond on the side of her nose. "I've always thought these were so pretty on you. You made them seem delicate, yet tough, like you."

"But this..." Alanso twirled the rhinestone in her belly. "Has always made me want to lick it."

"Not about to stop you." She arched her spine, offering him a taste.

"Except I think I'm going to discover something I want to play with more beneath this ridiculous excuse for a pair of undies." Alanso snapped the elastic of the thin strap against her hipbone.

"Why don't you find out?" Eli directed the stockier guy.

"You ready?" Alanso checked with her. "If I take these off, I'm not going to be able to stop myself from tasting you."

"Same goes for this bra." Cobra pried the edge of the cups from her grasp. "It's got to go."

Sally couldn't moisten her tongue enough to verbalize her response. Instead, she gave a curt nod. Work-roughed hands caressed her skin as they removed the last vestiges of her modesty.

It felt odd to be naked, or nearly so, with them. And yet, it seemed natural. Why shouldn't they see her body when they already knew the rest of her?

Slowly enough to drive her mad, Eli peeled the bra from her chest and tossed it aside. It draped over the bedside lamp, adding sultry shadows to the space.

The hoops in her nipples matched the ones in her labia.

Both Eli and Alanso offered up a small oath. Cobra plucked at the tips of her breasts, teasing the rapidly tightening flesh into rock-hard peaks while their lover toyed with the jewelry between her legs. She couldn't help but spread for him, granting him better access.

Their stares roved over every inch of her exposed body, making her wish they were displayed as prominently for her inspection. It was weird to know them so well yet, in this way, not at all. Strangers and best friends. Excitement mixed with nervousness made her long to hold them close. Soaking in their adoration was pretty great too, though.

"Holy shit, you're tan. You must have laid out every day." Alanso admired her golden skin. "You're almost as dark as me, *chica.*"

"And no lines." Eli frowned. "Where the hell are your tan lines?"

"Well, you see, in order to get those you have to have worn clothes." She grinned at his dilating pupils.

"You were roaming around like this in front of the crew?" The muscle in his cheek twitched. "The wives only, right?"

She shook her head. Let him be jealous. Served him right for the Fawn incident.

"The guys saw all this? Even my cousin, Joe? Before me?"

"Yep." She nodded. "Bare Natural *is* a naturist resort, you know?"

Alanso stared at her. "*Mierda!* You went naked? Like they do?"

"Did you fuck the crew too?" Eli was too still to be as relaxed as he pretended.

"It wouldn't really be your concern if I had. Would it?"

He looked away then back, and shook his head as if digesting a bitter dose of medicine. "Nope, I guess not. Considering you took off before I could make it *our* concern."

Good enough, she'd accept that. She didn't care to mislead him. "Whatever. I've been a part of this garage for almost a dozen years. You had plenty of chances. But no, unlike you dickheads, I don't bang people for the sake of a quick scratch."

"If it makes you feel better, the sex with Bambi sucked." Alanso groaned when she didn't crack a smile. "Even before the part where I got backhanded."

Sally blinked. "I still can't believe that bitch hit you. If I ever catch her too-much-makeup face around, she won't like what happens next."

"I'm kind of glad you didn't see that part." He hung his head.

"Or the ungraceful exit she made after Alanso dropped her on her ass on the garage floor when he staggered backward." Eli filled in the gaps.

"You didn't!" Salome couldn't help but laugh. She clasped her middle and rolled side to side as a flood of relieved joy spread through her. It wasn't Fawn's fault for fucking the two sexy guys. Disrespecting the bond between them was another matter.

"Well, not on purpose. But yeah, I did, *puta*." His wry smile belied the curse. "If you'd hung around just another minute or two, I'd have embarrassed myself more. It would have been worth it if maybe we wouldn't have had to miss you so bad. Please, don't leave us again."

Eli's jaw set so tight he risked cracking a tooth. She should have considered the impact her defection, even a temporary one, would have on him. His cheek was slightly rough beneath her fingers.

"I won't. And I'm sorry too. I should have been stronger. Hell, I should have stomped out there and run that hussy off so I could have taken her place." She smiled at the groan they both offered in response to that idea. "I was afraid too. I still am, a little. So could you guys please get naked already? Being the only one flashing all the goods is a little nerve-racking."

Eli's smile touched her hand. He angled his cheek to kiss her palm. When she glanced from him to Alanso, the engine tuner had already stripped to the waist. His gorgeous chest and the tattoos covering it made her mouth water. Not to mention his own nipple piercings. His barbells had always tempted her to flick them and see if they felt as good as hers did. He struggled a little with his fly, given the bulge behind it, which strained the fabric.

When he finally freed his cock, no underwear beneath his jeans today, his face went slack with relief. "You'll be lucky if I'm not permanently bent from hours of being trapped like that."

"Come here so I can kiss it and make it better." She held out her hand to him.

He kicked his jeans off and crawled closer to her head.

"Not too much." He hesitated outside her grasp. "I don't want to finish before we really get this party started."

"I think that could be a benefit of having sex with several guys." She wished it didn't sound as if she'd spent a zillion hours thinking about this, but even that was probably only half as much as she actually had obsessed about the possibilities. "I can please you. Let you be a little selfish. And there's still plenty more to come."

"Literally." Eli laughed.

"No, seriously." She knew that was a bit of a ridiculous request given her position flat on her back with her hand reaching and wrapping around Alanso's cock for the first time. God, he felt fine. Hard and smooth. Thick.

Nothing awkward about the way he fit in her palm.

Alanso uttered something reverent before his head dropped back and he leaned into her grasp.

"I'm waiting…" Cobra's smile tipped up on one side as she struggled to keep her thoughts in order when they distorted all her attention to them.

"Uh, right." What had she been about to say? "Oh! Yeah, I mean, sometimes giving a guy a great blowjob is sort of like shooting yourself in the foot if you want to get fucked worth a damn."

"Not if he does it right. Taking a nice long snack to catch you up and give himself time to refuel." Alanso closed his hand over hers, showing her how he preferred to be gripped with firm pressure. Their discussion helped ease their initial foray into intimacy. How could she be nervous when the friends she'd loved forever were here with her?

"I suppose." She shrugged. "Haven't met many guys interested in pursuing sex after they've blown their wad."

"The first time?" Eli looked confused.

"How many times do you guys plan to come in a night?" She paused, her fingers less certain on Alanso's shaft. Damn, she could hardly close her fingers around him, and his big balls bounced against the heel of her hand when she slid it to the base of his shaft.

"I can't count that high when I'm distracted by your fabulous tits and that pretty pussy." Eli shrugged. "But more than once or twice, that's for damn sure."

"Oh." She blinked.

While she mulled over the revelation, Eli performed an

impromptu strip tease for her. He unveiled his abs inch by inch until he shucked his shirt. Then he turned around and peeled his pants over his fine ass.

Alanso plumped in her hand. Had Eli let him in there? Oh, damn. She'd love to see that. Couldn't wait to watch them together. The desire was almost as strong as her need to feel them inside her, together, joining the three of them in a special bond. All she could picture was the look of pure bliss on Devon's face when her two men had teamed up to drive her wild.

Suddenly Eli was bare too. He faced her again, waiting as if for judgment beneath her appreciative stare. Her fingers traced the arched Hot Rods tattoo across his belly. Each dip and rise of his abs enhanced the lines of the script.

"I swear, I've fucked more in the past two weeks than in those early years when I first discovered the softer side of girls. And even all that fooling around with Cobra hasn't made me want you less. Nothing will." Alanso looked afraid, as if she might bolt again. "Still interested in playing our way now that you know we're sex maniacs?"

"Doubly so now." She winked at him. "In that case...can I taste you?"

"You never have to ask, *mi alma.*" He guided his cock toward her mouth.

Eli surprised her by running his thumb over her lips, opening her for his best friend. "Make him feel good, Sally. I'll do the same for you. Tell me what you like. Anything."

She opened her mouth and stretched her neck to close the gap between her lips and Alanso's cock. Eli slapped his hand on Alanso's abdomen and prevented the shorter guy from sealing the deal.

"No, no." He *tsk*ed at them. "She can't talk with her mouth full. I want to hear it. In that sexy rasp that tells me she needs us as much as we need her. What would you like me to do with you while Alanso becomes the luckiest bastard on the planet?"

"Lick me," she whispered.

"Here?" He tasted the column of her neck.

"Lower." She shoved his shoulders and begged Alanso with her eyes to give her something to work over. With him in her mouth, she'd at least have the satisfaction of knowing someone else suffered the bite of arousal with her. Suckling him would help her check her rocketing blood pressure too.

Being with Alanso always soothed her. There were lots of times they'd sat, quietly, staring at the fishpond in Tom's garden or watching paint dry on one of her projects. They didn't have to talk to enjoy each other's company, though they did plenty of that too.

"Like this?" Eli flitted along her collarbone with his mouth, tasting her skin as he teased.

"Lower," she repeated.

He obeyed in his own way, forcing her to admit to them both what she secretly craved. His mouth worked the slope of her breast, drawing ever nearer to the peak and the piercing there. When he bit and tugged just a little, a trickle of arousal squeezed from her pussy.

The spot where she truly craved his handiwork.

"Lower, lower, lower," she chanted as he kissed first her ribs then her belly and finally the spot just above her mound.

"Please, *Dios*." Alanso shivered above her, painting her knuckles with a smear of pre-come.

She released him long enough to sample the fluid, and him, for the first time. "I swear I can taste that dried pineapple you're always eating."

He gurgled when she devoured a second helping of him. "You'd better get down to business there, Cobra. I'm waiting exactly seven more seconds before I get my dick in her mouth. I've dreamed about this for too long to stop on the brink."

"Like this?" Eli humored them both.

The instant his mouth settled on her pussy, she squealed.

Alanso took advantage of the opportunity to insert his cock into her mouth. She surrounded him with her lips, welcoming him to her body, hoping he understood her open invitation. The weight of his thickness on her tongue, combined with the sweetness of him, acted like a drug on her.

She closed her eyes and drew on his cock as if it was a pacifier while Eli employed every trick in the book. Hell, he invented a few she'd never heard of to ramp her up. Flicks, circles and taps of his tongue had her eyelids fluttering closed. Her toes curled in the silky sheets and her hands sought her men out. With one palm she cupped Alanso's balls, holding him in place as she laved him from beneath. The other hand was filled with Eli's head and short hair as she pinned him to her body.

Arcs of her hips had her riding his tongue. She wasn't afraid to take what she desired from them. With another man she would have tried to be patient, let them exert their dominance. With her Hot Rods, she didn't have to tone herself down. She could be liberated. Undomesticated. And they would still tame the Mustang in her easily.

They made her feel dainty. Girly. And all woman.

Eli teased her piercings—the rings on either side of her pussy and the discreet barbell through the hood of her clit. She moaned around Alanso's shaft, making him groan too.

"This one isn't for decoration, is it?" Eli stopped pleasuring her long enough to ask about the captive bead ring at the apex of her slit. "It's functional, right?"

"Uh-huh." She wasn't about to stop sucking or she'd be screaming the house down beneath the added stimulation of Eli's fingers, which prodded her opening while his mouth returned to investigating the merits of her piercing.

It didn't take him long to figure out that sliding it up and down stroked her clit and drove her absolutely insane. Verging on painfully arousing, the stimulation required some distraction to bear for any length of time when activated directly. During intercourse, it provided that little bit extra she'd often needed to get off hands-free with an average lover.

Somehow she doubted Eli or Alanso would need such tricks. But the insurance couldn't hurt. Oh no, it did far nicer things than cause her pain.

Her suction on Alanso became irregular. He didn't seem to mind, adding tiny pumps of his hips to keep the friction going. Fucking her mouth, he joined her on the upward spiral toward rapture.

"Hurry, Cobra," he begged. "I want her to come with me."

Sally tried to tell him she wasn't close enough. She could detect the veins on his shaft creating more defined ridges, and he bulked up. The bad news was unintelligible with her mouth so full, however.

Just when she thought Alanso would lose control, her attention frayed. Eli inserted two long fingers as far as he could reach. The man above her began to chant her name. Sweat glistened on his chest and bald head. Knowing she inspired this pleasure in him enhanced the motion of Eli's fingers. They curled inside her, rubbing on a spot she'd never found herself.

Holy shit.

He pressed just enough, trapping sensitive nerves between his prodding digits and her pelvic bone. At the same time, he rolled the captive bead ring in her hood across his tongue several times in quick succession. And before she knew it, Alanso was having to catch up to her.

Without warning, she shattered.

Eli seemed prepared as he clung to her waist and pinned her where he pleased so he could continue his annihilation of her inhibitions. The immobility also kept her in place for Alanso to plunder her mouth. She shouted around his flesh, using all her spare brain cells to keep from biting him.

"*Joder!*" He grunted. The first splash of his come landed on her tongue. She swallowed, drawing more of his seed from his cock. Sweet. Salty. A potent combination. Mostly because it meant so much to have pleased him. Either of them. Both of them.

By being honest about what she wanted and how much joy they brought her, they were all winning. Alanso continued to pump jet after jet into her mouth. She suckled his pulsing cock until nothing remained except the traces of his ecstasy. And still her pussy clenched around Eli.

"Damn, you should feel this, Al." Their boss continued to pump her slow and steady. "She's tight and wet and so damn responsive."

Alanso sucked in air as if he'd run a marathon. He couldn't answer Eli. But his gaze told her everything she needed to know when it locked on hers. Allowing her to suckle him, a draw for every clench of her pussy, he stayed until he wilted in her mouth.

She sighed when he pulled out, leaving her empty.

Eli glanced between them, smug. "Was that fun?"

"Hell yes," they replied in unison.

"But weird to give a guy a blow job when I've never really kissed him before." She put one hand over her face. "We're doing this all out of order, aren't we?"

Not that she minded much when aftershocks tore through her, causing her to shiver violently.

"That can be fixed, you know?" Alanso practically collapsed beside her. He pillowed her head on his shoulder, then cuddled up.

She peeked at Eli and found him sitting on his haunches, straddling their intertwined legs. She'd swear he held his breath when he leaned forward, peering at two of his friends, who were about to make out.

"I think I'm going to like this part of us." Eli hummed as he stroked his hand idly over his rigid cock. "You two look hot together. So sexy. It makes me want to cut in on you both but also sit back and enjoy how beautiful you are."

Alanso winced a little at the description.

"Handsome." She patted his cheek.

"Thanks, Sally." He cradled her. From this close up, she could see a measure of contentment in his eyes that had been missing all this time. Until this moment, she hadn't quite noticed his underlying anxiety—he hid it well. The absence of negative stimuli allowed vulnerability to evaporate and leave only happiness in its place.

She lifted her face to his. He complied with her unspoken

wishes. Not by crushing their lips together and plundering the access she granted. No, he made love to her mouth with his lips and tongue as surely as he'd fucked it minutes before.

Unlike the guys she'd dated, Alanso didn't make her awkward. He felt right. Like a shelter from all her grief. Like a place to hide from a storm. With these guys and the rest of their gang in the living room, she would never be homesick.

With them was her place.

She'd never been so sure of it as when he traced her ear, tucking her hair behind it so he could caress her face. A sliver of guilt punctured her serenity when Eli groaned. The sound of his overpowering appetite had both her and Alanso pausing.

They turned their faces toward him. He rubbed his cock in time to the rhythm their mouths had set on each other. "Don't stop."

Chapter Six

"Let us take care of you." She glanced to Alanso, who nodded before trying to sit up.

"I said, keep going." Eli straddled their torsos, his long legs helping to bridge the bodies of his two lovers. He shoved Alanso's shoulder until the bald man fell back to the bed once more.

"Are you going to come on us, Cobra?" The engine tuner licked his lips. "Mark us? Claim us as your own?"

"Fuck yes." Eli's tugs over his impressive length weren't all even. He seemed extra affected when Salome trailed her fingers up and down Alanso's arm. "Kiss. More."

Sally imagined drawing his pleasure from him and allowing him to paint their bodies with the proof of his desire. She'd be his canvas any day.

A butterfly brush of Alanso's lips on her cheek broke her from her fantasy. He was so soft with her, so sugary. It caught her unexpectedly how much she really loved him. Not just as her partner at the shop or a roommate of nearly a dozen years. No, this was it. He was the one for her. And so was Eli.

They were the *ones*.

She smiled as he kissed her bottom lip, rasping his teeth lightly over the flesh swollen from his thrusting cock. And as if it heard her call, something stirred against her thigh. Already? He was revving up for another round?

They got a little carried away, their kisses turning insistent again.

"Slower," Eli commanded. And they obeyed. Anything to touch him, even if it wasn't physically.

Each press and glide of their lips on each other began to

feel like full-body contact. The slightest sensations were magnified until Sally wondered if she could have an orgasm just from kissing Alanso. The fact that her pussy had come to rest against his thigh didn't hurt either. She rode him just a little, with subtle twitches of her hips.

"Look how wet she is." Eli took the hand not pumping his cock and swiped his fingers through her slit. He gathered her moisture and put it on display, as though she would deny how much they turned her on.

Alanso broke free just long enough to pout. "My turn, please, Eli."

Sally quivered when Eli fed his fingers into Alanso's open mouth.

"That's right, suck them clean." Eli withdrew slowly, then scooped another dollop of cream from her. Like a baby bird, Alanso parted his lips. He cried out when Eli smeared the fluid over his tongue with gentle strokes of his fingers.

"Eli." She squirmed in Alanso's hold.

"Yes, Mustang?" The gleam in his eye proclaimed his knowledge of her struggle. Even if he wanted to tease her into begging. It didn't take much to twist her arm.

"Please fuck me." She spread her legs as best she could. Alanso adjusted his hold and positioned her for his best friend.

"Go ahead, *mi vida*." He swallowed. "You deserve this. Take her first, make her ours."

"Hand me a condom," King Cobra hissed at Alanso. "Quick."

Alanso's face fell. "I didn't have time to grab any from downstairs. Because of the party. We weren't expecting you until tomorrow, Sally."

With a curse, Eli backed away. His cock pulsed, spilling a bead of pre-come onto Alanso's thigh.

"I'll go get some." Alanso started to rise when Salome stopped him with her splayed palm over his heart.

"Not necessary." She winced. "Unless you've been unprotected with someone else. I'm clean and you know I get the shot. Why should we start with barriers between us? That's not what I have in mind."

"Me either." The man snuggling her dropped a kiss on her nose. "We're always safe. Even when we made dumbass decisions on who to fuck. Even the time I went to the gay hook-up spot. Never touched another person without a condom. Swear it."

"Hang on, you went where?" She felt the mini-quake of an aftershock or a pre-shock, she couldn't say.

"Oh." He blushed a little. "The night Eli and I fought, I checked out Chestnut Grove."

"No wonder he looked like...whoa...when you two came back that night." Sally's eyes went wide.

"I needed to know." Alanso hugged her tight.

"I get it." She shushed him with another kiss. "I just wish you hadn't had to resort to strangers and experiments. From now on, you come to me. We'll figure things out together if there's something you need. Okay?"

"You sound like Cobra." A grimace lined his face a moment before a colossal smile revealed his bright-white teeth and his killer grin. "I love that about you. Both of you. Thank you for giving me what I need."

"Eli?" Sally returned her focus to the man strangling the base of his cock.

"Need a second." He took a deep breath then another. "You came that close to having me shoot all over your sappy moment."

"No complaints here." Alanso licked his lips. Then he reached out. "But if you really want to be inside her before that, now's the time."

The sight of Alanso grabbing Eli's cock and guiding it toward her pussy had her arching her back to meet him. The tip of his erection made contact with her opening. They both cursed, though Alanso laughed at their desperation.

Not in a mean way. Instead, with pure delight. As if he couldn't believe anymore than she could that this was finally about to happen.

"Make it real, Eli," he encouraged his boss, his lover, his friend. "I've dreamed of this forever."

Alanso stared into her eyes as he promised her that and a whole host of other things she couldn't understand in his husky, rapid-fire Spanish. The words didn't matter. His intent rang clearly through his smile and his pounding heartbeat and his gentle hold on her as he presented her body to the other part of them.

Clumsy in his urgency, Eli's cock slid off her saturated lips and prodded her clit piercing. That alone was nearly enough to throw her into climax again. Coming to the rescue, Alanso corralled Eli's rogue hard-on and aimed it, straight and true.

Cobra pressed forward until the tip notched in the entrance of her pussy. He leaned in, blanketing her and parts of Alanso, who still held her close. He joined his mouth to hers and Alanso's, partaking in a three-way kiss she wouldn't have believed could be so powerful.

When he advanced, his cock tunneling inside her on one impossibly slow thrust, she forgot to breathe. He felt amazing. Long and thick and so damn hot.

"I know," Alanso whispered in her ear. "He's big. It burns a little, doesn't it?"

She couldn't answer as she considered how he'd gained that knowledge. Her heels drummed on the mattress.

"Relax, Mustang." They both cautioned her together.

Eli stopped moving. He stared directly into her eyes and smiled. "Hi there."

"Hi." The single syllable stretched her abilities at the moment.

"You're heaven around me." He nibbled on her neck, then wandered to Alanso for a kiss of his own.

The instant their mouths collided, she lost control. She couldn't help it. She bucked on Eli's cock. Stroking her clit piercing against the base of his shaft set her off in seconds.

It was surreal. Listening to Eli describe for Alanso how

hard she came around him as she squeezed him tight. Cobra split his attention between her and the man he kissed, inspiring waves of her pleasure. His hips ground against her as he fucked her deep and thoroughly for the duration of her orgasm.

"I can't believe you didn't come with her." Alanso stared at Eli.

Sally continued to shudder when Eli tested the firmness of Alanso's shaft. Apparently satisfied, he asked, "You're ready to go again, huh?"

"Yeah, Cobra."

Both men sounded like they'd eaten a gravel sandwich for dinner.

"Then you'll have to suck me. Get ready to keep me hard." He bit Alanso's neck, making Sally come again, or still. The stimulation of her body, mind and heart were more than she could resist.

The last round of spasms proved too much for Eli. He rammed his hard-on into her a few times before he withdrew. A feral cry tore from his chest as he jerked his cock fast enough to make his hand a blur.

The shout he gave of their names was the only warning provided before he launched a line of come at Alanso, hitting him in the chest. Mesmerized, she watched another aimed in her direction. It splattered on her breast and caught Alanso as collateral damage. On and on, Eli pumped himself dry, alternating which lover received his seed.

It didn't matter anyway because while Eli still massaged himself, Alanso turned into her and ground together. The slickness made their bodies glide. "Don't go anywhere, *mami chula.*"

Alanso left her with a kiss on the forehead and launched himself in Eli's direction.

They tumbled to the bed in a jumble of limbs, some lighter and longer, some darker and thicker. Just like their cocks. Eli sprawled on his back, punching the mattress as Alanso sucked the hell out of his sensitive cock.

Sally scrambled to her knees to watch the two men and the force of their attraction.

This time it was her who initiated a kiss. With Eli. She contributed to Alanso's heroic efforts by seducing their King Cobra's mouth. It appeared to work. Eli's cock stayed steely. For the most part. And when Alanso appeared a little unpleased, he drew off with a sloppy pop that had her peeking at what he intended next.

The butterflies in her stomach kicked up into flight when he fisted both their cocks in one of his hands and began to stroke them in unison.

Eli groaned. "Do that thing—"

Apparently he didn't have to elaborate for Alanso to understand.

Spanish rained over them as he held his cock around the base and began to swordfight with Eli. The bounce of their flesh against each other seemed to please them both as shockwaves travelled down to their balls, which jiggled and bounced before her eyes.

The bald man cursed and moaned as he rubbed the crown of his cock against Eli's. He smeared them together, coated in a combination of come from all three of them. And seeing their erections standing proudly together, Sally knew exactly what she wanted to make this night perfect.

"I need to have you both." She stalked the place where they intersected.

"You have us," Eli barked.

"Forever," Alanso added.

"Inside me." She looked to one then the other.

They paused.

"You're not ready. Anal isn't as easy as some of the girls we've been with made it look. I'm not rushing you on this. Especially not if one of us is in your pussy." Eli surprised her with the organization of his thoughts.

"I didn't say anything about my ass." She crossed her arms, pushing her boobs up. The motion distracted Alanso long enough for her to shove him backward. When he landed with a bounce, his flank pressed near Eli's and their legs wove together.

Balls met balls and shaft met shaft. When she collared the thick double-headed spear they made together, she had a few doubts as to whether this had been a good idea after all. Until she caught sight of Alanso's hopeful gaze, and Eli's.

"You're sure you're ready for this? No need to rush into the complicated stuff, Sally." Eli peered up at her.

"I've waited long enough." She refused to be deterred.

"Go ahead, then," he murmured. "Take us both if you can. Make us yours."

Salome knew that even if all the other Hot Rods were here with them now, sharing the event as the crew sometimes did, these two would have a special place in her life. They were hers. And she belonged to them. Completely.

She straddled them, sitting up tall as she hovered over their joined erections. Someday she'd have them like Devon with Neil and James, but it would feel right to hold them equally within her. Both of them surrounded by her, keeping them together.

Alanso wrapped his hands around her waist easily, helping her to control her motion and stay upright despite the spell they put on her, liquefying her insides and all her bones. Eli stroked her hair, which draped over her shoulders. He followed the strands to her breasts, cupping them in his hands as she lowered herself over them.

Pressure built on her pussy. She wasn't sure they would fit.

A needle of discomfort had her retreating for a second. "Alanso, let me borrow your lube."

"That's enough," Eli tried to stop her. "We can work up to this, Salome."

"Stop talking and let me love you." She ignored him as Al made quick work of slicking their shafts and her waiting flesh. Sally leaned forward to press her palm over Cobra's lips, stifling his objections. And when she did, the angle allowed him to slide in first with the bulge of Alanso's tip following after an inch or two. The gradual widening worked for her. And for them, if their moans were any indication.

And still Eli fought her. Until he could pant, "Do you? Love us?"

"With all my heart, King Cobra." She couldn't stop the silent tears tracking down her cheeks as she enveloped them jointly in her body. Glancing over her shoulder ensured Alanso was on the same page. He blinked rapidly when she held on to one of his hands at her waist. The other one she used to reach out to Eli.

Both men entwined their fingers with hers as she bonded them completely.

Their cocks stretched her so tight as they rubbed together within her that they tugged at the piercings in her labia and clit. Any additional pressure was more than she could bear.

"Don't hold back." Alanso let go of her waist to smack her ass. "Give us everything."

Eli used his free hand to pinch her nipple and tease the hoop there.

The duet they played on her body was accompanied by the love in their eyes and voices. It ensured she couldn't resist his order. Didn't want to either.

She relaxed her thighs consciously, allowing her men to impale her to the max.

The instant her clit piercing hit the pad of muscle above Eli's cock, she exploded.

Both of the guys joined her, flooding what little space remained around their shafts.

Colors and light danced in her vision as the most powerful orgasm of her life stole her consciousness. At least she heard both her partners proclaim their love one more time before a comfortable numbness encroached.

Her mind surrendered along with her body and she toppled forward, pitching onto Eli's chest.

Of course he caught her.

He always would.
They always would.

Alanso woke them both. The bed shook beneath the force of his bouncing shoulders.

Was he crying?

"Hey." Salome pushed onto her elbow, missing the heat of Eli's chest on her cheek. She dropped a light kiss over his heart then reached for their bald lover. "Are you all right?"

"Don't go feeling sorry for that fucker." Eli's sleep-roughened growl coiled desire within her. Damn, how could she still be horny after last night? "He's laughing. At me."

"What? Why?" She blinked to clear her eyes and shoved a lock of hair into place. And that's when she saw it.

Eli sported a shiner. Courtesy of her fist. "Oopsy."

"How bad is it?" He winced as he prodded the puffiness with the tips of his fingers.

"I bet no one notices." She tried to sound believable.

Alanso laughed harder.

"Don't make me spank you," King Cobra hissed. "Both of you could go over my knee at any moment, you know?"

"Really?" Sally hated that she sounded so hopeful.

A string of Spanish curses floated from Alanso. She wondered how long it would be before he drummed up some intentional misbehavior.

"Enough. Or we'll never get to work." Eli whipped the sheet off his lower body and escaped from bed in a hurry. As if that kept them from noticing his state of arousal.

"I could take care of that for you, boss." Sally licked her lips. "Bet it wouldn't take more than a few minutes."

"No deal, 'cause you're right." He grimaced. "But I want better for you. So get that ass up and in the shower. If we clear some of the backlog out, maybe we can take a long lunch."

"Shit." For the first time ever, work had been the farthest thing from her mind. Especially as she considered what she'd done, and what she hadn't told them. Maybe they should have known before… "Sorry, I lost track of my jobs. What's late?"

"Holden and Carver covered for you on the easy shit." Eli shrugged. "But the three custom designs need some attention. Our clients were understanding. Still, I'd like to churn them out this week."

"I'm on it." She hugged him as she passed, her heart trying to float and sink at the same time. "I have the art proofs set and ready to go. I'll stay until I'm finished. But, um, would you mind if I went to talk to Tom first?"

"Of course not." He smiled softly at her.

"Don't kill yourself. You'll need some energy tonight." Alanso winked at her. From the way he stretched as he rose, he felt the same delicious aches she did as she waddled into the bathroom with him trailing a bit behind.

"I can't believe Eli didn't open today. That must be a first. Did you set that up last night?" She raised her voice to carry over the shower spray she stepped into. It felt weird to use their bathroom, their soap and their razor. Smelling like them had advantages though. She liked the idea of being marked as theirs in some way.

"Actually, the bossman's loosening up some," Alanso responded quietly.

She tugged an edge of the shower curtain to peek at him. His tan, sculpted body leaned against the vanity. Thick fingers rubbed his chest, idly toying with the barbell in his nipple as she had the night before. And planned to do again.

"How so?"

"He's let Kaige open shop every day since you left. So we could have some time together in the mornings." Alanso cleared his throat.

Wow. Things were changing. Eli had never let someone else drive around here. He'd always worked the full schedule, even when the rest of them took shifts. When he was under the weather he'd still drag his ass out of bed to ensure the garage and the fueling station were opened and closed right.

It wasn't that he didn't trust them. She didn't think so anyway. More like the garage was his life. Could he really be ready to take other things as seriously? To make room for them at the top of his priorities?

If he could do the right thing, she could too. She had to. For all of them.

While Alanso was separated from her, even by the thin plastic barrier, she took the opportunity to say what she hadn't been able to last night. "I'm happy for you two. No matter what else happens. I'm so glad that you guys worked things out between you."

"Thanks." He cleared his throat. "I wasn't sure we'd ever get here. But you're part of my equation, Sally. You know that, right?"

"I'm hoping."

"I mean, who the hell else is going to dance with me?" He always knew when to build her up. "Certainly not double-lefty out there. And we both know talking isn't his strong suit. I always come to you for a chat. Plus I need you to draw me something. I want a tattoo for us. The three of us."

"You got it, as long as I can have the same one." The idea of matching him appealed immensely.

"I'd like that, Salome." He sighed. "A lot."

She rinsed her hair as he reminded her of all their commonalities. Those simple pleasures were powerful too. Maybe not caged lightning like the bond she sensed between the guys, but strong in their own quiet, steady way. Smiling, she stepped out of the spray onto the bathmat. "Go ahead. Your turn, *papi*."

He gripped the counter as if holding himself in place. The Hot Rods tattoo across his fingers distorted slightly beneath the pressure. "*Carajo.* You're fucking hot when you talk like that. Hell, when you look at me like that."

A shiver shook her as water droplets spilled from her breasts and trickled down her skin. "Actually, I'm kind of chilly. Would you hand me a towel? I'll go grab you a replacement out of the hall closet while you're in the shower."

"You could forget about drying off and join me." Alanso's stare scorched her as it swept up and down her body.

"I'd love to. But we wouldn't be quick."

"Speak for yourself." He took himself in hand and pumped a few times. "Either way I'm gonna have to take care of this or I won't be able to walk, never mind crawl around under the low rider I'm working on this morning."

"I don't want to let Eli down." She kissed him on the cheek, thinking of what needed to be done. "I'll take a rain check. Or two."

"More like a dozen." Alanso slapped her ass as she trotted past, snagging the soft, worn terrycloth from a hanger on the wall.

She dried her body quickly, only looking up when her senses began to hum.

"If that isn't a sight to behold." Eli shocked her. He'd returned to bed. Reclining, he turned to the side so he could watch the show she'd unintentionally put on. "Are you okay, Sally? You've got marks all over. I didn't realize we were so rough with you. Being with Alanso lately…maybe I forgot about having to be gentle."

"I could go for one of Kayla's massages. Or even one of James's. He's almost as good as her." She laughed when Cobra's sour face made it clear what he thought of the other guy's hands on her. "But otherwise I'm fine. Amazing, really."

"Yes, you are." He accepted her kiss when she leaned over him, bracing herself with a palm on his belly, just above the Hot Rods tattoo that arched across his rock-hard abdomen. He looked as if he might say more right before a clatter echoed from the bathroom.

"Yo, Al? You okay?" he yelled.

They both coiled for action.

"Ah, yeah." Spanish curses were chased by laughter. "I dropped the soap. Want to come help me find it?"

Cobra's eyes slitted. His cock twitched against his stomach.

She drew a finger along his impressive length from base to tip. "Go ahead, Eli. Play with him. I'd love to watch, but it's going to take me a couple minutes to dry my hair. You two have the advantage there."

"Work can wait." He rose, stretching his glorious body and the lean muscles decorating it nearly as prettily as his inked artwork. "You'd better go see my dad if you have something to discuss. I can see it in your eyes, Mustang. No more ghosts. Let's do this right."

"Who is this guy?" She grinned up at him. It was either that or bawl at how well he knew her. Did he suspect? "And where have you put my boss?"

"It's a fresh model year, Mustang." He beat his chest. "New and improved."

"I appreciate the offer. I promise I won't be long. Then I really should get back to my projects. I need some time in my studio." When she ducked her head, he lifted her chin with two fingers.

"Are you sure you're all right with everything that's happened?" He shifted closer, wrapping her in his free arm and resting his forehead on hers. "It's heavy shit to carry, I know."

"Yeah." She drew away to kiss the tip of his nose. "It's a ton. Of good stuff. But kind of like a hangover after a great party, I'm zoned out. And kind of sore. Need to recover a little, okay?"

"Of course." He rubbed his hand up and down her arm. "Whatever you need. We'll try to give it to you."

"I'm glad you feel that way. Because—"

This time the repetitive clatter made it obvious Alanso was playing soccer with the soap in a desperate bid for attention. They laughed so hard, she lost her train of thought and the moment to ask for more—for everything—passed.

"Go." Sally waved him toward the bathroom. "I'll meet you guys down there."

Rather than waste time walking around the bed, Eli bounded over it, bouncing in the middle of the mattress and making it to the bathroom in two strides. Alanso's growled, "Fuck yeah," nearly changed her mind about getting ready for work.

But part of her didn't care to intrude. This was new for all of them, and the guys should have some time to themselves. Another insidious voice insisted she didn't deserve them for essentially lying. That mistake had to be fixed. Pronto. She swiped the towel over her body hastily then wrapped it around her hair turban-style.

A groan followed her, filling her imagination with plenty of fodder for the rest of the day. Engrossed in her daydreams, she didn't hear Kaige and Holden trekking down the hall from their rooms until she rounded the corner and nearly plowed into them.

Her first instinct was to cover herself with her hands. Then she realized how ridiculous that was. She hoped someday to display herself proudly for them. Not just in her nudity but in ecstasy as well.

Alanso and Eli were the stuff of fantasies. But their web of affection extended beyond the three of them. Maybe not in the forever-and-always-soul-mates way, but like Devon, James and Neil with their crew, they were bonded by their common experiences.

In their case, the sharing would only help them build security in a world that hadn't always treated them kindly. They'd been dealt bad hands, yes. This was the trump card they'd been waiting to play to show life they refused to quit. They could come from nothing and end up having it all.

Salome was sure of it.

If only she could convince the rest of them.

"Whoa." Holden stared at her for a solid five seconds before slapping a hand over his eyes. Carver politely faced the wall. While their reactions might have eased her mind a month ago, now they deflated some of her elation. "I see someone had a nice night."

"What the hell did they do to you?" Carver stared at the ceiling. "That's a lot of love bites for two men and less than twelve hours. Did you sleep at all?"

"Jesus." Holden discretely adjusted his package.

Okay. So maybe they weren't completely immune. But as much as she wanted to test the waters, there was work to do and her responsibilities to Eli came first. "Sorry, guys. I didn't think anyone else was still home. Things are good. No, great. I'll be downstairs in a couple minutes, promise."

"Don't worry, I think our boss likes you," Carver snarked. He and Holden cracked up as they continued down the hall, shaking their heads.

"Sally..." Holden called out to her though they didn't turn around.

"Yeah?" Part of her longed to draw them back.

"We're glad you're home," Carver finished for his friend.

"And happy," Holden added.

"Thanks guys, that means a lot to me." She struggled to speak.

"See you in a few." Carver closed the door on their emotions before they got out of control. He was good at coping like that.

The guys raised their hands and kept walking.

They could discuss the rest of the guys' involvement tonight, right?

They could have.

But they didn't.

Chapter Seven

Sally couldn't believe it. She'd gotten what she wanted. And it looked like it might be a recurring pleasure. *Holy shit.*

So why couldn't she enjoy the ride, pretending—like they had—that everything was cool?

Something ate at her, spoiling her euphoria. Why hadn't she taken the road block more seriously before? It didn't seem like it mattered when she was solo, but now...she felt like she was lying to herself and the guys. Had she waited too long to mention it? Would they feel violated? Like she'd intentionally misled them?

Alanso and Holden, at least, were somewhat religious. Maybe some of the other guys less openly. Not in the strict sense or the shove-it-down-your-throat way, but she knew they believed in some form of higher being who organized the chaos around them. Alanso had said many times he thought it was divine intervention that had brought them together when they'd needed each other most. The permanent cross on his back was a quiet statement of his faith.

She loved that he'd never tried to dictate his beliefs. She'd had enough of that bullshit growing up.

What if she'd caused them to transgress? It wasn't their fault, they hadn't known, but it might be hers. She couldn't stand the thought of them hating her. She'd have to tell them. Soon. But maybe she could fix it first. Without entangling them in her mess.

Only one person would understand. Well, maybe the crew ladies would too. She'd considered enlisting their help during her stay, but...this was too personal. Too much.

She needed Tom.

After throwing on her coveralls, she sprinted across the lawn to Eli's father's house. Her dash made it seem as if she were a spy or some action hero in the movies her Hot Rods loved so much. She didn't want any of the other guys dropping in on her little talk with the only man she'd ever really considered a true father.

So when she raced up to the door, she knocked a little harder than she intended.

In no time, he opened his home to her with a smile, just like he always had. "Sally. Come on in."

"Tom." She hugged him hard. What if what she told him changed his mind about her? It seemed kind of farfetched, considering the way he'd stood by their sides despite their unconventional relationship and the evolving bonds they were developing.

But the brainwashing she'd endured as a child still sometimes reared its head.

No one will believe you.

This is the way God wants it to be.

You've been chosen for greatness.

Turning down His gift would be unforgiveable.

No wonder she'd left religion to others.

"Hey there, kid. I'm so glad to have you back." Tom chuckled as he patted her. Until he caught on to her clinging, which lasted a little too long for simple greeting. "Ah, shit. What's wrong? Are those boys of mine treating you bad? Do I have to go kick some asses? Those young fools don't know what they're doing with a lady like you."

"You're not that old, Tom." She smiled against his chest. "But no, it's not the whippersnappers this time. I'm kind of afraid I fucked up. And I don't know how to tell them. Or if I should."

"Well, I find that honesty is generally the best policy." Tom led her to the bench seat of his rustic table. He'd made the set himself and the gorgeous grain always tempted her to run her fingers along its curves and lines. "Why don't you fill me in on what's got your panties in a bunch so I can make a true call, though?"

"Could I maybe get a cup of tea?" She worried her lip.

"Damn, this must be bad, honey." He squeezed her shoulder as he put the kettle on, then rummaged a chipped cup and saucer from the cabinet. Eli's mom had been the last tea drinker around these parts before Sally had picked up the habit. Nothing soothed her like the warm, sweet brew.

She rested her head on her crossed arms to try and think of the best way to explain.

A few minutes later, Tom neared. He paused with the teabag half-immersed as he stared at her pale face. "Sally?"

She glanced up at him, blinking back memories.

"I just thought of something. Are you pregnant, honey?" He set the cup down then sank onto the bench beside her, covering her hand with his. "It's okay if you are. I'm sure the guys will be thrilled. It doesn't matter who—"

"Jeez. No. Tom, stop." She waved him off, a little horrified. She hadn't even gotten that far ahead in her whirlwind thoughts yet. "I'm not knocked up. Nothing happened until last night…"

"Whew!" He scrubbed his free hand over his weathered face. "I mean, it wouldn't have been a disaster if you were, but I hoped you kids would have more time to yourselves first. To really iron out this thing between you. Okay, okay. I'm good. What *is* it?"

There was no good way to say it.

"Eli and Alanso love me. They mean for this to be a forever thing."

"That's bad news?" Tom's face lit up. "To have you as my daughter officially? And Alanso my son?"

He looked like he might bounce to his feet and dance.

"Tom, wait." She swallowed hard. "I'm not sure I can do that."

"What?" He jerked backward a bit. Exactly as she feared his son might if he unearthed the relic of her past. "Why not? Sure, you couldn't technically marry them both. It wouldn't matter. You know what's in your heart. Plenty of groups believe in..."

He trailed off as he realized what he was about to say.

"Yeah." She tried to swallow the knot in her throat. "Just like Utah. Lots of wives. One husband."

"It scares you because it reminds you of that place they kept you as a child. That prison—"

"It's nothing like that, Tom." She shook her head. "Cobra and Al never forced me. Hell, I've had to practically twist their arms."

Maybe that was TMI, but too fucking bad. She needed help.

"Then I'm confused." He rubbed his temples. "I must be slow today."

"I can't commit to them because *I'm married.*"

"The fuck you are!" Tom stood in a rush. He glowered, his face turning red.

"Oh shit. See. I knew it was bad." Tears started to gather in her eyes, blurring the disgust in his usually affable features. "I'll go. I'll tell them we can't keep going along this road..."

"Sit your ass down, Salome." His tone was cold. The fact that he'd used her real name meant he wasn't fooling around either.

She plopped into her seat again, preparing herself for his fury.

"There is no way you're married. You were a baby when you came to us, no matter how grown up you acted." He swiped the liquid trail from her cheeks with the hem of his shirt.

"I was fifteen and six days old when I made it this far east and that truck driver I hitched with dropped me off at the shelter." She drew in a ragged breath, trying to struggle through the story she'd never fully told anyone.

"Fuck no, Sally." He rubbed her back. "Is that why you ran?"

She nodded. "I didn't want him. The man they chose for me. They told me I was special, I was his first wife. Hell, Tom, he was hardly much older than I was. He was nervous. I think he might have gone into the bathroom to be sick when we were finally left alone for our wedding night."

Tom had gone pale.

"The instant he disappeared from the bedroom, I went out the window." She sobbed. "But they put guards around the house. His older brothers were waiting. Making sure."

"Fuck!" The man banged his hand on the table, causing her to jump. "The fact that they needed reinforcements means they knew what they were doing was wrong. Coercing kids into their culture. This is bullshit, Sally. We'll have it annulled."

"Tom, I tried that. The records are all sealed and I'd have to go in person. I don't think I can. What if they find me? What if they come for me?" She trembled uncontrollably despite her best efforts to remain calm. "They don't allow people to walk away from that life."

"No one is going to steal you from us. You think I'd let them? You think Eli or Alanso would? The rest of the Hot Rods?" He'd never looked so mad in all the years she'd known him. "They'll be lucky to live if they fuck with a single hair on your head or…"

She couldn't ask him to continue.

"Sally." He used the name she'd adopted when she shed her old life. "Did they rape you? Like they did mentally to the boy they brainwashed into attacking you? Both are horrible things to do to a child. Unforgivable."

"No!" She hurried to reassure him. "The brother standing below the window—he was always someone I'd been friendly with before they separated boys and girls. When he got old enough. All the children stayed together until they turned fifteen. Then they disappeared. Got married. Had families of their own. Repeating the cycle over and over."

Tom cursed again.

"I told him I didn't want this. I begged him not to force me. We'd heard horror stories of girls who resisted. How the new husband's brothers would hold them down and humiliate them until they gave in. If they didn't, it got physical. They'd beat her.

Rape her. How a husband would treat a disobedient wife versus a compliant one. I knew which path I was headed for." She shuddered. "It didn't matter. I couldn't do it. I just...couldn't lay there and take it without a fight."

"And that's why we love you, Sally." Tom didn't touch her, but she could tell he wanted to. "Your spirit. Your strength. Your unwillingness to compromise on your morals. They're all amazing characteristics. You should never feel bad for that."

"I know that now." She honestly did. Any crisis she'd had about who she was had been resolved long ago. By the Hot Rods. Though they hadn't understood what their acceptance did to transform her. "I got lucky. So damn fortunate. He let me go. He couldn't help or they would have gone after him and his wives too. No one in his family would have been safe. Not even his children."

"Son of a bitch." Tom closed his eyes for a second.

"The rest of the story I told you guys is true. I didn't lie about that," she assured him.

"So you got picked up by a trucker. An honest guy. Someone who saw a gorgeous, broken woman-child running and decided to do the right thing." He paused. "If that doesn't make you believe in God, I'm not sure what would."

She'd never really thought of it like that before. But it was a nice perspective.

"I don't want to tell them, Tom." She sighed. "I don't know if I can. I don't want my past to influence the future. Haven't I already lost enough to risk them too? Especially over something they might not understand? They're always doing what they think is right for me even if it's totally wrong. I can't tell them. They'll abandon me, just when I've got them, to put us all in danger. But I don't want to lie to them or make them do something they wouldn't otherwise. What if they don't want me anymore?"

"Hey, hey." He shushed her when she began to hyperventilate. "You'll tell them someday. When you're all ready. I know it in my heart."

They both looked at their joined hands. "But if you're not

there yet, that's your call. I'll help you of course. We'll get the documents. Do research. Hire a lawyer to get this mess straightened out. It might take time and money, but we'll do what we have to so you can make my boys the happiest guys in Middletown."

"I don't believe in God anymore, Tom." She fidgeted beneath his stare. "But the Hot Rods have different opinions. What if I make them do something unforgiveable by their own standards? Even if they don't know it? Will they hate me when they find out?"

"Honey, if there is a God out there, whatever kind it may be…do you really think it would condone what those bastards did to you? Or tried to do?" He tipped his head as he let her think it over. "Is that the kind of being you'd give a shit about pissing off?"

She laughed. Only he could make it so simple. "I guess not."

"Damn straight." He nodded. "And my sons will say the same. We'll be lucky to keep them from hunting those bastards down."

"Another reason to keep it quiet for now." She sighed, exhausted and a little bit relieved. With Tom's help, they might be able to clean up her dirty past before it could destroy her future.

"How about I go look stuff up online? Probably only have a little while more before they start missing you and come looking. Tonight, swing by after dinner. When they're playing those damn video games or something." He hugged her. "It's going to be okay, Sally. We've got you."

"I hope they'll keep me." She laid her head on his shoulder for a few seconds before rising and heading toward the front door as he took a seat at the desk in the corner of his living room.

"You know that's what Eli said the day you came looking for a place to stay?" Tom laughed. "Like you were a kitten who'd lost its way. 'Can we keep her, Dad?'"

"I've never been so glad I said yes to him in my life. Even

though I had no idea where we'd put everybody back then." He shrugged. "Thank goodness for the garage."

"No, Tom. Thank goodness for you." She stared him straight in the eye. "You saved my life. So did the Hot Rods. Even if you didn't know it. You restored my faith in people. I love you."

"I love you too, kid." He blew her a kiss then got to work on saving her.

Again.

Chapter Eight

"Hey, Dev." Sally waved to her new friend over the screen of her computer. Video conferences might not be as perfect as the lunches they could have shared if they lived in the same city, but at least she had someone to bounce ideas off of these days. The crew women had been first in line to hear all about her developments with Eli and Alanso.

They offered lots of advice and tips for seducing two men that she'd put to good use.

On that front, things were progressing. Terrific. Sexy nights left her too exhausted to talk much about her lingering interests in the rest of the Hot Rods, and she couldn't find the willpower to forsake the pleasure they offered—especially to substitute a potential argument about her secret or her desires for their friends—when it was so new and shiny.

Being the center of their attention was heavenly. Falling asleep in their arms made dreams come true. Watching the two of them love each other had brought her to tears the first time. And several after. Finding that their friendship, easy laughter and work relationships were only enhanced—not hindered—by their bedroom gymnastics blew all her doubts out the window.

She adored every aspect of their relationship...except one.

Business as usual during the days and untamed nights continued for weeks, until Salome knew she had to do something to drive them all forward. No way would she make the same mistake twice.

This time she was running toward her Hot Rods instead of away from them.

Soon she'd have to act instead of waiting another decade for the guys to make a move.

And that was where Devon came in. She had to help formulate a plan. One Sally could stick to once the sun went down and her guys' clothes came off. Willpower, she would find some.

All she needed was some reassurance about the five other men roaming the garage each day. They acted as if everything was status quo, although her entire life had blossomed into something even more fabulous than it had been before she hit the romance lottery.

Even her fears about her ridiculous marriage seemed to be lessening as she and Tom made slow but steady progress, contacting a few more authorities and requesting records each evening. Juggling a new relationship while avoiding the potholes of her past and managing her longing for *everything* wasn't easy.

"It's bizarre. Either I'm going nuts or…there's something happening I don't know about." Sally sighed and flopped onto her stomach. She tried hard not to pout. Probably not entirely successfully. It was weird to be in her room again. She only used it for storage—and private calls—these days. "Like this morning, we were all eating breakfast. Just hanging out like usual. And, I swear to God, Roman and Kaige were looking at me like they wanted to throw me on the dining table and go to town. Circling like sharks. Or barracudas, I guess. But no one made a move. Not even when I sat on the edge of the butcher block and let my skirt ride up. It had to have been obvious to Carver and Holden, who were sitting there eating their damn cereal, that I wasn't wearing panties either."

"Uh, yeah, pretty sure the crew wouldn't have resisted if one of us teased them like that." Devon scratched her chin. "Do you think Eli's declared a no-fuck zone?"

"I'm starting to think so." Sally sighed. "But why? For his sake? Alanso's? Or some misguided bullshit about what he thinks I need?"

"*Ding ding ding.*" The other woman clapped. "I think we have a winner."

"Aren't we done with this phase yet? When is he going to

realize I'm a big girl?" Anger infiltrated her confusion. Maybe she'd been right to hide her marriage fiasco after all. "I don't need him to protect me. Half the time it only ends up hurting worse than whatever he thinks he's saving me from."

"Maybe that's a discussion you need to have." Devon winced.

"Or maybe I'm delusional and I should be satisfied with the two studs who love me and are banging me into oblivion every night—and sometimes at work—instead of reaching for all seven I'm in lust with?" She smacked her forehead with the heel of her palm. "Am I crazy?"

"Maybe just a little. Five is enough for this girl." Devon giggled as she aimed her thumb at her chest. "No, but seriously, I think this is about way more than sex. It's the network of ultimate trust and devotion that comes from sharing that you're missing. Still, guys will respond better to the physical aspect than the emotional one at first. So, it's time to turn up the heat. They can only resist so much if they're hoping to get it on half as much as you are. If it's too hard for the guys to talk it out...get devious."

"Hmm..." She liked the direction they headed. "Any ideas?"

"Weren't you going to plan an annual fundraiser for the youth shelter?" Devon must have had this thought on tap. It came too fast to be a random light bulb. "We were talking about it last night. The crew said something that perked my ears up. They were debating going into town for a car wash. Then they tried to sweet talk me and the rest of the ladies into wearing skimpy clothes and..."

"Oh my God." Sally knew exactly where she was going. "You're a genius! That's legit. Rides will be lined up halfway to town with ladies hoping to spy the Hot Rods on display. And I can convince them they need to have their cars cleaned to contribute to the cause. I'll do a *really* good job."

"Let me know how it goes." The pixie winked. "I'm guessing your problems will be history in no time. Plus you're using your best assets to help out the kids. Win-win!"

They laughed together for a while then talked of the crew

babies' latest feats, shopping and some helpful hints on surviving a massive ménage before Devon began to yawn.

"Let's go find our guys. It's time for bed." Sally smiled, knowing she wouldn't sleep until she joined her pair in Alanso's room. It'd become their middle ground. Hell, she'd likely not doze off until long after that, but at least she'd be relaxed. "Say hello to your couple and the rest of the crew."

"Do the same from me."

"I will. And thanks, Devon."

"Anytime. Go get 'em, Mustang."

When the next weekend rolled around, everything was in place.

Sally had solidified her nerves, planned the event and bought the skimpiest string bikini she could find, surprised that it also flattered her figure. Who would have guessed the tiny triangles of neon fabric could make her boobs look pretty decent and her waist seem thinner?

Probably she should have done some nude sunbathing. Without the protection of the crew and their woods, she didn't think it'd fly. Too late now, in any case.

As predicted, a line of cars snaked down their country road, *more* than halfway to Middletown by most accounts. And that was before nine o'clock in the morning. She was nobody's fool. Plenty of women in town would pay top dollar for the right to stare at the Hot Rods, shirtless and soapy, just inches away as they worked over the exterior of their minivan mom-mobiles.

She didn't blame the ladies. Even if they did spend the entire seven minutes of their wash and wax lost in an overdose of sexy muscles and tattoos. Sally understood completely.

And if putting the guys on display—and herself along with them—profited the youth center, she was willing to sacrifice. Not to mention how she'd be able to steal some eye candy to nourish herself all day long.

She really should have considered the side effects of all that yummiliciousness.

Because by lunchtime, she was ready to slam Alanso onto the hood of the late model Honda she serviced and let him ride her like her namesake. Probably the ruckus they caused would draw Eli and he'd join them where all the other guys could see.

And from that moment on, she knew what she'd do once they cleared out the last of the customers for the charity event.

Fortunately, Tom gave up and went inside sometime before dinner. It was exhausting manual labor, but the thought of her reward kept Sally going strong.

Finally, the last person rolled away.

Kaige tugged the hose into the circle cast by the spotlight that illuminated the parking lot in the twilight. "How'd we do, Mustang?"

She pretended to flip through the cash she'd already counted and fudged the figure just a teensy-weensy bit. "Damn! We're ten dollars short of three grand. That's only one more car wash. Come on, somebody pony up."

"I'll pitch in a hundred and ten so long as I don't have to pick up that sponge again." Kaige glanced sideways at her.

"What, you have dishpan hands?" She wrinkled her nose. "Fine. I'll do the washing. Pull your green monstrosity around front."

He eyed her up and down, his eyes narrowing when he caught sight of her palms pressed together in front of her as if praying…or begging.

"Fine. But I'm not getting in my baby like this." Before she realized what he meant, he'd started stripping. And she didn't look away. His boots and saturated cargo shorts were followed by a sexy pair of sky-blue briefs.

Somebody issued a catcall and a whistle or two as he sauntered around the corner to the pile of towels they'd stocked and snagged his keys from the pegboard by the door. He did have a fine ass and the contrast of his golden dreads and his black and white tattoos had her drooling just a little.

Please let this work.

She tried not to wring her hands while she waited for the roar of his engine. The rest of the guys had collapsed on the pavement. Leaning up against the garage, they nursed the bottles of beer she'd passed out like candy on Halloween.

"You're crazy, Mustang." Bryce shook his head. "Let's wrap this and order some Chinese. We could be watching a movie and resting up."

"Or we could be helping a good cause." She guilted them into staying, although she did believe escalating their bond was one hell of a thing to fight for.

Super Nova's headlights turned the corner, temporarily blinding her.

Alanso whistled when her figure was limned by the glow. Maybe this would work after all. She crossed her fingers as Kaige rolled to a stop beside her. Naked inside the cab of his Chevy, Kaige flashed her a wink. His devilish smile might mean he'd scorch her as surely as the flames she'd painted down the sides of his neon green ride.

Time to put up or shut up.

She toted her bucket to the hose and bent at the waist, intentionally displaying her ass in the tiny string bikini bottom for the Hot Rods. Eli might have growled, hard to say from her outpost. But there was no missing Alanso's Spanish curses or even Holden's guttural utterance, "Have mercy!"

Sally grinned. She peeked up at Super Nova and Kaige smiled back. He nodded subtly and prepared for her special treatment. Both of him and his car.

She made sure to overdo the soap.

Foam cast bubbles into the air. An *accidental* mishap had her dropping the sponge and splashing suds all over herself. She giggled as they dripped down her body. They really did tickle her breasts and her stomach.

"Son of a bitch," someone muttered.

She made sure to duck her head. The black strands of her hair that had come free of her ponytail cascaded over her cheeks, hiding her smirk. She sauntered to Kaige's studmobile and laid herself out over the hood, reaching as far as she could, to start her scrubbing.

Her ass wiggled as she made sure to swing her arm far and wide.

When she bent to the bucket to rinse her sponge, several comments were exchanged low enough that she couldn't catch them. Rising tension made the night even more balmy.

Sally moved on to Kaige's windshield, pressing her wet breasts to the glass.

The cool surface soothed her even as it hardened her nipples.

Super Nova must have had his fill. He rolled down his window and called to Eli. "King Cobra, you should check out the view from in here. You're a lucky bastard."

Salome didn't turn around. She didn't need to. Sensing Alanso and Eli had become second nature and the raised hairs on her arms ensured they were stalking her.

"What game is this, Mustang?" Eli fisted his hand in her hair, keeping her bent over Kaige's car.

Alanso's fingers glided up the back of her thigh and over her slick, soapy ass. The crack his wet palm made on her clenched cheek had her yelping. "Are you trying to tease us to death? As if today wasn't enough, *mami chula?*"

"And what about the rest of the Hot Rods?" Eli shrugged. "You're not planning on leaving them exhausted *and* horny are you, cruel girl?"

She followed the direction of his hand as he pointed at the rest of the guys.

Bryce, Holden, Carver and Roman looked as if their tongues might slip out of their mouths at any second.

"I don't want to." She shook her head. "It's nice to see they're not completely grossed out by me, though."

"What?" Kaige tore from his car, slamming the door. "Does this look like I'm repulsed? You damn near killed us today."

She followed his gaze down his chiseled chest to the thick length of his erect cock. "Oh."

"Damn straight." He stomped off, making her heart fall again.

"I may not have a fancy college degree, but I'm no dummy." She propped her hands on her hips, loving the way Alanso's gaze fell to her accentuated breasts. "I've been putting myself on display for all of you. And no one's made a move. That's usually not a sign guys want you."

"*Mierda.*" Alanso scrubbed his hands over his head. "Cobra, I told you. We're not doing this right."

Eli stood really still.

Sally's heart galloped a million miles an hour. What if he didn't appreciate her promiscuous side? What if he thought their equilateral triangle was perfect the way it was? What if he didn't approve of her wanton behavior lately, and definitely not today?

"You want to be shown off, Mustang?" He stalked so close they were pressed together from head to toe. His ripped abdomen warmed her breasts and the hardness she hadn't seen in the shadows nudged her belly.

"Yes." She didn't plan to deny it now.

"And you want to see what you do to guys? These guys?" Alanso chimed in.

"Hell yeah." She shivered.

"Fine." Eli wrapped his hands around her waist and lifted her from the ground. "But not out here. Enough of Middletown has gawked at what's ours today."

He marched into the garage and the guys filed behind him through the single open bay. The last one through hit the red button to close the door.

"Don't be mad, Eli." She clung to his frame. "I just want to show them how it is."

"I think they already know." He paused, dipping down to kiss her. Firm yet cautious.

"I'd like to see," Roman interjected.

"Same here." The rest of the guys agreed, with Kaige as their spokesman. "God knows we hear enough of your fucking. I think we deserve a visual to go with the racket."

"I'm curious." Carver didn't let them turn the serious exchange into a joke or something crude. He had the courage to be honest, and Sally loved him even more for it. "I wonder what it could be like with…more than one person."

Hope radiated through Sally. Maybe all of them would edge from inquisitive onlookers to something more in time. For now, she thought they should have the same informative experience Eli and Alanso had gained when they'd visited the crew and walked in on their sharing. Or the firsthand knowledge she'd gleaned when Devon, James and Neil had offered her their little demonstration.

Because the truth was…she sought them all. Not in the soul-searing way she needed to bond with Alanso and Eli, inseparably, but in the spirit of the honest sharing she'd witnessed from the crew. It was so hard to define. Impossible to put into words.

But once her guys had witnessed it—and her too, later—there'd been no going back.

It worked for the crew and it would work for them.

She knew it to the depths of her soul.

They were meant for this. If only she could show them what they were missing. Artificial boundaries kept them apart. No more.

"Please," she whispered against Eli's lips. "My King Cobra. Show them."

Chapter Nine

He stared into her eyes for endless seconds, then crushed his mouth over hers. She wrapped her legs around his waist as he walked her to the hood of his car. It surprised her when he laid her out over the rich blue paint. Did he prize her more than the Shelby, to risk scratching her finish?

"Alanso," he barked.

"Yeah." The other man was never more than a step behind their Cobra.

"Get that ridiculous bathing suit off her." He ravished her neck as he issued commands. "That thing should be illegal. You flashed your ass and tits at everyone today. Hell, I think John McCormick came through the line four times. Do you want us to have to beat guys off with a stick?"

"No." She gasped when Alanso ripped the skimpy bottoms down her legs, past her sneakers, then attacked the barely-there bra. "The show was for you. All the Hot Rods."

"Brava," Bryce muttered.

"I swear my cock is aching from how hard it's been all day." Holden unbuttoned his shorts, seeking relief. Several of the others followed suit.

"See what you do to them, Sally?" Eli nipped her collarbone.

"Not quite." She struggled to keep alert. To fight for what she really wanted. Getting close and burning out now would be like Icarus, crashing when he flew in a drive-by too close to the sun. "They still have their pants on, mostly."

"I could fix that in a second." Roman slid his hands in his waistband and tilted his head while staring at Eli.

King Cobra looked to Alanso, then to Sally. He swallowed

hard and returned his gaze to Alanso. "You ready for this?"

"Hell yeah, Eli." The bald man groaned. "You're killing me with this we-have-to-wait bullshit. I can't go any slower."

Suspicions confirmed.

Sally wanted to be pissed that Eli had dictated the snail's pace of their evolution. But she couldn't find the energy for anger when all of her fizzed and bubbled in anticipation.

"Rebel, go grab the lube out of my desk drawer." Eli looked over his shoulder at Bryce. "The rest of you strip. If you're going to have a ticket to this peep show, it's only fair we see you too."

A purr ripped from Sally's throat as the Hot Rods revealed themselves one by one. Loud tattoos, sexy piercings to rival her own and enough six packs to have her drunk on their forms. It was like visual Christmas. For an artist, that was nearly enough to have her coming on the spot.

She took a mental picture and filed it away for show and tell later.

Bryce jogged back, shucked his shorts, sneakers and socks. He joined the rest of the guys resting against stacks of tires. With one hand he snicked open the cap of his prize, poured a drop of gel in his palm and began to stroke his cock before handing the bottle to his neighbor, Kaige.

They all followed suit before Roman tossed the tube to Alanso. "Enjoy, kids."

"You know we will, *cabrón*." The bald man didn't bother to apply any to his shaft. That wasn't Eli's intent. They all knew it.

Sally shivered.

"Cold, Mustang?" Eli's wicked smile curved up on one side. He was so devilishly handsome she could hardly stand it. His short blond hair and luminous blue eyes offset the darkness encroaching outside.

With these men, her future was bright.

She reached for each of her guys with one arm, tugging them close. Alanso greeted her with long, languid kisses until Eli cut in. His lips were a little rougher, a little bolder, a little more direct. She savored both flavors of lovemaking they seasoned her life with.

"Damn." Roman appreciated their connection, at least.

"You haven't seen anything yet." Eli shot over his shoulder. "Wait until they fuck. They're gorgeous. Both of them. Together."

He sat on the bumper and gave them free rein to play as he temporarily donned a spectator hat, like his friends. They performed for their King.

Sally opened her arms and Alanso went into them. He felt so solid in her grasp. She adored his honest passion and the loyalty he'd always shown to her and his garage rat brothers.

"I could watch them for hours," Eli murmured, idly stroking himself. "Sometimes I do."

The chorus of wet skin on skin from the sideline made Sally all too aware that six men now pleasured themselves while observing her get it on. One a little more closely than the others.

"Hi." She ran her hands over Alanso's bald head.

"Hi, Mustang." He kissed her nose. "Welcome back."

A giggle escaped. "Sorry, they're hard to ignore. Does it bother you?"

"Nah." He smiled. "I love to get you off, however I can. If that means you come apart while staring at the Hot Rods, no worries, I get it. Plus, I'll be the one inside you."

A shiver ran down her spine as she recalled his gentle invasions of these past several weeks. She loved loving him. "Could you maybe step on the gas with that whole screwing thing?"

He ran his hands down her body, outlining the contours of her breasts and hips. "I'm afraid you've pushed me beyond my limits, *mi vida*. I'll make this up to you later."

"Deal." She squirmed, trying to get closer to his cock. Stocky, he filled her so well. She couldn't wait to feel him again. And again and again and again.

And then she didn't have to wonder what it would be like to be fucked while a whole host of other guys watched on. Because he slipped inside her and dropped low, fusing their torsos. His heat battled the cold of the metal on her back.

A perfect balance, just like her guys.

Alanso put one hand behind each of her knees and folded her legs up while he glided in and out of her pussy, working himself deeper, incidentally stroking the captive ball ring through her hood. It teased her clit, making her whimper as he rocked over her.

"They're amazing, right?" Eli leaned closer, inspecting their connection.

"Hell yeah," Carver grunted. "Perfect."

"Not yet." Sally sighed. "Almost."

She reached up and drew Cobra to them. She guided his mouth, not to hers but to Alanso's. Watching them make out got her every time. This was no exception. Their lips locked. Teeth and tongues warred. As they really got into it, Alanso began to plow into her pussy.

The groan that escaped her drew their attention.

"Sorry." Alanso blushed.

"I liked it." She patted his cheek, then angled her face toward Eli. He smiled as he neared.

"Having fun yet?" He bussed her lips, then allowed her to respond.

"So good," she moaned. The presence of the rest of the Hot Rods amplified the natural arousal her guys inspired. She loved knowing the gang had their backs and that they weren't alone. They shared this, like everything else important in their lives.

It felt natural. It felt right.

Eli tapped Alanso on the shoulder, pressing until the shorter man stood up straight. Sally whimpered at the loss of his radiant heat and the contact of their lightly perspiring skin.

"You don't want me to help him out?" Eli dragged his open mouth down from hers, over her chin, along her neck to her breasts. He matched the flicks of his tongue to the pace of Alanso's steady lunges. All of her pulsed in time to their dual assaults.

"Fine, fine." She panted. "Go ahead."

Holden cracked up, though his laughter was strained. "You show her, Cobra."

Eli only made it more intense when he traveled lower. Eventually his mouth hovered at the intersection of her body with Alanso's. His breath washed over her clit and the top of her pussy.

"*Mierda!*" their Cuban lover cursed. "I can feel that on my balls, Cobra. Don't fucking tempt me."

"Having a hard time controlling yourself?" Eli reached around and smacked Alanso's ass.

"That isn't helping," he growled.

A grunt from Carver's direction made Sally wonder if he'd feel the same way. She'd seen Eli spank Alanso plenty. It always impressed her how hard Al was afterward. How excited. How ready to fuck.

Roman surprised her when he called out, "Do it again, Cobra."

Eli glanced up, a grin spreading over his beloved face. "Sure thing, Barracuda."

This time he administered several open-handed blows to Alanso's ass. Sally knew the man's cheeks would be a pretty salmon color when his tan skin mixed with the rush of blood just below the skin.

She tightened around his cock, which massaged her from the inside out in the most delicious way possible. "Damn, Eli. I have to come. Please, help me."

He never tortured her for long. Today was no exception.

She buried the fingers of one hand in his hair and urged him lower until his tongue collided with her clit. Sensations sparkled through her veins. Her eyes flew open. They looked first to Eli, then Alanso and next to the crowd of men touching themselves as they surveyed her escalating debauchery.

Carver met her stare full on. He swallowed hard enough to make the flex of his throat visible from ten feet away. She didn't blink when she admitted, "I love when they fuck me like this."

"Jesus." Roman gripped himself harder.

"They make me feel so good," she confessed to Holden.

Bryce took a deep breath and held it.

"Is there room for more?" Kaige asked. "For us?"

"I'll always have a parking spot in my heart for you guys. All of you." Tears sprang to her eyes as they nodded in agreement.

"Same goes, Mustang." Kaige reassured her.

Eli's mouth performed magic on her. Either that or it was the affirmation of their gang's acceptance that shoved her over the edge into orgasm.

Alanso worked harder to penetrate the spasming rings of her muscles and Eli thrashed her mercilessly with his tongue. She loved every second.

As soon as she relaxed a little, Eli raised his head. His gaze seared her as he zoomed in for a quick yet fierce kiss. "I love you, Sally."

"I love you too. Both of you." She glanced to the rest of the Hot Rods. "All of you."

"You sons of bitches," Roman snarled. "You've been keeping her all to yourselves. Look at her. She's fucking amazing. No wonder you can hardly walk most days."

"That might have something to do with Eli." Alanso shut his eyes and shivered between her legs. He never once stopped fucking her. Slow then fast then slow, as if his control wobbled on occasion.

"Don't pretend you don't crave me in your ass." Eli addressed Al, though he dusted one last kiss over Sally's mouth before rising. He circled around behind Alanso and rested his chin on the shorter man's shoulder. It bobbed as his partner kept burying himself inside her as if he couldn't ever get enough.

Thank God, because neither could she. Already the initial relief they'd granted her morphed into renewed need.

"Shit, look at Sally." Bryce called the Hot Rods attention to her. "She's getting hot again."

"Damn." Holden seemed reverent.

Alanso traced her hard nipple with the tip of one finger. He flicked the hoop there before moving on to the other.

"You didn't answer me, Alanso." Eli used his midnight voice. "Do you want me to fuck this tight ass? While our friends watch you give it up to me?"

"Yes!" The bald man shouted. "And next time I'll return the favor so they can see it goes both ways, *mamalón*."

"Seriously?" Kaige asked.

"Don't knock it 'til you've tried it," Holden saved Eli from responding.

"We should make this car wash an annual event," Roman added.

"In favor." Carver backed him up, as usual.

"Shut up and give it to me already." Alanso reached behind him with one hand, fishing for Eli's cock.

"Patience, Al." Eli bit his lover's shoulder, harder than he would have dared with Sally.

"We've stalled long enough, don't you think?" Sally stared into Eli's liquid gaze. The blue pools had her drowning before long.

"Yeah, I do." He reached around Alanso's hip to squeeze her hand, then turned his concentration on the man sandwiched between them.

When Alanso's thrusts became uneven and his eyes widened, she knew exactly what had happened. Eli had breached his ass. Every time, the man's heart rate sped and a tiny muscle in his cheek ticked. Yet some part of him relaxed. As if he never quite believed it could be true until they proved it again. Someday he wouldn't doubt. Soon, if she had any say in the matter.

"Breathe, Alanso," she coached him. It couldn't be entirely painless. She should know—she too had taken them both there in recent days. "Deep."

"It looks pretty fucking deep from here." Kaige got smacked upside the head with Carver's free hand. "Damn, Cobra. Give the guy a minute."

"No!" Alanso chased Eli's cock when he began to retreat. The motion stole him from Sally. They both whimpered at the loss.

Eli fucked deep, tucking tight to Alanso's perfect, round ass. "Get back in there."

Sally sighed when he filled her to capacity once more. Holding him like this satisfied her on so many levels. She adored giving him pleasure while Eli took his own. Alanso had admitted this was his favorite position, taking and giving simultaneously.

"Don't let that cock slip out again." Eli smacked Alanso's ass a few more times, though they knew his threats were only for show. "You make sure our Mustang has everything she needs to come with us. Got it?"

"Yes, Cobra." Alanso groaned as Eli slid home again. The thrusts from their leader transmitted through the man between her legs. They ground his body against Sally. Every single contact brought her pleasure. A gift from them both.

Alanso rocked between them, sliding into her, then onto Eli's shaft. Soon he began to shake. The veins in his forehead and neck stood out. His fingers gripped her thighs hard enough to bruise, but she didn't call him off. The possessiveness of his hold thrilled her.

"He's on the edge," Roman called to their King Cobra. "You're going to lose him in a second."

"Never." Eli wrapped his arms around Alanso's waist. He caressed the other man's chest and abdomen. Then he peeked over the bald man's shoulder at Sally. "Are you with us?"

"Of course," she gasped. "Always."

"They're going to come together," Carver shouted.

"Shit! Me too." Holden seemed moved by their unity. His fingers flew over his cock faster, one hand skimming up his torso to pinch his nipple while he took in every nuance of their session.

"I'm there," Bryce grunted.

And the others didn't have time to give their agreement. Instead it just happened.

Alanso kick-started the domino effect. He jerked in her arms and in Eli's. He flooded her pussy with pulse after pulse of come while he wrung the same from the man behind him. The transfusion of warmth and energy set Sally off. She looked from her men to the Hot Rods scattered on the garage floor nearby.

She let them observe the pure rapture in her soul when she flew apart, confident that her guys would piece her back together, time after time. And as she writhed on Eli's Cobra, she stared at the Hot Rods surrendering together.

Spurts of pearly come shot into the air and a few rogue strands made neighbors collateral damage. Instead of being shy or letting the barrage detract from the relief they found together, the proof of their simultaneous release seemed to egg them on.

Holden gaped at the line of Bryce's come on his forearm and pumped another three or four blasts from his own shaft. Carver went as far as to reach over and swipe a drop of Roman's seed from his thigh to sample the flavor.

Sally continued to be racked by endless ecstasy until their chain reaction burned itself out and left them all smoking in the wake of the powerful feedback loop. She shuddered as Alanso pulled out and wetness trickled down her ass.

"Damn, that'll ruin your finish." Sally tried to wrest from her men and slide off the hood of Eli's car.

"Good thing I know the best painter in the country." Eli held her in place. "I love having you on my car, Mustang. And you, Alanso."

They exchanged a three-way kiss, their lips and mouths saying everything they didn't know how to translate into speech. Nothing could be as powerful as their love.

And when she surfaced, she realized the rest of the Hot Rods were tucking themselves away. What would they think of her now? Exposed, she squirmed from Alanso.

"Where do you think you're going so fast?" Eli caught her in his arms. He looked from her to Alanso. When the bald guy nodded, he grinned. "Here, hang onto her for a minute. Let me grab it."

"Grab what?" Sally could hardly orient herself to the universe around her. She didn't complain when he transferred her to Alanso, who held her tight.

"Patience, Mustang." He nuzzled their noses together. "It's a good thing, promise."

Then why did he look so nervous?

The guys huddled around them and Eli's car in a semi-circle. Roman had his poker face on and Carver bit his lip. *No.* No way would she let another one of their schemes ruin the best evening of her damn life. Not when she'd hoped to have an even better night.

"Kaige?" She intentionally singled him out. Probably the most romantic of the guys next to Holden, he hated secrets.

"Pay attention. You'll see." He jerked his chin toward Eli.

She peeked up at Alanso, who had tears in his eyes, alarming her more. But when she wriggled, he didn't budge. He trapped her close to his heart.

Eli returned in under a minute, though it felt like an eon to her. The Hot Rods parted so he could cut through their ranks. What had he retrieved from his office?

"Can you stand?" Alanso whispered into her hair.

"Of course. I've been fucked half to death, but I'm still kicking." She snorted. "In fact, if someone doesn't start talking in a second—"

Her threat faded as Alanso set her feet on the garage floor, then knelt by them. Eli joined him. In his hand was a tiny box. Or maybe it was just his strong, broad fingers that dwarfed the velvet stamped with the name of her favorite jeweler.

"Holy shit." She swore her whole body went numb. "What are you doing down there?"

"What does it look like?" Eli seemed offended.

Alanso cracked up. "Chill, *cabrón*. She doesn't know you've been practicing this speech for weeks. Roll with it."

She clutched her bare breast, hoping her heart could stay in place long enough to do what she had to. She tried to stop them, but they were set on their course. And so damn gorgeous she couldn't interrupt their pledges of devotion.

"Salome Rider, I have loved you since I was fifteen years old." Eli took her trembling fingers in his.

He kissed them as Alanso joined in, "We might not have understood everything that meant right at first."

"But we're older and wiser...sometimes..." The head of their garage smiled. His dazzling grin nearly knocking her off her feet. When had she ever seen him so happy? So unburdened by caution and fear?

"You can say that again," Kaige reached out to muss Eli's hair, earning a glare from one of her lovers.

"Today is one of those times." King Cobra stared at her as though she held the key to the mysteries of the universe. "We love you. Forever. We want to make it official, as best we can."

"Let us give you everything we have." Alanso reached out to hold her other hand.

"Everything we are." Eli nodded.

"We'd be honored to accept you in return. All of you, Sally. This..." Alanso waved at the guys around them. "Or not. Whatever you decide you want for the future. Even your cute little snoring."

"I do not snore!" She couldn't help the instinctive denial.

Roman laughed out loud. "All of us have passed you taking a nap in the common area. You snore, kid."

"And we love that too." Eli drew her attention back to his beloved face. "Sally, will you marry us?"

He cracked open the box, but she scrunched her eyes closed to avoid temptation.

There was no way she could say what she needed to if she saw a glimmering token of the much more valuable promises their souls made to hers.

"I love you both with all my heart." She sniffled a little, trying to maintain her composure. "Hell, all of the Hot Rods."

Alanso squeezed her fingers, lending her strength.

"That will never change, even if you decide to take back what you just said—"

"Never," Eli insisted.

"Not when I tell you how very sorry I am that I can't accept your proposal?" She covered her face with the hands both men dropped so fast she wondered if she'd seared them with the white-hot agony ripping through her like lightning strikes.

"Wh-what?" The confusion in Cobra's question kept her from looking at him. She'd shatter if she did.

"I *can't* marry you, Eli. I'm so, so sorry." Tears ran in rivulets down her face. When she finally blinked her eyes open, the whole garage was a blur.

"It's okay, Cobra." Alanso turned to Eli. "We knew it might take some time. We'll convince—"

"No. You won't." She shook her head as she staggered away. Tripping over someone's coveralls made a handy break. In a flash she'd robed herself with the way-too-big clothes. "Please. Can we just forget today ended like this? Please? Don't let this ruin what we *can* share. I'm so sorry. I can't."

Seven men stared at their Mustang like she'd grown hooves or maybe a horse's ass.

Though she'd promised herself she'd never do it again, she turned and fled from them. If she'd spoiled what they'd given her, she'd never forgive herself.

In the sanctuary of her room, which now felt like someone else's home, she flung herself onto the bed face down and cried until she couldn't breathe. When everything inside her went as numb as her body had earlier, she tumbled into darkness.

Chapter Ten

Eli slammed the drawer on his toolbox, deciding he needed some manual labor to burn off his frustration. It didn't make any sense. A month had passed since the car wash and his disastrous proposal. Full of sex, and *love*, and perfection. Passion and friendship, easy living and satisfying work they all enjoyed.

So what the hell was there to think about?

How the hell long could a man wait before he started wondering what the fuck was wrong with him?

Had Sally turned them down because he hadn't truly given her what she desired most? Was she afraid he never would? Fuck work. He knew what he needed to do.

She'd shown him over and over that she could handle herself. Sally didn't need him to be her bulletproof vest or make her choices. Fine. Let her say no if it was too much. The guys would respect her call.

"Alanso." He nudged his lover with his knee. The guy leaned over the front of a 1937 Mercedes-Benz 540K Special Roadster. It was a thing of beauty and a big deal for the shop to work on. A once-in-a-lifetime car. Alanso had been talking about the machine non-stop—at breakfast, to Tom and even in bed. Yet Eli knew he'd drop it in a second for a chance at Mustang and the gang.

"Yeah?" His bald head peeked out from beneath the hood. The instant he caught sight of Eli's face, he set down his tools and peeled his gloves off. "Ah, shit. It's eating you too?"

He looked as miserable as Eli felt.

"What can we do to convince her, Cobra?" Alanso pinched the bridge of his nose.

"We can get the rest of the guys together and unleash them." Eli didn't hesitate. They'd been chomping at the bit since the car wash. Not to mention all the other shows the trio had put on for them in the common area of their apartment. Sure, they'd gotten off on watching, on being part of the fringes of their lust, but...maybe it was time to quit hedging.

"You think *that's* what she's waiting for?" His forehead wrinkled as his eyes narrowed. "It could be. I know I'm ready for it. I'm dying to see her win them all over. As if she hasn't already. Hell, they've adored her since she came to us."

"It's time." Eli nodded.

"Whatever happens, Cobra, you've got me." Alanso held out his fist until Eli bumped it. "I love you; nothing's going to change that."

"I never mean to act like that's not enough." He winced. "It's everything. I just—"

"I get it." Alanso waved him off. "It's the same for me, you know."

"I'd never have survived without you." He dropped a fierce kiss on his best friend's mouth. "Not in my younger days and certainly not now. I love you, Al."

"So let's go get the guys and blow our girl's mind." He grinned. "I've had enough of her holding out on us."

Eli flipped the sign on the office door to closed, locked it, then hit each of the red buttons on the rolling bay doors as Alanso went down the line, rallying the troops.

Or at least he would have if a well-dressed suit hadn't come knocking on the glass.

"Sally!" Eli bellowed from the garage.

She couldn't fault him for his recent crankiness. Her sham forced them apart more by the day. But she and Tom were close to finding a solution. When it was all said and done, then she'd go to them. She'd apologize and explain after the ghosts of her past had been exorcised so that they could no longer hurt her guys if they went all overprotective on her. Brute force would only snarl knots she and Tom had nearly finessed apart.

Setting down her brush, she wiped primer on her coveralls and jogged from the paint booth to try her best to settle Eli. Maybe he'd respond well to a blowjob behind his desk. She licked her lips in anticipation.

"What do you need, Cobra?" She tipped her head at the worry lines crinkling his eyes. She hadn't seen those in a while. Not even after her refusals.

"There's some dickhead in here about to get his ass kicked." Eli canted his head in the direction of the office.

"Why?" She tucked close to him—loving the heat and scent of her mate—for a peek around his torso. When she caught sight of the tall, handsome man in a traditional navy suit, she froze.

"The fucker claims he's your *husband*."

She wobbled, grabbing the doorframe for support. "Phillip."

The hoarse scratch of her plea must have alerted him to the danger she faced. She'd brought trouble to all the Hot Rods.

Eli glanced at the crumpled business card in his fist for confirmation. "Shit, Sally. How do you know his name?"

"He's not lying." She stared up at Eli in horror. "We *are* married."

From behind her, Alanso's cry ripped her soul in half. She tried to reach for Eli, needing his support. But her lover stepped aside, avoiding her touch as if it would shrivel his cock, turn it black and make it fall off.

Instead of comforting her, he rushed to Alanso's side and lifted the man from the concrete floor. He glared at her over his shoulder as he attended to their lover, who spouted endless Spanish.

"Get the hell out of here. Go talk to your *husband*." He sneered. "Don't forget to mention that you love to fuck me and Alanso raw. How you claimed to love us. Hell, how you let the whole garage watch us bang you and hoped they'd join in someday soon."

"Enough." Roman stepped between Eli and Sally. "Stop talking, Cobra. You can't take angry words back."

The defense from their hardest member, Barracuda, stunned her almost as much as seeing the man she'd escaped standing in her haven.

"Go, Sally." The oldest Hot Rod nodded to her as he corralled Alanso and Eli out the back door. "Fix this. Fast."

She braced herself on outstretched arms that still clung to the doorjamb for the duration of two more breaths. Then she drew herself up and marched into the office, using Alanso's agony as motivation to conquer history.

Bryce and Kaige stood guard, flanking the proper-looking man. He didn't seem like he'd broken a rule in his whole life, never mind shown aggression toward a woman. Then again, if he'd heard even a fraction of what Eli had shouted, he'd know she was no kind of lady.

At least Cobra had left her to clean up her own mess. Maybe because he didn't care about her anymore. She couldn't really blame him after the engine block that'd just dropped on him like an anvil squashing an old cartoon villain.

"Salome." Phillip breathed her name, making his guards stand straighter like junk-yard dogs about to pounce. "Look at you. So different. Yet so beautiful."

"I'm not going back to Utah." Sally set her feet shoulder width apart and faced him squarely. "You can forget that right now."

"That's good to hear, Salome." Phillip smiled softly at her. "I wouldn't recommend that to anyone, having been gone from there myself for nearly eight years."

"What?" Nothing could have shocked her more.

"It took me longer than you to get brave enough to make the break, but yes, I left the commune." He shook his head sadly. "I've been searching for you a long time. You hid well. I was afraid you…didn't make it."

The fight leeched out of Sally as she stared into the gentle eyes of the boy who hadn't been able to rape her as he'd been taught was his right. She swallowed hard.

Turning to Kaige and Bryce, she tried to make them understand with one look. Sure she failed, she asked, "Would you mind if Phillip and I take a little walk? To Tom's garden?"

Would they trust her or try to smash this obstacle for her like she knew Eli would have if she'd entrusted him with the truth?

"Are you sure it's okay, Mustang?" Bryce's chest puffed up. "You know we'd never let anyone hurt you, right? We'd *crush* any asshole who tried."

Phillip held his hands up and laughed. "Do I look like the kind of guy who could take her on and win? I'm not stirring up trouble. I promise. Though I'm glad to see Salome has found a family who loves her and will protect her so fiercely."

When she peeked toward the open door to the garage, hearing nothing, Bryce opened his arms. She went to him and accepted his hug. "It's going to be okay, Sally. I'm not trying to intrude or make you feel like you can't handle this, but I'm going to stand by the window inside Tom's house and watch to make sure you're safe. That's the best I can do."

"Sounds fair." Phillip nodded to her as he patted his inside pocket. He must have been sweltering in that outfit. Still, he didn't appear disheveled or rumpled. He'd grown up pretty nice himself. "This won't take long. I have your papers. I just...I'd like to talk first."

Bryce gave them about a twenty pace head start before tailing them toward Tom's place. When they rounded the back porch, he let himself inside. Within seconds, Tom burst from his home, sprinting for the Hot Rods' apartment above the garage.

He nodded in her direction, hopped the railing, then kept running toward his sons.

They would need him to explain.

"I imagined a lot of different greetings I might receive today." Phillip chuckled. "I promise you, that wasn't one of my scenarios. I'm not quite sure what to say next."

Sally smiled up at him and took his hand. She squeezed it lightly, remembering the boy he'd been and how they'd had a friendship once. They sat on a stone bench beside the waterfall. A manmade stream led toward the rocks she'd painted in memory of the mothers both her lovers had lost.

"Sorry about that." Sally shrugged. "I don't even know where to start."

"Just tell me that you're happy." He seemed earnest. "I've worried for so long. Guilt ate at me after you left. I tried to find you. I didn't have a lot of resources at first, but I did my best. Actually, it was because of you that I became interested in law."

"You're a lawyer?" She reevaluated his suit. It had a nice cut despite its simplicity.

"Yes." He nodded. "I take cases like ours. Kids who are fighting for emancipation from parents who don't deserve them."

"Huh." Sally found she liked Phillip. Maybe a little too much. He reminded her of Eli in a lot of ways. Strong. A leader. Someone others would trust. Decent. Maybe they could have had something under different circumstances. "My...boyfriend...and his dad volunteer at a youth shelter. They took me in after I ran away."

"You've been with them the whole time? All these years?" Phillip nodded. "It makes sense that they love you so much, then."

Sally didn't bother to go into details. When she simply sat there and blinked up at Phillip, he nodded. "I kind of hoped I might convince you to see what might have been if we'd grown up somewhere normal. But I see that ship has sailed. Too bad, Salome. You're even more fascinating to me now than you were back then."

"Thank you, Phillip." She patted his hand. "I can't tell you how surprised I am to see that you did the right thing."

He choked on a laugh.

"Shit. I didn't mean it like that." She ran her fingers through her hair, flipping it over her shoulder.

"I understand." He smiled. "I wasn't very strong. Until I saw more. Learned more. The things they wanted from me, I simply couldn't go along with. It wasn't a choice. And I had you as my role model. You made me believe it was possible to opt out."

"That's *exactly* how I felt." She stared up at him. "I'm so glad you came."

"Me too. And I can't tell you how much it pleases me to give you the last of your freedom." He handed her a thick envelope. "You would have gotten it annulled if I hadn't responded soon, I know. Besides, the compliance with early marriage protocols were suspect at best in our community. You could have fought and won. But I hope this makes your life just a little easier."

"That's all I can ask. And I'm glad I can do the same for you." She didn't question her instincts when she leaned over and hugged him. "You're going to make someone a fine husband, Phillip."

"Maybe now I can concentrate on finding the right woman." He nodded as he rose, dusting off his expensive pants.

Crap, she hadn't even considered that. Her coveralls suffered no damage from the natural surface.

"Would you mind if Bryce takes you back to your car?" She glanced up at the windows to the great room of their apartment. A shadow near one made her sure there was a reason the hairs on her nape stood up.

"Not at all." He touched her cheek. "Be happy, Salome."

"I'm going to try my best. Have Bryce give you one of my business cards. I have yours. Keep in touch?" She smiled when he nodded.

"You'll just have to make sure your guys don't rip my head off. Deal?" He grinned.

"Deal." She leapt in the air, pumping her fist as she took off for home and the people who made it special.

Please don't let me have ruined it all.

Eli, Alanso, I'm coming for you.

Chapter Eleven

Eli stared into the garden, sickness climbing his esophagus when Sally hugged her *husband*. "I can't believe she told my dad and not me that she was fucking married."

"Cobra, don't deck me." Kaige took a step out of arm's reach before he admitted, "I kind of get her logic. You haven't always let her fight her own battles."

"That was before." He gritted his teeth, hating that the fucker made sense.

"And you'd have done what differently this time, son?" Tom wasn't afraid. He approached and laid his hand on Eli's shoulder. Eli welcomed the infusion of strength from his dad. "I'd bet my house you'd have piled in that Cobra of yours with Alanso and driven for days straight to the ass-end of Utah, muscles blazing."

"Maybe." He rubbed his temples. "I still can't believe they'd do that to a kid!"

Alanso stepped near, ducking under the arm Eli flung around his shoulder. He barely managed to chime in, probably because of the bear hug from his best friend and boss. "It pisses me off the most that she considered anything about that mess valid. *Mierda*, it's not like what we proposed would hold water in court. It's about the commitment behind the label. *That's* what counts. The spirit behind the promise never existed for her before. I think it does now."

"Unless her refusal was about more than some dumb paperwork." Eli laid his cheek on Alanso's crown.

"It wasn't." Tom spoke with authority.

Better than Tom's hearsay affirmation, Sally stepped through the door they'd left ajar—in case she or Bryce hollered for help—and met his gaze directly. "It wasn't."

The largest of their gang snuck in behind her and took his place in the crowd of concerned mechanics.

She displayed a sheaf of papers. "I'm sorry this didn't happen sooner. I never meant to hurt you. Any of you."

Eli wasn't sure he trusted himself to speak. So he swallowed hard and nodded instead.

"I have some good news." Sally clutched the documents to her chest and lowered her head. She sidled closer, as if afraid they would reject her. Like that was ever a possibility. "Eli. Alanso. I'm officially available. I'm divorced. I'm so sorry if sleeping with me...before...compromised your values. I didn't consider it real. It wasn't from my heart. Nothing like what I have with you two. You know that, right?"

"Was that even a worry in your mind?" Alanso tipped his head as he observed her fingers tapping on the folder she held in a death grip.

"I'd say that's a yes." Eli rubbed at his chest, aching for them all.

Sally inhaled deep enough she might have floated away under less heavy circumstances. "I think I can finally leave all that shit behind me. If you can..."

Her enormous grin lit up his world.

"Dad?" Eli didn't take his gaze from the woman of his dreams. "I love you, but would you mind going home?"

Tom patted his son's chest then Alanso's bald head.

He turned, whooped and lifted Sally from the floor to spin her around. "We did it! Why don't you kids take the rest of the day off? I've got the station under control and I'll call your clients. It's not every day some of our Hot Rods get engaged."

"Uhh," Kaige piped up from across the room. "I didn't hear her say yes yet."

"I haven't asked again." Eli didn't take the opportunity to do it right then either. "We've got a few matters left to sort out."

"Right, right." Tom rolled his eyes. "Sort away. I've got you covered."

The door shut loud enough behind him to make sure they were alone. All eight of them.

"Sally, get your pretty ass over here. Right now." Eli tried to stay still, relaxed. He was sure he did a shitty job when she hesitated.

"Are you angry?" She set the papers on the table by the door then twisted her fingers together.

"Some." He didn't bother to lie. Those days were far behind them. Besides, he knew to his core now. She could handle all of him. All of *them* and whatever the world tossed at her. The list of things she required from him didn't include being a force field between her and reality.

She nodded. "I'm so sorry. I should have told you. Your dad tried to convince me to, by the way. I just..."

"You were afraid he'd flip his shit or go off half-cocked." Alanso came between them. "I've been there. In the hiding days. It's not a nice place to live. I'm sorry that you didn't feel safe enough to confide in us. In *me*."

"I didn't want to put you in the middle." Their girl went to Alanso and hugged him tight. "It wouldn't have been right."

"We can discuss that later," Eli growled at her.

"Uh-oh, he's got his fuck face on." Kaige got smacked upside the head by Bryce. Holden and Carver laughed while Roman simply smirked.

Sally looked up from her place in Alanso's arms and read Eli's expression. "He's right. You *do* have your fuck face on. I love it when you get bossy. All growly and shit."

"I don't know what the hell you're talking about." Eli tried not to bark at them despite his frustration. "But yes, I plan to stake my claim right here, right now. You belong to us. You said so yourself. If you feel differently today then you need to pipe up. Otherwise, it isn't only me with my fuck face on. We're all going to remind you who you belong with. Not because you're forced to stay. No. You *chose* us. And we chose you."

The Hot Rods stepped closer, encircling his girl with their strength and love.

"No more pacing ourselves. No more taking it slow. Everything I've warned them about is off the table. You're right. You're a big girl. You've got this, don't you?" He whipped his shirt over his head and was delighted to see her gulp.

"I think so." She took shallow breaths, excitement flushing her cheeks. "I'd like to try. I've wanted you for so long. Eli, Alanso, I love you both. Forever."

"*Te amo, mi corazón.*" Alanso let her off the hook right away. Or so she thought. "Now get rid of those clothes before I rip them to shreds. You're ours. And we want to share you with our brothers."

Eli had never seen a woman get naked so fast. He groaned as her paint-spattered coveralls hit the floor followed by her T-shirt and underwear. Before he knew what he intended, he'd strode forward, scooped her into his arms and hauled her toward their enormous sectional sofa.

"What are you waiting for?" He scolded the rest of the Hot Rods for their sluggishness. This was not the time to hesitate. Despite her bravado, Sally could balk if they didn't burn her rational side alive. What woman wouldn't be a little nervous at the idea of entertaining seven men?

Even though she adored each and every member of their gang.

Alanso took the instruction to heart. The man was buck-naked by the time he reached the couch, a step or two before Eli.

He deposited their woman onto the peninsula chaise that stuck out from the rest of the seating area. The armless sofa allowed them to surround her.

On either side of her, at shoulder height, Eli and Alanso stood. The rest of their friends stripped off denim and work shirts left and right. Each man stepped forward, prepared to make her theirs once and for all, offering part of themselves in return.

When Sally reached for her pussy, Eli snatched her hand away. "Hell no, you're not touching yourself. You've got plenty of guys around to do that for you."

"I'm so turned on it hurts." She whimpered and squirmed, trying to press her thighs together.

"So ask one of them to help you out." Alanso jumped in, surprising Eli with his lack of restraint. He could get used to this. The feral gleam in the bald man's eyes turned Eli on even more. If his cock got any harder he'd probably break his zipper.

He stripped as fast as he dared, moaning when she said, "Kaige."

"Yeah, Mustang?" The inventor slash mechanic dropped to his knees beside her. His dreads bounced as he settled in, letting his fingers trail from her breasts to just above her pussy. She gasped at the initial contact.

"They call you Super Nova for a reason." She winked. "Show me."

"Pretty sure it has something to do with my temper. But I'll see what I can do." He didn't waste time. Instead he latched on to her breast with his mouth, worshipping her as he glanced up at Eli then Alanso out of the corner of his eye. It wasn't easy to translate his question considering his mouthful of tit but Eli managed. "You two still okay?"

Alanso groaned. He watched another man please Sally and his cock grew harder with each pump of his giant heart. "Hell no. That's so hot, Nova. Sally, you look so pretty. I'm about to have a heart attack. Coño."

Eli could relate. They might have to be less than sedate during this first cruise. If the sparks in Sally's eyes were any indication, she wouldn't mind that much.

"You guys going to let Kaige have all the fun?" Cobra prodded the rest of the Hot Rods though he couldn't fault their wide-eyed stares, which fixed on his lovers and their friends.

"Shit, no." Holden caved next. He descended on the opposite side of Sally, treating her other breast to similar delights. Both men appeared fascinated with her piercings and the pretty Hot Rods tattoo surrounded by flowers and vines at her hip.

Roman and Carver approached together. The two best

friends—one dark, one light—took up a post on either side of Sally's knees. They spread her apart, running their hands up and down the length of her thighs reverently. The extension of their friendship seemed perfectly natural.

That left Bryce standing between her feet at the foot of the couch.

"Guess you're the lucky one." Eli nodded to the big, gentle guy. He was glad the well-mannered Hot Rod would be up first to show Sally how much they all cared for her. For men who'd had rough lives—and maybe doubly so for the girl who'd been brave enough to strike out alone—this bond meant everything.

They would never abandon each other. They never would ostracize someone from their gang. Their individual beliefs were their own, respected even when they conflicted with someone else's, though that didn't happen often. In this case, they aligned with one goal. Giving Sally as much pleasure as possible while absorbing some of her ecstasy for themselves. What pleased one of them, impacted them all.

She'd always been their sunshine, even during the darkest of nights.

Knowing now the full magnitude of the dangers and disappointments she'd escaped, Eli held her in even higher esteem. How had she grown into such a loving, accepting, expressive woman after being raised in a stunting environment?

She gave him hope. If she could overcome her past, they all could.

Every last one of the Hot Rods looked desperate to demonstrate the pride they had for her. The respect and desire. It all mingled into a perfect storm of passion.

Bryce sank to his knees. He approached Sally slowly, giving her plenty of chances to object before he reached the apex of her thighs. She didn't utter a peep. Well, except for the cries and moans carried on the bursts of her unsteady respiration.

The fissure between them diminished until she had to be able to feel Bryce's breath on her pussy. Their Rebel hovered there, making her dance between all the men supporting her. Each twist in one direction only granted someone better access on her reverse side. When the pleasure he gifted became too much, she shifted into the clutches of another Hot Rod.

Sally cursed at Bryce and tried to force him to eliminate the fraction of an inch separating them, but Eli and Alanso each grabbed one of her hands and pinned them to the cushion above her head as if by tacit understanding.

The motion arched her back and made her small yet perfect tits irresistibly presented to Kaige and Holden. The guys licked and sucked at her nipples, toying with the rings there for their amusement and Sally's rapture.

Roman and Caver traced the lines of her gorgeous tattoos up her hips, then swept inward to her belly. Though her tan had faded some, Eli had to admit he preferred her totally pale skin, which allowed the bright colors of her artwork to take center stage. He loved how vibrant she was beneath the surface too.

Welcoming, accepting, she became a vessel to collect the attention and admiration the guys lavished on her. She held them together and allowed them to join with each other in a way they'd never dreamed possible. Especially for the guys who hadn't explored their less-than-ramrod-straight sides…yet.

Eli felt closer to the men than he ever had before. He never wanted to let go of this moment, this magic.

"Please, Bryce," she whimpered. "It's too good. It hurts."

"I've got you, Mustang. You have no idea how many times I've imagined this." He didn't torture her anymore. He nuzzled her mound, drawing a sigh from her and a groan from several of the other men.

"*Joder!*" Alanso shouted, using his free hand to grab his cock. The stiff erection already leaked as he witnessed his friends imparting bliss on his lover. The woman they planned to keep forever. Hell, the whole group had no choice but to stay now.

Finally, something deep in Eli's soul relaxed. The Hot Rods were here. They were his and they were welded into one unit. Eternally.

He stared at Alanso, who watched the action below them while mumbling in Spanish. Eli couldn't resist. He reached across the couch to his best friend and tipped the guy forward. Alanso folded, lunging through the canyon. Bent over, they met in the middle, making out above the glazed eyes of their mutual lover.

Sally tried to express her approval, but her words were garbled when Bryce escalated his contact from soft brushes of his cheek and chin to long laps of his tongue over her slit. The Hot Rod cursed after he discovered the piercing in her hood.

It didn't take him more than an instant to investigate the effects of manipulating the curved metal through her most sensitive flesh.

Sally jolted as if someone had pinched her ass with a jumper cable.

Ten hands held her in place to receive the full gluttony of bliss the Hot Rods imparted. Eli and Alanso broke apart, panting, when Sally arched. In less than two minutes, she dissolved. Eli beamed when she showed the guys just how responsive she was. And how gorgeous.

They petted her all over as she crested and returned to their gathering.

"Sorry," she whispered.

"What the hell for?" Bryce lifted his head, licking his lips. His chin glistened with her release.

"Wanted it to last longer." She glanced to Eli. The drowsy satisfaction in her brilliant green eyes had him dying to stake a claim. Except he knew it would please her more if he waited. He'd give her anything she needed.

"You think you're off the hook already?" Alanso laughed. "Hardly."

Eli nodded to his partner. "Get the condoms."

He didn't need to be told twice. Alanso leapt the couch back and raced for the hall closet. He returned with one hand over his stiff, waving cock and the other clutching a glass jar. Condoms of every color filled it like candy in an old-fashioned drug store.

The shiny metal lid clattered as Eli flung it to the floor. He reached inside for a clear plastic packet and tossed it to Roman. "Go ahead, old man. Take Bryce's place."

Eli had always had a ton of respect for Barracuda, who'd chosen a higher path than the one he'd been set on when they'd met. It took a lot to change. The more mature guy had sometimes seemed uncertain of his friends, even years after he'd left his life of petty crime behind. He wanted the man to know Eli would trust him with even the most precious parts of his life.

"You're sure?" He ripped open the condom but didn't roll it over his impressive cock. He stood there, looking between Alanso, Sally, Eli and—for some reason—Carver. The two of them had always been close, from the very first day when most of the Hot Rods had voted to kick Roman's ass for attempting to steal Tom's truck.

Carver had stepped in front of the guy, keeping the gang in line. Eli wondered how long it would be before Barracuda and Meep, who drove a Roadrunner, admitted they had more in common with Eli and Alanso than wanting to fuck their Mustang.

When they were ready, he'd help them navigate what would likely be a rocky course.

Eli's gaze traveled across dark tattoos. Skulls, flames, dice and cards, devils, guns, booze—you name it, Roman had it. Even one mysterious purple blotch that looked like a permanent bruise over his ribs. He'd never cracked under the Hot Rods' teasing about the artist's mistake to tell them what it had been intended to represent.

Eli was afraid he knew the answer.

But now was not the time for their troubled pasts. This was their future. And it was bright. Blazing with lust and love that could cauterize even the rawest wounds.

"Of course he's sure," Sally answered for Eli. "He loves me, and this is what I've dreamed about. You. Come on, Roman. Suit up."

Sally opened her heart and arms, unafraid of the Barracuda's reputation. His big teeth didn't frighten her one bit. Bryce swapped places with the guy and took up where he'd left off, massaging Sally's thigh and hips, keeping her comfortable and aroused so they could all indulge their fantasies.

"Go ahead, Roman." Carver cheered on his roommate. Since the rooms above the garage had already been built out by the time Barracuda joined them, Meep and Roman had ended up bunking together. Though Eli had offered to renovate through the years, neither seemed to mind doubling up.

"Fine, fine. I'm fucking her." He dropped onto his hands, his palms bracketing Sally's shoulders.

She reached up to hug him and laugh. "Don't act like it's such a chore, asshole."

"That's not—" Roman's denial cut off. Carver reached between his roommate's legs to position Barracuda's tool at Sally's entrance. Given Roman's stance, supporting himself on the couch, assistance was warranted.

"Don't mind me. Just lending a hand." Carver winked up at the couple as he smeared moisture from the opening of Sally's pussy over the latex-coated tip of Roman's cock. "Nothing to see here. Keep bickering. You know it makes me hot to see her beat down arrogant bastards."

"*Uhhg*," Roman groaned.

He dipped his head to kiss Sally with a tenderness Eli hadn't known him capable of. Once he'd gotten his fill, he thrilled them all by thrusting through Carver's grip. Burying deep, he pressed into the paradise Eli could attest waited for them between Mustang's thighs.

Sally squeezed Eli's fingers, which were still entwined with hers. Alanso's grin made him sure the same was true for the other pair.

"Yeah, Mustang. Take him." Carver coached her from his excellent vantage point. "You've got almost all of his cock. Just a little more."

"Who're you calling little?" Roman growled.

They all laughed. Eli swatted the other man's ass. The bunched muscles there attested to his restraint. "Concentrate, Barracuda."

"If I think about this too much it's not going to last very long." He shook his head, cursing. "She's fucking tight. Haven't you two been stretching her out? What the hell have you been doing to keep us all awake night after night?"

"Just lucky. She's pliable. And resilient." Eli grinned. "Actually, we kind of like to fuck her together. Talk about tight."

And the joke was on him, because the thought alone had him curling his toes in the carpet.

"I don't believe you." Roman clenched his jaw, gritting his teeth. "You're no pencil dick. She can't take you both."

"That sounds like a dare." Eli glanced down at Sally. "Want to go higher? Can you take more?"

She was grinning up at him between moans and sighs. "Please. You know I love it."

Alanso pouted. "And me?"

"Someone's got to keep me from screaming. Don't need Tom rushing in here anytime soon." She reached for Alanso's cock and tugged until he shuffled closer. He sprang onto the couch and knelt over her head, feeding her his shaft.

She took him in her mouth eagerly. Eli could relate. He craved the taste of both of his lovers.

"Wait." All of the mechanics paused when his stern command echoed off the high ceilings and concrete floors.

A heartbeat passed, then two, before he smiled. "Let me underneath her first."

The guys chuckled and clapped him on the back as they helped the trio arrange themselves. Sally cried out when Roman slipped from her grasp.

"Just a minute, Mustang." Eli lifted her, then slid onto his back in her place. Having the Hot Rods standing around him like pillars made him feel secure. He understood how they gave Sally the strength to submit to their adoring gazes. He rearranged his woman on his chest. "There, better?"

Mustang Sally

"Uh, no." She squirmed. "Your hard-on is jabbing me."

"It hasn't even started." He laughed into the hair at her temple, nuzzling her as he reached around them both to notch his cock in her pussy. Then they ground together until he was buried deep. To the base of his shaft. It hadn't taken them long to learn how they fit best. "There. *Now* I'm jabbing you."

She whimpered.

Alanso spouted another stream of Spanish from where he hovered over them. Eli and Sally responded in unison. She took care of his shaft while Eli reached up and lipped the other man's balls.

"Riiiiight. I think *that* might have been part of the riot they were causing." Holden's jibe held a healthy dose of envy.

"You haven't heard anything yet," Alanso struggled to inform his friends. "Come on, Roman. Get back in there."

"Are you sure I'm gonna fit?" The other guy sounded incredulous.

"Hell yeah." Alanso shouted, whether in response to Barracuda or because of the fancy doodles Sally drew on his cockhead with her tongue, none of them could say.

The rest of the Hot Rods searched for purchase, contributing anything they could to the barrage of pleasure they levied at Salome.

"*Mámame!*" Alanso growled. "*Mámame, por favor.*"

Sally stiffened.

Even if Eli hadn't felt the pressure of Roman's cock on his own as they were squeezed together in his woman's sheath, he would have known Barracuda had invaded her from the reaction of his lovers. Alanso's begging for Sally to suck him could only mean she'd paused. Though not for long if the bald man's satisfied grunts were any indication. He might have worried if she hadn't proven she could take both him and Alanso. Not just could, but that she loved cradling them both inside her.

"Holy shit," Carver murmured. "That's impressive."

All at once, Sally bucked. Eli was ready for her. He hugged

her tight to his torso and let her ride out the rapturous assault. Roman bulged along Eli's length, as far as he'd embedded himself, while Sally's orgasm squeezed them both in regular pulses. The poor guy didn't stand a chance.

He thrust deep in one stroke that reignited Sally's spasms, then shot over and over into the condom he wore. Eli swore the heat of the other man's come scalded his own cock, though it might have simply been his imagination. It took every ounce of willpower he possessed to keep from joining the Hot Rod.

But he was dying to please Sally and make this the best experience of her life. Nothing else would suffice.

"I think that might be a record." Kaige slapped Roman on his heaving back. "Better luck next time, buddy."

"Oh, yeah." The winded man didn't seem too upset. How could he be when he'd come so damn hard? "I'd like to see you do better, Nova. I bet you fucking live up to your name and explode in a minute or less."

"What're you willing to wager on it?" Kaige scrambled to his feet, snatched a condom from the jar and covered himself before Roman had managed to retreat from Sally's quivering pussy. She whimpered around Alanso when her newest lover withdrew then laid a kiss on her thigh in thanks.

"A blowjob." Barracuda sighed as he sank into Kaige's spot near Sally's breast. He leaned forward and pressed kiss after kiss on the subtle mound, showering her with reverence and gratitude.

"I doubt I'm gonna be able to get it up again after this." Kaige slid his middle finger into Sally's pussy beside Eli's cock, testing the flexibility of her body. Eli groaned around Alanso's nuts when the bastard bent his knuckle to swipe across the crown of Eli's dick.

"Fine, you can blow me tomorrow. Or some other time. *When* you lose." Roman wrote a check his mouth might not be able to cash. The familiar competitive streak they all had in common reared its head in new circumstances. The energy they generated ramped Eli up even more.

This. This is what he'd been missing. Alanso too, if the

other man's happy groans told the full story. And he intended to make the most of it. They had to convince Sally this was where she belonged.

They were the only men for her.

Well, the seven of them.

Chapter Twelve

Sally squirmed, opening her thighs wider. After the intensity of the two orgasms she'd already had, Eli might have been surprised by her endurance if she hadn't shown him and Alanso every night just how much capacity she had for loving. Amazing. Beautiful. Rare.

He loved everything about her.

"Whatever, Barracuda." Kaige inserted the head of his cock and proceeded to work his length along Eli's. "You're on. Start the clock."

Alanso gurgled. From his angle, Eli thought he saw Sally take him full to the back of her throat. "She likes that, Super Nova. Give her everything."

"Working on it." Kaige shuddered, his entire body flexing as Sally welcomed him.

Carver, Holden and Bryce stared, transfixed, as their buddy slid home. They never once stopped caressing Sally, lavishing attention on her to ramp her excitement higher, over and over.

"Not so cocky now, are you?" Roman's smug smile had Eli chuckling.

Sweat broke out on the other guy's brow as he burrowed deeper and deeper until he'd maxed out his penetration. "Shut up, Barracuda. I'm busy."

Sally giggled around Alanso's cock, making the man cry out. His hands clenched, one in Sally's hair and one in Eli's. The slight pinch must have turned her on, helping her to climb the spiral of rapture once again. She tightened around Eli and Kaige, making the guy on top work harder to drill into her pussy.

Eli sighed as the thick shaft massaged his own, both of

them rubbing Sally together. In counterpoint, then in unison. They drove into her over and over.

Bryce paused his exploration of Sally's lips to call the bet in Kaige's favor. An instant later, the man broke. His thrusts turned jerky and short, ramming him into Sally all the way. The contact of his torso with her clit, especially given the ring in her hood, was too much for her to resist. She screamed as she shattered this time.

Alanso backed away temporarily. Maybe to watch. Maybe to avoid being bitten. Most likely to keep himself from erupting down Sally's throat before he was ready.

Eli didn't blame the man. After all, Cobra was doomed. At the bottom of the pile of libertine revelry, all he could do was enjoy the ride. The separation from Alanso, his balls now out of reach, allowed Eli a better vantage to view Super Nova's detonation. Sally lifted her head to witness his synchronized pleasure too. She reached up to press her hand over the mechanic's heart. The affection in that single gesture lured them all.

Several of the men cursed. Kaige's quaking renewed. The complete destruction of their inhibitions guaranteed he couldn't hang on another moment. He tried to warn Salome or Alanso—anyone, really. But the guys didn't help him regain his composure. Instead, they switched their petting from Sally to him.

Alanso contorted himself to kiss Eli, and nothing could stop him from coming then.

Kaige groaned as Eli hammered upward, filling his mate and thrilling the other man still snugged inside her. He swore his back was about to break as he arched, strung tight, then released. Come bubbled in his balls and rocketed from his cock. No condom prevented him from flooding Sally with every drop of his seed. The scalding hot liquid must have been apparent to Kaige, even through the condom.

He yelled and jerked a few more times.

Through it all, the Hot Rods held their vulnerable members in place. They made sure they were protected as they surrendered to the heat of the moment, years in the making.

And when Eli finished coming, still in the wake of the most violent climax of his life, they lifted Sally from him and dragged him out of the way. Her limp form might have alarmed him if she hadn't mewled and made a grab for Carver's cock.

"Eli." Alanso nudged his shoulder.

"Mmm." He couldn't manage more, the sights surrounding him nearly as pleasurable as his epic orgasm had been.

"Remember the porn link I sent you a couple weeks ago?" Alanso's arms, chest and shoulders were ripped. The blood filling his muscles, and pumping him up, made him seem twice as big as usual.

Eli licked his lips. "Which one?"

His brain was fuzzy.

"*The* one. Where the woman took *three* guys at once." Alanso seemed urgent. "I think it's time. She's ready. So am I."

"What are you boys plotting over there?" Sally blinked as if to clear the haze of arousal from her mind. "I miss you."

Alanso rushed to her side. "I want to try something we saw."

"Anything, you know that." She reached up to touch his cheek with her fingertips.

And suddenly Eli knew what they were about to attempt. "Shit. I don't know, Alanso. She's small."

"If it hurts, you promise to tell us, right?" Alanso peered into Sally's eyes.

The link between them warmed Eli's heart. At least if something happened to him, they'd have each other. It made him feel safer about loving them so completely. They wouldn't have to be alone...like his dad.

He shook his head, clearing the morose thoughts.

One thing was sure to burn only the pleasurable memories into his brain from this afternoon. Alanso was right as usual. When he looked to Holden, Carver and Bryce, he knew the trio would never be able to wait their individual turns anyway.

It was now or never.

Eli rolled onto his knees on the floor, coming to rest by Sally's side, close enough that he could kiss her—face, brows, nose and lips. "You ready to play hard?"

"Thought I already was?" She moaned as an aftershock wrung her body.

"Just one more time." Eli prodded her to reach for the stars. He nodded to his friends who still sported painful-looking hard-ons. "You're going to take all three of them at once."

"How?" She tried to do the math. He didn't blame her when her foggy mind refused to cooperate.

"Trust me?" He smoothed her hair from her damp brow.

"Of course. You're my King Cobra." She smiled then leaned up to capture his mouth in a scorching kiss. "I love you."

"I love you too, Salome Rider." He scooped her from the couch. "So you're going to ride for me. For us."

Alanso groaned. With his head tipped back, he played with the post in his nipple and rubbed his abdomen. Anything to keep his hands off his cock, Eli suspected. Not yet.

"Bryce, you're the biggest. Lay down on your back. Where I was." Eli didn't expect him to hesitate and he wasn't disappointed. The big man draped his frame over the couch.

Eli flipped Sally and handed her to Rebel. "Take good care of her."

"Always, Cobra." Bryce hugged Sally and pillowed her head on his shoulder.

"Holden, roll a condom on him." Eli was thankful he'd come and could have a clear mind to ensure his partners got everything they deserved. He kept them safe while they experimented. Their willingness to try whatever he had in store made him proud.

Their trust humbled him.

Swinger obeyed. He ripped open another packet, adding to the growing pile of wrappers, and slid the rubber over Bryce's fat shaft without so much as a flinch. Then he went one step farther, tipping the man's cock toward Sally, helping him get settled in the drenched warmth of her pussy. Eli's come would ease the way for his friends.

She gasped, the sensations nearly too much after an entire parade of lovers.

"You've got this, Mustang," Eli whispered to her. The guys rubbed her shoulders, back and ass until she relaxed again.

Good thing too, because when Eli scooped fluid from her saturated folds and painted it over her back entrance, she might have rocketed into space without their assistance. Holden sheathed himself, then assisted his friend as Carver edged near to the action.

Both men cursed when Eli's finger sank into Sally's delicate portal and massaged her ring of muscle until she relaxed. After long nights of loving both him and Alanso, she'd taken to anal play better than he could have imagined. Most of the time she preferred to watch her guys when it came to that, but every once in a while…

This seemed to be one of those times.

She moaned, then bit Bryce's neck. Not in an attempt to get away, but in an effort to stay still and take him deeper. Alanso bolted from the couch. He returned with a mostly-empty bottle of lube. The guys teased him, but he didn't give a fuck as he provided the last ingredient they needed to unite them all together.

Eli slicked his palm, then held it out to Holden. The man stepped nearer until Eli wrapped his fingers around the thinner yet longer erection his friend sported. Perfect for this. They all had their places. Their uses. And this one was Holden's.

Without needing to be told, Swinger climbed onto the couch, squatting over both Sally and Bryce. He pressed the head of his cock against her tight ass until he began to sink inside, making Eli sure this wasn't his first time around the block. He fucked into her gently and with enough finesse that he calmed Eli's uneasiness. Alanso stared, transfixed.

Sally cried out. It wasn't pain he heard in her scream. But pleasure.

Lots of it.

Mustang Sally

"Get your cock in her mouth again, Alanso." Eli directed his best friend, his lover and his mate. He knew that's where the man wanted to be during this show. And Sally would feel better having him near.

The two men filling her now began to rock in time, providing every inch of satisfaction they could. Behind them, Carver stroked himself. He seemed in another world as he watched Holden's and Bryce's shafts disappear into their partner's body.

"I have to fuck, Eli." The guy's stare snapped to his boss'. "Let me have a turn. Holden? Please."

"No turns." Eli shook his head. "Stand between Bryce's knees. Get his and Sally's legs around you. You're tall enough to make this work. You're going to slide in with Bryce. Between him and Holden. The three of you are going to take her together."

"Are you fucking crazy?" Carver's hand froze on his shaft. Even Bryce and Holden stuttered in their rhythm.

The spent Hot Rods perked up, a few of them rubbing themselves as if they might opt for a second round in their own palms.

"Hey, it's Alanso's idea." Eli shrugged, confident his lovers could handle it.

Sally lifted her head from Bryce's chest to stare at the Cuban man in front of her. "I knew I loved you for a reason."

He smiled as he dangled his index finger in front of her face. She opened her mouth and sucked on it. "I'll give you my cock back if you promise not to hurt me when you're fucking all three of them at once."

"Like you could keep it out of her mouth now." Roman snickered from his spot on the floor. He might have been relaxed, but he stared at the men and woman piled in front of him without blinking.

"Shit. You're right." Alanso kneeled on the couch and fed her his erection. While she was distracted with her treat, Carver approached.

"Are you sure this'll work, Cobra?" He rubbed the covered head of his dick against her pussy, at the junction of her and Bryce's body.

"Hell yes," Eli reassured him.

"He told you to get in there," Roman barked at their spare-part guru. "What the hell are you waiting for, boy?"

Carver's eyes rolled back in his head a little. He advanced, nudging Bryce's balls with his cock then sliding up the base of the thick, mostly embedded shaft until he tucked against Sally's pussy. All of them groaned when they connected.

Tentatively, he began to wedge himself inside her. The additional pressure had her moaning. And when she lurched, she dislodged him.

Alanso immediately tended to her, calming her and preparing her for another attempt.

"You were close." Eli nodded to Carver. "Again."

"Do it," Roman added.

Carver didn't mess around. He grabbed Holden's shuttling hips for purchase and clung with one hand. The other he used to align his hard-on with Sally's pussy. Bryce paused, allowing Carver to worm his way inside the tiny gap remaining. Carver's pupils dilated as her body expanded to encompass all three men. Bit by bit, he pressed inside her.

Bryce's fists balled on the sofa.

Eli, Roman and Kaige focused on soothing Sally, who'd been reduced to unintelligible moans and cries. She wasn't fighting them, though, unless it was to rock back and take the Hot Rods deeper.

Alanso stared into Eli's eyes when he looked up. "She's about to suck my cock off. She wants this. More. I can't hang on much longer."

Sweat trickled down his chest and rolled over his washboard abs.

"You won't have to," Eli promised him. "They'll come when she does. She's close. So close."

He knew because she'd started grinding on Bryce in the

primal dance he'd come to know so well these past weeks. God, he loved her. He loved driving her wild. Beyond civilized responses. This is who she was. This is what she wanted. And he would do anything to be the man to give it to her.

One of them anyway.

In awe, he signaled for the men to let loose. To take what they needed too. All of them were aligned. Their passions complimentary.

Holden rocked deep within her, plundering her ass with gentle yet complete possession.

Bryce and Carver found their own cadence. It seemed to work wonders for Sally as the two cocks in her pussy rubbed each other as well as her from every possible angle. She gobbled Alanso's dick. Sloppy and noisy, none of them minded her gusto.

Least of all the man in her mouth.

"*Mierda*. You're so beautiful." He praised her, mostly in rapid-fire Spanish. And finally it was too much. When she swallowed him to the root and cupped his balls in her fingers, Alanso went stiff as a board. He hung on the edge for seconds that probably felt like millennia, then went into a frenzy. Animalistic grunts and curses fell from his lips along with words of devotion and love.

He pumped his release down her throat and she didn't spill a drop despite the three men rutting on her, granting her wishes and fulfilling their own simultaneously. There was no room for misunderstanding. She had to know she was the center of their universe—beloved and precious. Awe inspiring.

Eli knew how long they'd all waited for this moment. He understood their quiet desperation and their utter abandon. With time, control and grace would come.

Not today.

As if the taste of Alanso triggered Sally's orgasm, she shattered around the men impaling her.

And not a single Hot Rod stood a chance at resisting that ultimate tautness.

Eli wished there was room for even his pinky beside one of the three cocks she took so that he could experience her stretched like they could. Next time it would be him inside her like this. Or maybe even if they took her pussy with three guys instead of one in her ass. Someday soon, it would happen.

When Alanso evacuated her mouth, come still spilling from his cock, Eli angled her head to face him. "I love you, Salome."

Her eyes glassed over, a contented smile on her face.

Holden, Carver and Bryce launched jet after jet of come into the condoms, still buried in their littlest member. She proved to them again that size didn't matter, unless it was the scale of your heart and soul. Sally welcomed them all and held them while they were obliterated.

Roman got to his feet. When Carver would have fallen backwards, he was there to catch the smaller man, whose cock slid from Sally, squeezed out by one of her lingering aftershocks. Kaige lent Holden a hand in climbing from their Mustang, who'd given him the ride of his life. Eli collected Alanso and moved him out of the way so that Bryce could lift Sally.

Eli and Alanso accepted the precious bundle she made as she curled into their chests and they sandwiched her between them. They blanketed her in kisses and slathered her with praise.

Though he half expected her to black out or drop into a sated slumber, her eyes popped open and fixated on his. Green gaze to his own blue one.

Alanso whispered his appreciation from beside them.

"Ask me to marry you, Eli," she demanded.

"Again?" he teased.

"I'm ready this time." She bit the corner of her lip. "Unless this changed your mind?"

"*Hijo de puta!*" Alanso elbowed Eli in the ribs.

"Hell no, Mustang." He rubbed his nose on hers. "I love you even more tonight than I have before. More than I thought possible. I want you with us for the rest of our lives. I can't live with less."

Eli handed her to Alanso for a moment. He lunged for his discarded jeans. From the pocket, he withdrew the box he'd been dying for her to accept.

He took a deep breath and prayed this time he'd do this right.

Sinking to his knees, Alanso joined him. The other man held his hand as he flipped open the velvet casing.

For the first time, Sally took a good look at the ring they'd commissioned for her. A big diamond, the exact shade of pink as her car, nestled between two gleaming white stones. One for him. One for Alanso. Five smaller pink baguettes completed the unbroken circle around the band. Rainbows danced on her pale skin as the many facets reflected the halogen lights above them.

The entire gang of Hot Rods closed rank around them, forming a tight circle that protected the trio at the center of the group.

"Salome Rider, will you marry Alanso and me?"

"Hell yes!" She flung herself at them, bowling them over.

They laughed together as they cuddled close. Alanso plucked the ring from the box and slipped it onto Sally's hand. She peered at it, then dashed tears from her cheeks before kissing first Eli, then Alanso. She made out with him some more, then Eli again.

The Hot Rods congratulated them one by one. Someone flipped on the faux fireplace at the end of the rug the threesome lounged on as they left the room. The trio lost themselves in each other and the complex relationship they'd forged.

It may have taken a long time to cure, but it would never break.

Sally raised her head and promised them both, "I'll love you forever."

"Hot Rods for life," Alanso whispered.

Eli settled for simplicity. "I'm yours."

Epilogue

Kaige grinned as he filled in the five guys and their women, who anxiously huddled around the camera on the other end of the video chat, even if not all of them were visible on the limited screen. "Yep. Looks like Eli and Alanso are chained for life. Or will be. Soon."

"If you really believe they haven't already been committed to her—to the Hot Rods—for years, you're crazy." Morgan shook her head.

"Are you paying attention over there, Super Nova?" Even Dave got in on the lecture.

"Yeah." He dropped the smartass act for just a minute. It'd been his shelter for so long he wasn't sure how to let go sometimes. "It's good. They're changing. We all are."

"I hear Eli's giving you a lot more responsibility on the business side of things," Mike chimed in. As the operation owner for the crew, he had a lot in common with Cobra. "That's a damn fine idea. You've always had an eye for strategy and new leads. Don't let this screw with your head. Trust your gut. When you're all working together, only good things will come."

He nodded. "That's not what's worrying me."

"Ah, now we're getting somewhere." Kayla leaned forward in her husband's hold. "Finally going to admit everything isn't fine in paradise?"

"That's the thing, Kay." He sighed. "It *is* perfect. I'm afraid I might mess it up."

"And not on the garage stuff," Neil supplied.

"Hell, no. I've got that under control." Kaige scratched his eyebrow. "It's the other shit. I mean, this is great for now. But what if I find someone I want to be with? You know, a woman?

How the hell did you guys make that work? There are no other chicks here. Just Mustang. She's amazing, but she's not going to be enough for us all. She'll always belong to Cobra and Al first."

"Why can't your group grow?" Mike hugged his wife and their daughter tight to his chest.

"I don't know if we're ready for that." Kaige grimaced. "It took this long to get where we are with people we've known all our lives."

"Well, do you have someone in mind?" Joe narrowed his eyes.

"Nah, nothing like that." Kaige shrugged. "Just thinking ahead, I guess. This means too much to me to get down a road I can't finish driving."

"Why not enjoy the ride for a bit?" James encouraged him. "You've already got one Eli—you don't need two worriers. Besides, hasn't he proved that the best-laid plans don't always work out like you thought? Sometimes you've gotta roll with what you're handed."

Kaige nodded. "I suppose you're right. I just have this feeling..."

"I get that sometimes too." Neil adjusted his crotch. "You'll get used to it. Go find Mustang and her guys. They'll fix you up."

"Ug. Not *that* kind of—" Kaige cracked up. It wasn't often he got kidded by another kidder. "Okay, okay. Right. But when my time comes, you better get your long distance minutes ready. I'm gonna need some help."

"We've got your back, Nova." Joe nodded. "And so do your Hot Rods. Now put my cousin on the line so we can congratulate him properly."

"For that you'd have to come in person." Kaige extended the invitation that was always open.

"We may do that sometime soon." Mike smiled. "Certainly for the wedding."

"All right, then. Hang on." Kaige strode out of his room and into the main area of the Hot Rods apartment. "Yo, Cobra. There are some people here who want to talk to you."

He plopped the laptop on the coffee table and covered his ears as the nine-member crew, plus their kids, squealed and shouted their congratulations while Eli, Alanso and Sally grinned on their side of the screen.

A smile crossed his face as Mustang showed off the ring they'd helped Eli pick out.

His friends were happy. That made him happy too.

For now.

About the Author

Jayne Rylon is a *New York Times* and *USA Today* bestselling author. She received the 2011 Romantic Times Reviewer Choice Award for Best Indie Erotic Romance. Her stories usually begin as a daydream in an endless business meeting. Writing acts as a creative counterpoint to her straight-laced corporate existence. She lives in Ohio with two cats and her husband, who both inspires her fantasies and supports her careers. When she can escape her office, she loves to travel the world, avoid speeding tickets in her beloved Sky and, of course, read.

What will grow from the seeds of desire?

Hope Springs
© *2013 Jayne Rylon & Mari Carr*
Compass Girls, Book 2

Hope Compton never considered her parents' unconventional relationship a dangerous thing. Until, after a few too many drinks in a crowded bar, she admits her desire for a ménage to her college boyfriend—and uninvited guests try to turn her fantasy into a nightmare.

When Wyatt catches some thugs harassing the pretty daughter of his bosses, he doesn't hesitate to call on his partner Clayton to kick some asses. But then he realizes what a temptation the sweet, sheltered Hope presents. Especially her naughty wish to unleash her inner vixen—with both of them.

Hope has no doubt her playmates want to fulfill her every desire, but something's holding them back. She has an idea what those *somethings* are. With luck, and a little help from her Compass cousins to hold her fathers off, she'll find what she needs in the shadows of the past—and convince them she's found two men of her own who are worthy of her love.

Warning: Compass books bring love in every direction and every season. But not all of life's moments are filled with joy. Take the good with the bad, and the steamy.

Available now in ebook and print from Samhain Publishing.

Relationship, no…but threesome, hell yes!

How to Love
© 2013 Kelly Jamieson
San Amaro Singles, Book 2

Ever since Jules's new neighbor moved in, she's been undressing him in her mind. Mike is the fresh inspiration she needs to make her erotic photography studio a success, if she can convince him *and* his equally buff roommate, Carlos, to strip for her lens. And maybe indulge in a little off-camera fun as well.

But Jules isn't too worried. She doesn't do relationships, but she loves men and sex—and in her experience, most men are okay with that.

Judging from the raw emotions leaping from the images in Jules's gallery, Mike senses there's a lot going on beneath her flirtatious, slightly cynical exterior. He and Carlos are happy in their committed relationship, but they've always felt there's a piece missing. They want a woman. Jules could be that woman.

A threesome with two committed men? Sounds like an emotionally risk-free dream come true for Jules. But when they make it clear they want more, her deepest fears push to the surface. Straining bonds forged in incredible heat to the breaking point…

Warning: The book features two hot men brave enough to climb cliffs, strip naked for erotic photographs, have sex in a portrait studio and on a cliff, and who have the courage to teach a commitment-phobic woman how to love.

Available now in ebook and print from Samhain Publishing.

It's all about the story...

Romance

HORROR

www.samhainpublishing.com

Made in the USA
Middletown, DE
10 September 2016